HONOR YOUR FATHER. *HURT* YOUR MOTHER

Christabel believes it's her sacred duty to protect her teenage daughter, Samantha. Never mind that Sam can be aggressive to the point of violence. Never mind that she refuses to return Christabel's love.

Inevitably, in a fit of rage, Sam knocks her mother unconscious. During her recovery, Christabel finally concedes that tough decisions must be made, and she and her ex-husband Ravi register Sam in a group residence. Ravi is relieved, but Christabel is guilt-stricken. Somehow, though, with Samantha securely rehomed, sparks of the couple's old romance reignite.

Too bad that their budding love is built on deception. Worse, that their daughter reveres her manipulative father and shuns her generous mother. More horrifying yet, something evil is happening in Sam's group facility and Christabel must intervene before an ominous situation turns into a disaster.

Editorial Reviews

"A surprising, disturbing look into small town utopia that had me turning pages at warp speed. ***Fountain of Evil*** kept me up past my bedtime, both because I couldn't put it down, and because I couldn't let it go."—***Cat Skinner, author of Bump and Grind***

"Sally Basmajian tips her quill into darker ink for this creepy, twisty story of motherhood and marriage gone off the rails. Readers will root for the protagonist stuck in a Stepfordesque setting until the very end."—***Lena Scholman, author of Between Silk and Wool***

Excerpt

Samantha: Where's Daddy?
Nurse: He will visit again tomorrow. With your mother, who is always here for you.
Samantha: Want Daddy.
Nurse: Your parents are so happy you're using more of your words. As am I.
Samantha: [She is still smiling but she closes her eyes]
Nurse: Well, there we go. Another day, and such a pleasant one it was, too. I'll wish you sweet dreams now, Samantha.
Samantha: Good night.
Nurse: Sleep tight.
Samantha: Give Mommy a great big bite. [Grinds teeth and laughs]

FOUNTAIN OF EVIL

Sally Basmajian

Moonshine Cove Publishing, LLC

Abbeville, South Carolina U.S.A.

First Moonshine Cove Edition Sep 2023

ISBN: 9781952439650

Library of Congress LCCN: 2023914836

This book is a work of fiction. Names, characters, businesses, places, events, conversations, opinions, and incidents are either products of the author's imagination or are used fictitiously. Any resemblance to actual events, locales, conversations, opinions, business establishments, or persons, living or dead, is entirely coincidental and unintended.

Cover and interior design by Moonshine Cove staff.

About the Author

Sally Basmajian is an escapee from the corporate broadcasting world in Canada. Before fleeing the business, she was Bell Media's Vice President and General Manager, Comedy and Drama.

She completed her Graduate Certificate in Creative Writing at Humber College in 2019 and holds a Master of Arts in Musicology from the University of Toronto. In January 2023, her first Women's novel, *So Hard to Do*, was published by Creative James Media. California Bookwatch described it as "not just a different kind of love triangle, but a different growth experience that will lead patrons to laugh, cry, and ponder." The lifestyle website, *divine.ca*, commented, "This is such a gentle, relatable book on so many levels. It explores people on the spectrum in the kindest way possible. As a reader, you will be laughing with them, but not at them."

In addition to her long-form projects, Sally Basmajian also writes short-form memoir pieces, several of which have appeared in Canada's national newspaper, *The Globe & Mail*. In 2022, she won prizes in the Gulf Coast Writers Association and the Northwestern Ontario Writers Workshop international contests for non-fiction. Her fiction shorts have been selected for a number of anthologies, such as *UnCommon Bodies* and *The Year's Best Dog Stories 2021*.

In Fall 2023, her rollicking children's fantasy, *Apprentices in Magic*, will debut. She hopes it will counterbalance the soul-deep darkness she mined for *Fountain of Evil,* with both books scheduled for publication within the same season.

sallybasmajian.com

Chapter 1: May 14

Christabel picked up the abandoned party hats one by one, stacking them together like ice cream cones. She glanced at the "Happy Sweet Sixteen" plastic topper that lay on its side next to a partially devoured white slab cake. Someone had tongued off the last few sugar roses.

In the doorway to the entrance hall, Ravi put a finger to his lips as he backed away, his dark eyes solemn behind the thick lenses of his designer glasses. She went to him and held on to his hand a fraction of a second too long, absorbing its reassuring warmth, before easing the door shut behind him. Dependable man, her ex-husband, today at least. He'd been the first guest to arrive and the last to leave.

Now it was quiet, except for Samantha's low humming, barely audible in the peaceful house. Yes, there it was. *Sesame Street*—always the theme from *Sesame Street.* Christabel crumpled up a handful of wilted crepe paper and sighed.

It had been an unusual celebration for a sixteen-year-old. In its own way, successful. For once, Sam had stayed calm.

Christabel turned to look at her daughter. Sam sat cross-legged on the floor, combing the hair of one of the many Barbies she'd received that day. For an instant, Christabel wanted to weep. Not one classmate had come. Sam had been the only person at the party under the age of forty. Poor kid, shunned by her peers again—and by their wary parents, too.

Christabel moved around the room, picking up a plastic fork here, a half-melted candle there, depositing the debris into a green garbage bag. She took care not to rustle as she glided from spot to spot.

After she secured the drawstring on the bulging sack, she shortened the table and pushed it against the wall. No sound. Ravi had paid for the padded wall-to-wall after Sam had had one too many head-banging rages against the underlying hardwood.

Christabel guided the cushiony couch back into its usual location in front of the picture window and stood up straight, massaging the small of her back with one hand. She cast a glance through the fingerprint-covered safety glass and was momentarily dazzled by the last rays of the May sun as it set over their uptown Toronto neighborhood. Time for Sam to go to bed. Only then could Christabel pour herself a glass of well-deserved pinot.

"Honey?" Christabel pitched her voice to a soft alto.

Sam was stroking her doll's hair. Blond Barbie seemed to be her favorite. Sam had dressed and undressed it a dozen times. Most of the others lay naked and scattered about on the rug in a plastic orgy of unrealistic curvature– except for red-headed Barbie, who hadn't even made it out of the package yet. Christabel touched her own shoulder-length auburn hair, wondering if her daughter was sending her a message. Hawaiian Barbie, who looked the most like Sam, apart from not wearing prescription glasses, sat stiff-legged next to the teen. Together, they surveyed the assembled doll population with unblinking almond eyes, like heartless judges at a nudist beauty competition.

Christabel counted silently to ten.

"Sam?"

A hummed melodic fragment, from the *Sesame Street* theme song. The line about the clouds going away, maybe.

Patience. Composed mother, well-behaved child.

Christabel rubbed her forehead. She began to count again, struggling to get all the way to fifteen. *One, God help me; two, please Jesus; three, I'm losing it; four ...*

"Samantha?"

"Heard you the first time." Sam did not look up. Her long, black hair hung in tentacles.

"All right. Well, you had a lovely party, sweetie. So many people came. You must be exhausted."

"Nope. Not tired. Not one bit."

"Really? Well, I certainly am." Christabel laughed. In her ears it sounded false, as hollow as she felt.

Somewhere, deep inside, compassion and love existed. She concentrated on igniting those twin sparks of empathy and smiled at Sam.

"How about we start getting you ready for bed? Tell you what: no bath tonight. If you like, we can read one of your books."

"Said I'm not tired." Sam cast blond Barbie aside and picked up her Hawaiian doppelganger.

Together, doll and girl looked up at Christabel with unwavering stares. With a grubby finger, Sam pushed her black-rimmed eyeglasses from the tip of her nose back up the long bridge. Her jaw jutted forward.

Christabel forced herself to breathe. In through the nose, out through the mouth. Hands at her sides in a non-combative stance, all muscles relaxed. She stood and waited, just like the latest psychiatrist and Adolescent Development Center's behavioral counselor had told her to do. *Defuse the situation before bad things start. Go with the flow; never push Sam unnecessarily.*

But it had been a grueling day. Christabel's back was killing her. How long could she stand here, hoping her hopped-up-on-sugar-roses daughter would put the doll down, and opt for bedtime?

Thirty excruciating seconds plodded by. Still, Sam stared at her, holding Hawaiian Barbie up as if to bear witness to Christabel's substandard mothering. The girl's expression was as blank as the doll's.

Christabel was so tired. With all her might, she clung to the last filaments of self-control. Sam's happiness, particularly on her birthday, came first. Laying a gentle hand on her daughter's shoulder, Christabel opened her mouth, intending to say some soothing but persuasive words.

Words that never left her lips.

With superhuman speed, Sam used Hawaiian Barbie as a bludgeon, striking Christabel's knuckles with a vicious crack.

"Get offa me!"

Christabel recoiled. Hot tears pricked her eyes. She choked back an angry rebuke.

Sam dropped the doll and unspooled from her cross-legged position on the floor. Although her face was serene, she radiated a freshly-wakened malice. This was the Sam very few people ever saw—the one who terrified even her mother.

No sudden moves. Keeping her eyes locked on her daughter's, Christabel took a cautious backward step. Sam had a slight weight advantage, not to mention a robotic will to dominate.

Christabel slunk back another pace. Then a third. If she could make it to the staircase, she might be able to dash up the steps to her bedroom and lock herself in. Sam's emotional storm would pass, and they'd both be safe.

Now or never. Christabel turned and ran, inches ahead of a furious, inarticulate hiss. As she approached the landing, she felt a tug at her ankle and fell forward. Raising her arms to shield her face, she clipped her sore hand and groaned.

Sam paid no heed. She yanked her mother back down the stairs. Chillingly, in rhythm with the bumpy descent, she hummed the *Sesame Street* theme song.

Christabel cried out as her temple bounced off the newel post. Light shot through her vision—incandescent, laced with searing pain.

She was on the floor. Her head felt like someone had taken an axe to it. Fighting waves of nausea, Christabel peered up. Sam was hovering above her. Not the maniacal version, but good, sweet Sam, dark eyes filled with innocent concern.

Sam leaned closer, and the inky curtain of her long hair spilled onto Christabel's face. The whole world suddenly smelled sickeningly of pink icing roses. Agony bloomed in her right temple, full force. Still, Christabel lifted her head and attempted to smile reassuringly up at her daughter.

The effort was too much.

As Sam kissed her on the cheek, everything went black.

Chapter 2: June 3

Christabel stood on the sidewalk and squinted through the shroud of her dark lenses. From what she could make out, the lawn and gardens were lush, and the building looked more like a posh residence than a psychiatric facility.

She walked a few paces to a shady spot beneath a mature maple and blinked to clear her vision. Dr. Apigian had warned her to avoid bright light while she recovered from her concussion. Noisy environments and stress were verboten, too. Christabel repeatedly promised him she'd do her best to comply.

Ravi had tried to keep her cocooned while he took charge of her recovery. At first she was an obedient patient, but, with her strength returning, she became increasingly restless. After a few days in the hospital, she insisted on going home, ignoring her ex's plea to convalesce under his roof. She needed to be with Sam, the girl she loved more than anything else on earth—ninety-five percent of the time.

Only Sam wasn't at home anymore. Ravi had arranged for her to be admitted to Treffian House, a luxurious fortress in the small town of Graysville, about a two-hour drive from Toronto, in decent traffic. Treffian House was an all-ages facility where his mother had spent her last confused years. As far as these types of places went, it was the crème-de-la-crème for staff and facilities, and it offered a full range of treatments, ranging from rehab to Reiki. Ravi, a member of its Board of Directors, swore he'd get Sam the highest level of attention.

Christabel had signed the sheaf of documents, but she'd been out of her head, in a post-concussive world of haze. At least, she hoped she had an excuse for agreeing to hand over her only child to strangers. The weight of black guilt told her otherwise.

She gazed across an expanse of well-tended lawn at the building. It screamed Victorian excessiveness, all gables and turrets and wraparound porch. Not like an asylum at all.

Christabel chided herself. Of course it wasn't an asylum. It was a residence. A *home*. For older teens and adults who were lucky enough to come from well-to-do families. Families who could afford to warehouse their inconvenient relatives—drop them off and throw away the key. Until now.

She'd be surprised if Sam hadn't taken an immediate dislike to Treffian House. Christabel had heard from her neighbors that Sam had had to be forcibly restrained by the crew who had come to get her the night of the incident. They'd arrived in something that looked like a cross between a hearse and an ambulance, painted a nondescript gray. No siren or flashing bubble on top. Designed to glide unnoticed through quiet residential streets.

Christabel took a deep breath and walked across the grass to the building. Knowing Ravi's more than comfortable financial status, she wasn't surprised at the opulence of the place but she was taken aback by its antiquated look. The Ravi she knew was all high tech and gleaming modernity, and this was the flamboyant opposite of that. Maybe when it came to finding a lock-up joint for your mother and your kid you prioritized security and let architectural design take a back seat.

She gave herself another mental slap. Ravi had come to the rescue. This group home was leagues above what she'd be able to afford. It had been the right decision, though, hadn't it—giving up the job she loved? Advocating for Samantha had become a full-time gig so long ago, she could barely remember her teaching days at Oak Ridges Middle School.

Fortunately, Ravi was generous in the divorce settlement and always came through when there were additional expenses. Guilt money, perhaps, but it was essential. Appreciated, too, even though she never enjoyed having to cash his checks.

Enough negativity. Christabel breathed in the fresh air. It was a glorious late spring day and she was bathed in golden sunlight. How long had it been since she'd last had the luxury of solitude? And it was beautiful here. The gardens were immaculately groomed. Maybe some of the residents helped with the maintenance.

She tried the door, even though she figured it would be secure. It didn't budge, the well-polished hardware unassailable. There'd be no escaping from this place. Somehow this made her feel better, then immediately worse, but her hand was steady as she rang the intercom buzzer.

"Welcome to Treffian House," a polite, disembodied voice said. "Could you please look into the camera and tell us your name and who you would like to see?"

"Christabel Mistry," she replied, peering into the discreetly located camera and wondering if she appeared calmer than she felt. "Samantha Mistry's mom."

There was a slight pause. Then, "Please enter and take a seat, Mrs. Mistry," and the heavy click of the lock.

The transition from sunshine to artificial lighting was jarring. Christabel removed her sunglasses and put a hand to her temple, still sore from its encounter with the newel post. The buzz of fluorescent tubes and the whistling of too-cold air conditioning irritated her raw nerve endings. She wondered how Sam, with all her sensory issues, was coping with these aggressive stimuli.

Christabel sank into a chair. The entrance area was set up like a doctor's antechamber. Not cozy Dr. Apigian's, back in the city; his family practice office was scuffed and bordering on shabby. Here, everything was luxe. Stuffed leather chairs and loveseats in gray-browns were grouped around a colorful area rug. Reproduction abstract prints on the walls picked up the same upbeat shades and made Christabel feel cheerier, until she realized that the room had no windows.

Unless you counted the one in the door opposite to where she sat. She rose to her feet as the shutter slid open, revealing the face of a woman behind thick glass. Bulletproof, Christabel bet. Escape-proof, too.

"Mrs. Mistry, please come in." The piped-in transmission had a high school PA quality to it.

As Christabel approached, the door swung open and a blocky woman moved forward to greet her. She wore a no-nonsense tweed suit, the skirt hitting her mid-calf, and a white silk blouse, high to the neck. Her eyes were a faded blue, and her short, wavy hair was gray. Agatha Christie's Miss Marple to the life.

"Hello, Mrs. Mistry. I am Mrs. McKay," the woman said, with a faint accent.

British for sure; likely Scottish. It coordinated perfectly with her appearance.

"Very nice to meet you, Mrs. McKay. I'm here to–"

Words deserted Christabel as an odor, sneaking through the antiseptic overlay, invaded her nostrils. It wasn't exactly the scent of mothballed old people nor was it the sickly smell of kids' unwashed hair. It was a hard to define, subtle reek, almost concealed by the fragrance of a high-class cleaning solution that featured natural overtones of lavender and hints of sage. Almost, but not quite.

Mrs. McKay was scrutinizing her. Christabel forced herself to swallow, and pinned on a smile. It probably didn't extend to her untwinkling eyes, but Mrs. McKay seemed reassured.

"This is one of our common areas, Mrs. Mistry. Bright and attractive, isn't it?"

Overcoming her gag reflex, Christabel nodded and moved into the center of the room. Mrs. McKay was correct. If you erased the clutch of blank-faced residents, both old and young–some sitting in wheelchairs, others collapsed in lethargic slumps on Barcaloungers–and just focused on the décor, it was a pleasant enough setting. The walls were an optimistic yellow, and horizontal windows, positioned well above eye level, let in ample light. Leather recliners, in shades of black, gray, and forest green, were arranged in clusters. There was an obscenely large high-definition television in one corner tuned to a slick reality program, but it was blessedly silent. Someone had turned on the closed-captioning, and a few elderly residents in wheelchairs stared at the screen, transfixed. Were they actually following the action or medicated to the brink of oblivion?

She shook her head, trying to jettison the negative thoughts—and dislodge the smell.

A teenaged boy and girl entered the room, accompanied by an orderly, the boy chattering away in a reassuringly normal manner. Christabel felt her shoulders relax. Maybe there were elements of sanity here, after all. On closer look, though, the girl's posture was saggy and she stumbled rather than walked. Poor young thing—she could be an extra in a *Walking Dead* episode.

Christabel locked eyes with Mrs. McKay. "Where's Sam?"

"One of our staff members is bringing her down. Please have a seat," Mrs. McKay said, waving in the direction of some unoccupied chairs.

"Can't I see her in her room?" Christabel clasped her hands around her purse, holding it against her body like armor.

"Soon, but not today. We find our new residents need time to adjust to their surroundings. They can become agitated when loved ones come into their personal space. Please don't worry, Mrs. Mistry, she's on her way."

With that, Mrs. McKay moved toward an exit. She said something at a low volume into the intercom, and stood back as the automated door opened.

A male orderly supported Sam into the room and transferred her hand from his forearm to Mrs. McKay's. She gave Sam's shoulder a pat, and together they moved forward, stopping in front of Christabel, who remained frozen.

"Well, now, here she is. Say good afternoon to your mother, Samantha."

Christabel tried to stand up, but Mrs. McKay shook her head, placed both hands on Sam's upper arms, and pressed the girl into a chair opposite.

"Now, why don't the two of you enjoy a nice catch-up? I'll give you a bit of privacy, shall I?" With that, Mrs. McKay departed, leaving Christabel alone with her innocent, developmentally delayed child.

Of their own accord, Christabel's arms opened for a hug. Sam seemed oblivious, and after a moment or two—like the gates of hope closing—they dropped.

Sam looked combed and brushed and tidy. She was dressed in a blue acrylic sweater over black leggings and she had some kind of institutional booties on her feet. Puffy and soft and probably difficult to escape in.

Across the room, the teenagers had started to argue. Sam seemed not to notice as the volume of their fight crescendoed to a shrill pitch that twanged Christabel's nerve endings. It faded as the orderly hustled them out of the common area.

Sam hadn't so much as twitched. Her eyes were looking up, the irises rolling back into her head. The corners of her mouth drooped.

"Sammie?" Christabel tossed her handbag onto the ground. She reached forward and took her daughter's hands in hers.

"Uhh." Sam did not return her mother's squeeze.

"Sweetie, are you all right?"

Silence. Sam's head lolled on her neck and she began to pitch forward. Christabel caught her daughter's shoulders, wedged her securely back into the chair, and ran to the intercom, brushing by a bored-looking aide who was pushing a moaning old man in a wheelchair.

She stabbed at the button, calling, "Mrs. McKay? Are you there? I need help, fast!"

"On my way."

An instant later, Christabel grabbed the woman's arm as she entered the room.

"Please! Come quickly! Sam's not herself."

Sam was still sprawled in the large padded chair, glasses perched low on her nose, eyes heavenward. A string of drool crept down her chin. With a small *tut-tut*, Mrs. McKay whisked a tissue from a box on a side table, and wiped it away. Sam's expression didn't change.

Christabel waved a hand in front of her face. "She's totally out of it!"

"Mrs. Mistry, please. Samantha has been through a traumatic experience. Her relocation to Treffian House was made under challenging circumstances, and she has expended much emotional energy during this adjustment period. She will need more time to establish a level of comfort here."

"But she's not even fully conscious! I mean, just *look* at her!"

"Yes, Mrs. Mistry. I do see her. As I have seen many other residents, young and old alike, make a similar transition to a communal living facility. This is quite typical."

"Not for Sam, it isn't." Christabel struggled for words, a flash of pain sizzling behind her eyes. She raised her hands to her temples.

Dr. Apigian had warned her not to underestimate the aftereffects of her concussion. Dizziness and nausea. Brain fog.

But a mother needed to put everything aside when it came to protecting her child. She *had* to intervene.

She raised her eyes to meet Mrs. McKay's. "What kind of drugs have you put her on?"

"Mrs. Mistry, please calm down."

Instead, Christabel's pulse accelerated. "I want to know why my daughter looks stoned."

Mrs. McKay frowned. "An unfortunate choice of words. When Samantha failed to settle down, Dr. Cheung administered antipsychotics."

"Antipsychotics? Are you kidding me?" *Breathe, Christabel, breathe.*

"The doctor will monitor her behavior closely, of course, and reduce or change the prescription accordingly. It's standard procedure. Rohibital has been safely used here and at other reputable institutions and group home settings for decades. It's quite safe."

"But Sam doesn't take drugs." Christabel scrubbed away a teardrop with the back of her wrist. This was no time to break down.

"I'm afraid you and your husband have signed documents allowing us to make decisions when it comes to Samantha's health and well-being. And Dr. Cheung decided that for her safety and the safety of others, Rohibital was the wisest course of treatment."

Christabel stared at the woman in disbelief. Mrs. McKay reached out and stroked Sam's head.

"There, there, my dear, you're doing very well." She directed a gaze at Christabel. "Maybe this has been enough excitement for today?"

Christabel slid out of her chair, onto her knees in front of Sam. She took her daughter's beautiful face in her hands, gently guiding Sam's eyeglasses into position on the bridge of her nose.

If only she could go back to the night of Sam's birthday party. This time she'd handle things differently, never mind her weariness.

She hated herself for signing over her parental rights, but there was no doubt she'd done it, even if she'd been recovering from a concussion at the time. And Ravi had said this was the best possible setting for Sam. It wasn't just an old folks' home; there were plenty of kids Sam's age and not all of them appeared to be drugged out of their minds.

It could be that the annoying Mrs. McKay was right, and she and the other experts knew what they were doing. Christabel had failed miserably on her own. And surely, after the introductory period, Sam's meds would be adjusted.

Christabel made a silent vow. She'd see to it that her daughter was treated with dignity and compassion. She'd be there daily to provide all the love and reassurance in the world.

As Christabel leaned forward to kiss her daughter's cheek she could hear the merest mosquito-like droning. Humming. *Sesame Street.*

Sam's spirit was in there, somewhere—the good Sam.

And the one who had put her mother in the hospital, too.

Chapter 3: June 11

From the official records of the late Mrs. Audrey McKay (MSW), formerly of Treffian House

Transcribed from recorded session with Samantha Mistry. Handwritten notes indicated in italics

McKay: Samantha, how are you today?

Mistry: [No response]

McKay: You seem to like blond Barbie very much. Is she your favorite?

Mistry: Mmmmmm [humming]

McKay: She looks elegant in her ball gown. Is she going somewhere special?

Mistry: Mmmmmm

[A minute elapses. No vocalization other than Samantha's constant humming]

McKay: I see you have Hawaiian Barbie sitting beside you. I like her lei—her flower necklace, I mean. The colors are very pretty.

Mistry: [No response, but the humming stops. Samantha picks up Hawaiian Barbie and turns it face down on the floor. She continues to play with the blond doll. Humming recommences]

McKay: Poor Hawaiian Barbie. I hope she's able to breathe.

[Samantha shifts her weight so her buttock is firmly pressing down on Hawaiian Barbie. Humming continues. Two minutes later, a bell chimes]

McKay: Well, Samantha, that's our session for today. I'm afraid it's time for me to say good-bye.

Mistry: [No response]

* * *

Observations: After a difficult, month-long transition period, Samantha Mistry is at last adjusting to her placement at Treffian House. She is still nonverbal, but she no longer experiences psychotic episodes requiring physical restraint. One troubling aspect is that visits from her mother are usually followed by periods in which Samantha manifests restlessness and makes inarticulate, distressed noises.

After lengthy and sometimes heated discussions I have convinced Dr. Cheung to reduce the administration of Rohibital, which I felt to be a higher than advisable dosage for a 120-pound teenage girl.

This is not the first time I have questioned his use of pharmaceuticals to elicit behavior modification in young people. I have assured him I will monitor her behavior closely.

I will also monitor his.

Chapter 4: June 17, morning

Christabel lugged the last suitcase into her new bungalow-style condominium and heaved it onto the living room couch. As she entered the kitchen, wiping the perspiration from her forehead, she smiled at the sight of her older sister, who was roosting on a stool at the breakfast bar, checking her email. Grace looked as cool and crisp in her summer frock as she'd been two hours earlier when she'd picked Christabel up for their trip to Graysville. Every strand of her auburn hair, so like Christabel's but professionally colored, was in place.

"I'll be right with you, Chrissie. Just need to get back to my OCD boss about the latest crisis." Grace tapped away at the miniature screen. It was a wonder she could type at all, given the length of her curved red fingernails.

"Never mind. That was the last of my baggage. We're done."

"Really? Well, that wasn't so bad, was it?" Grace put the iPhone down and looked up with a grin.

In spite of being overheated and exasperated, Christabel laughed. While she'd been toting boxes and bags, Grace had been texting, phoning and even taking extended bathroom breaks in order to avoid doing any hard labor. But at least she'd shown up on time with a borrowed car and chauffeured Christabel to her new home, gabbing animatedly the whole way. Maybe Grace hadn't flexed a muscle, but she'd provided plenty of much-needed moral support.

"Do you want to unpack a few things or should we head over to visit Sam first?" Grace asked.

Christabel picked up her phone and checked the time. "Too early. Visiting hours are between two and four o'clock."

"So prepare me. What should I expect?"

Christabel sat down beside Grace, closed her eyes and pictured her daughter. It had been two weeks since she'd first seen Sam in her new residence. Since then, Christabel had traveled to Graysville almost every day by bus.

Ravi had offered her the use of one of his cars, and if she hadn't been under medical orders not to drive, she would have taken him up on it. But she knew it was too dangerous. She was still experiencing occasional starbursts in her field of vision as well as random jabs of pain.

The grueling bus trips had been worthwhile. Recent visits hadn't exactly been heartwarming, but they'd been encouraging. Sam was adjusting to her new surroundings and, while she remained non-verbal, she was no longer in a state of drooling vacancy. Lately, she hadn't shown any signs of agitation—until a few days ago when Christabel had attempted a hug and Sam had growled and shoved her away. A tight-lipped Mrs. McKay had stepped between them, and escorted Sam from the room.

Grace gave Christabel a nudge. "Well? How is she?"

"She looks healthy. They keep her clean and well-groomed—I hate to admit it, but better than I was able to manage. She was always shaking me off when I tried to brush her hair."

"So she's neat and tidy. But what about her spirits?"

"God, that's a tough one. She isn't talking yet. Mrs. McKay says it's all part of the adjustment period. The good news is that Sam seems a lot less angry."

"That's somewhat reassuring." Grace had a worried look in her eyes.

"I wonder ..." Christabel leaned forward, gripping her hands together.

"Stop right there. No, she should *not* leave Treffian House. Sam almost *killed* you a few weeks ago. You're lucky she knew how to dial 911. Otherwise you'd be dead."

"You're being melodramatic."

"Sam has attacked you more than a few times. Don't deny it. And it's my job as your big sister to see that it never happens again."

For as long as Christabel could remember, Grace had bossed her around. As soon as little Christabel had been capable of carrying anything, her ten-year-older sister had treated her like a cross between a favorite puppy and a sturdy pack mule.

"Okay, so let's have lunch first and visit Sam after. And, hey, this condo of yours isn't half bad," Grace said, stuffing her iPhone into her Dior bag and securing the clasp. "If only it weren't located in this crappy little town."

Christabel raised her index finger. "I'll have you know, sister dear, that Graysville is one of the highest per capita income regions in the province." She arched a delicate eyebrow at Grace, who attempted to mirror the gesture but was too Botox-impaired.

"And the most elderly spot on earth," Grace said. "You're going to be like jailbait."

"Ah, jealousy won't get you my spiffy new condo, girl."

"Ravi has to be good for something, damn him to hell and back. His withered old mother probably haunts this place."

"Grace! Don't talk about Mama Mistry like that. Besides, she didn't die in this condo."

"She would have if her spooky ass hadn't been carted off to the Domicile for Rich-Bitch Dementos." Grace broke off. "Chrissie, I'm so sorry. I didn't mean that. About Treffian House, that is."

"I know you didn't. But the jury's still out. Which is why I'm staying put in Graysville until I either spring Sam out of there—don't give me that look!—or make sure it's suitable."

"Sweetie, you need to have a life, too. Sam will be fine. It's the very best that Ravi's gazillions can buy. You'll see."

"Hope you're right." Christabel twisted the emerald-studded band on her right ring finger. It had been their grandmother's and Christabel had always hoped to pass it on to her own daughter. Emeralds were Sam's birthstone.

"Meanwhile, check out your swanky new condo!" Grace swept out her arm in a theatrical arc. "It appears Ravi didn't economize when it came to Mama's comfort. Thank God he didn't get around to putting it up for sale last year when she croaked."

Christabel grimaced but just said, "It's nice enough here."

The place had been decorated with wheelchair access in mind. One room led into the next through wide archways. Standing in the shiny white-and-red kitchen, she could see into the airy living room with its well-spaced furnishings. Beyond that, there was a gracious bedroom and an en-suite bathroom, the only two rooms with interior doors.

It was tasteful and immaculate. Best of all, she was within easy walking distance of Treffian House.

"You'll be living the high life," Grace said, trailing her hand over the white marble countertop.

"If you'd save even a fraction of your humongous salary ..." Christabel said, knowing she was wasting her breath.

And who was Christabel to offer anyone advice? She was a full-time mother without a child at home, living off her ex-husband's largesse.

She put a hand to her temple. *Stay calm. Doctor's orders.*

"It's getting late," Grace said, standing up and stretching. "If we're going to see Sam this afternoon before I vamoose, we should grab lunch now. Maybe find our way to the main drag and locate a restaurant?"

"You bet. Ravi's treat." Christabel rooted in her handbag and held up her wallet. The Visa Black card inside was brand new and fully backed.

"I'll be sure to order at least two of every item on the menu," Grace said. She took her sister's unmanicured hand in her own well-tended one, and together the sisters left to explore Christabel's new hometown.

* * *

Grace motored down Graysville's main street without sparing a glance to the left or right.

Christabel nudged her. "Hey, there's the famous fountain."

Grace squinted at it. "According to which experts?"

"All of them. Let's park and check it out."

Grace muttered something rude. Still, she braked and maneuvered the car into a tight parking spot, with only a slight rebound against an adjacent SUV.

Christabel hopped out. She ran her finger along the paintwork of each vehicle before joining her sister, who was standing in front the fountain, her head tipped to one side.

"So, what's so special?" Grace asked.

A realistic bronze figure of a woman posed on a pedestal inside a shallow marble basin. Her head was lowered, her eyes were almost closed. Tears streamed down her cheeks, dripping onto the bronze letter she held in both hands, and falling into the basin beneath her.

"Not exactly the Trevi," Grace said. "But maybe a step up from the peeing boy of Brussels." Her tone mocked, but as she leaned forward to examine the sculpture more closely, she shivered.

Christabel finished reading the plaque located next to the statue. "Graysville's young male population was decimated in the early twentieth century, by the war and then by the influenza epidemic."

"So this is the universal mother?"

"Or wife."

Christabel reached out a fingertip to catch a teardrop. It was bitingly cold, and she immediately shook it off.

A pair of giggling, university-aged girls burdened by cumbersome backpacks joined them.

"You didn't actually touch that water, did you?" the shorter one asked with pseudo solemnity, as she adjusted one of her backpack's straps.

"Why?"

"You're not nearly old enough. This is Graysville's fountain of youth. At least, that's what we tell the tourists."

The taller girl took a giant step back from the fountain's perimeter, tugging her friend along with her. "My mom says the water's cursed. Or at least, it only works on super-old folks. It might actually *hurt* the two of us." She let go of her friend's arm to make the sign of the cross over her heart. She looked meaningfully at Christabel. "And, sorry, it won't help *you*, either."

The two girls giggled again, and wandered away.

"Stupid superstitious nonsense," Grace said. Still, she stuck her own fingers under the flow of simulated tears, before turning and leading the way back toward the car, her hand trailing droplets.

Behind them, the fountain trickled and tinkled musically. In addition to the tuneful effect of water hitting metal and stone, though, there was a sorrowful undertone that evoked the plaintive sound of weeping and the pain of loss.

* * *

"What can I get you two lovely ladies?"

The waitress's voice went well with her dimpled cheeks and gold-flecked hazel eyes. She appeared to be in her late forties or early fifties, with dark, bobbed hair beginning to show a few white threads. Surely too old to be called Bunny, no matter what her name badge might say.

Grace ran a nail down the laminated menu. "I'll bet your toasted western sandwich is great."

The waitress wrote something on her pad. Turning to Christabel she said, "And for you, hon?"

Hon? Okay, she'd take it from Bunny, who had such a kind smile. "I'll have the same, please."

"And don't tell us the side salads come out of a plastic bag," Grace said.

Bunny pointed to the menu with her pencil. "The coleslaw was prepared fresh this morning, and it's delicious."

"Make that two coleslaws, then," Grace said, and Bunny bustled off to place the order.

The diner was furnished with booths that appeared to be straight out of the saddle shoes and jive era. Behind the counter there were old-fashioned milkshake machines and a Bunn coffee maker. Not an espresso machine in sight.

"Do you feel like we've traveled back in time?"

"Chrissie, it's not just this restaurant. It's all of Graysville. Like an upscale Mayberry—look, there's Aunt Bea with an eye job!"

"I guess the locals do look a bit unnatural."

"It's wonderful what years of savings and juicy pensions can buy." Grace sounded almost wistful. She began to fidget with the packets of sweeteners.

Christabel studied the crowd. At least they were up to date as far as trends for the elastic-waistband set went. The room buzzed with chatter, and Christabel found herself nodding in approval.

Soon Bunny re-emerged, bearing heaping plates.

"Two westerns, hold the bagged salad." She winked at the sisters.

"May I ask you a question, Bunny?" Grace asked.

"Sure, hon."

"What does someone our age do for excitement in this town?"

"Go to Toronto. Once you've taken a photo of our fountain, there's nothing else to do here."

"What keeps you here?" Grace poked at her coleslaw with a fork.

A shadow passed across Bunny's face. "Well, I have my job. And, of course, family." She opened her mouth to add something, then snapped it closed. Abruptly, she turned on her heel and hurried to the cash register.

Christabel's skin prickled. "What do you suppose *that* was about?"

"Just more of the general weirdness of Graysville." Grace picked up her sandwich and took a bite. An expression of bliss rippled across her face. "At least the cook in this diner knows how to make some good greasy chow."

She didn't say another word until every morsel was gone. Christabel ate with much less gusto. For some reason, she was having trouble swallowing.

They left Bunny a generous tip and exited, Christabel carrying a take-out box containing most of her lunch.

"And you'd better eat it later," Grace said, turning the key in the Mazda's ignition. "I don't want to be the more gorgeous but much fatter sister."

"I'll do my best."

Christabel placed the carton carefully on the car's floor and buckled her seatbelt as Grace pulled away from the curb, narrowly missing an elderly jaywalker. The man jumped onto the sidewalk with the agility of a hurdler and shot them a dirty look. Grace chuckled and kept driving but Christabel turned around and gave him an apologetic wave. He shook a hostile fist at them. Still, she was relieved to see he was marching down the sidewalk, unscathed.

Walking like a young man, in fact.

Chapter 5: June 17, afternoon

The pain in Christabel's forehead plagued her less often these days; really, it was only bad when she saw Sam. Still, she was willing to take a whole lot of agony before she gave up visiting her only child.

She felt Grace wriggle out of her clutch. "As much as I love you, Chrissie, your hand is dripping with sweat."

Christabel wiped it on the leg of her capris, ignoring the pained look Grace shot her. "Sorry. I get nervous coming here."

"You must know what to expect by now."

"This place is just a glorified jail. And Sam's so unpredictable. God, the last time I saw her, she pushed me away."

"Well, here's a recommendation from someone who loves you: get yourself some therapy. Sam's got a good set-up here. She's A-OK. You, on the other hand, need help."

"You're probably right."

"Say it like you mean it." There wasn't a hint of the usual sardonic sparkle in Grace's eyes.

"Okay. As soon as I can set up an appointment." Christabel offered up her little finger for a pinky swear but Grace waved it away.

A youngish man with slicked-back black hair arrived in reception and buzzed the women in. Christabel hadn't met him before. Treffian House seemed to employ a large staff—she hoped it wasn't because there was frequent personnel turnover.

The orderly led them on the route that was now so familiar Christabel saw it nightly in her dreams. They crossed the main communal living space, past a Broadway-warbling octogenarian who was being unsuccessfully shushed by her irritated peers, to a quiet corner where Sam sat on the floor, surrounded by her collection of dolls.

Mrs. McKay watched from a nearby chair. "Good morning, Mrs. Mistry, and ..."

"Grace Newberry. Christabel's sister." Grace reached down and gave Mrs. McKay's square hand a brisk one-two shake.

The woman didn't rise from her chair. "Of course. The family resemblance is unmistakable. In fact, it's curious ..." She closed her mouth. The twin vertical lines between her eyebrows deepened.

Sam hadn't looked up. She was dressing a blond Barbie in a virulent pink ball gown that was on the raggedy side. Christabel was going to have to supplement the dolls' wardrobe soon.

"Please, ladies, sit down," Mrs. McKay said. "Remember, Samantha requires personal space."

Christabel chose a gray lounger and perched forward on its padded seat. After a moment, Grace sank to her knees in front of Sam.

Mrs. McKay inhaled sharply.

"Sammie! It's been ages," Grace said to the crown of Sam's bowed head, looking directly at Mrs. McKay.

Christabel held her breath.

Grace had been the one to teach Sam to swim, staying by her side in the pool and catching Sam's slippery, wriggling body only when the little girl needed help. Just weeks ago, she'd taken Sam shopping, returning home with logoed bags of summer clothes, pink for both of them, and for Barbie, too.

"Mrs. Newberry, I really must ..."

"Ms. Or just plain Grace," Grace said, edging closer to Sam.

"*Ms.* Newberry." The Scottish burr in Mrs. McKay's voice was more prominent. "Samantha is making great progress but she does not care for sudden movement or physical proximity, especially when she is playing with her dolls."

"I'm willing to take the risk. *But* of course I'll move away—if her *mother* asks me to."

"Mrs. Mistry? I must insist ..."

"That's all right," Christabel heard herself say. "Let's give them a chance."

"I know you're in there, Sammie." Grace hunkered lower, but Sam kept her focus on the doll in her lap.

A minute passed. Sam's low humming carried to Christabel's ears, along with Mrs. McKay's short, angry breaths.

Christabel's headache was gone. It made such a difference being here with Grace, her brave big sister.

"Sammie? It's me. Auntie Grace. Can you say hi?"

Sam paused in Velcroing Barbie's fake fur shawl. She was motionless for five seconds, before reaching out and picking up a pair of miniature, hot pink stilettos. She held them in the knot of her fist before pushing the shoes onto her doll's feet, one at a time, a look of fierce concentration on her face.

"Girl after my own heart, that Barbie," Grace said. "Beauty before function."

Sam put down her blond doll. She sat still, cross-legged on the rug, staring down at a spot in front of her. Slowly, she raised her head, her features emerging from her long black hair as if she were in the deep end of a pool, surfacing for air. She lifted her eyes and pushed back her glasses. Behind the smudged lenses, her gaze was serene.

Christabel slid to the very edge of her chair. Grace was connecting. If only Sam would say something, even show an expression or make a gesture that the old Sam, the *real* Sam, might make.

"Now, then, Samantha, I think that's enough for today." Mrs. McKay stood up.

"Wait a sec," Grace said, stretching out her hand.

But the moment had passed. With machinelike movements, Sam placed her toy collection into a short-handled, straw tote bag and rose. Her head drooped; her hair veiled her face. She shuffled after

Mrs. McKay like a heifer along a slaughterhouse chute. The safety door closed behind them.

Grace leapt to her feet, her eyes flashing. "What the fuck?"

Christabel couldn't control her grin. "You were brilliant!" She threw her arms around her sister.

"Yeah? Then why did I just get scorched by that fire-breathing dragon of yours? I mean, and I'm sorry, but what the *fuck*?"

"We have to take things step by step. Sam can get violent."

"Don't tell me you're on the side of that snooty Scottish bitch?"

"The only side I'll ever take is Sam's."

Grace's cheeks flamed. After a moment she smiled, warmth returning to her eyes.

"Sorry. But, holy hell, I was close there. I could almost taste it."

"I could, too."

"I won't be able to visit again for a while. Maybe a couple of weeks."

Sigh. "Yes. I know."

"And you're not allowed to do what I just did, with your concussion. And Sam's history."

"Crummy mother that I am."

"Kiddo, you're the best mom in the world. And we should know from shit mothering. If you'll cast your mind back to our own screwed-up childhoods."

"Mine wasn't so bad, Grace. I always had you."

"Brat that you were. So now listen to me. Don't lose faith."

"I won't."

"And don't take any risks. Sit back and let the sturdy Mrs. McKay be on the receiving end of anything physical."

"All right. And, Grace?"

"Yes?"

"I can't tell you how much it means that you came."

"I'll visit again, as soon as I can."

"Please do," Christabel whispered.

The two women walked to the security door and were buzzed through. They linked arms and exited Treffian House together, escaping into the late afternoon air.

Chapter 6: June 17, evening

Mama Mistry's condo was spotless, but after Grace left, Christabel worked until well past dinnertime scouring all the accessible surfaces. She'd never admit it, but she wanted to eliminate every last trace of her ex-mother-in-law.

Later on, in the shower, she tried to be positive. Be grateful for the use of this condo, so close to Sam. Do her best not to think about the old lady who used to use this tub.

Mama Mistry had never lost an opportunity to express her disappointment with her only son's choice of bride. The superstitious old woman had claimed the Jyotisha charts from her favorite Hindu astrologer told her that their marriage was bound to be cursed.

"You were full of bad intention in your past life," she told Christabel. "Papa-khatri is present on the bhava."

Whatever that meant.

As for children—the stars clearly indicated such an event would compound the bad omens. A girl child would be particularly disastrous.

Spooky old witch.

Christabel had fallen hard for Ravi. She loved his quiet authority and his intensity. He was only four years older but he seemed so much wiser, and when he held her, she felt empowered and beautiful, like a rose in sunlight. It didn't hurt, either, that he was so good-looking—tall, with skin the color of oak leaves in autumn and eyes that snapped with intelligence behind the lenses he wore to correct his extreme myopia.

"Why are you even hesitating?" Grace had demanded. "The boy has it all: strapping muscles, charm, and deep pockets. Great posture. Clean fingernails. Let's not forget, he adores you."

"But his mom—"

"You're not marrying his mother."

"I kind of am."

"Maybe she'll have the decency to die, like ours finally did."

"Grace!"

"Don't 'Grace' me. As you'll recall, Mommy Dearest was always hammered and our dad was an enabler. You've got a wonderful, sober, generous man at your fingertips. Now reach out and grab him."

And Christabel took her sister's advice.

They had a city hall wedding, with only Grace and her beau du jour in attendance. Ravi didn't tell his mother, and Christabel's dad had been AWOL for years.

"Do you take this man to be your lawfully wedded husband?" the official asked in a crackly voice. Shaggy terrier brows obscured his eyes, and he smelled faintly of whiskey.

"Yes!" Christabel's simple affirmative rang with certainty and joy.

The kiss that followed was unrestrained. Theirs was a union no person could break asunder.

But a little over a decade later, a small person named Samantha had done just that—and Mama Mistry hadn't been heartbroken when things fell apart.

The thought of her ex-mother-in-law jolted Christabel back to the present. She turned off the water and stepped out of the bathtub, frowning as she recalled the mother-in-law problems she'd experienced from the earliest days of her marriage. As she dried herself off, she felt her stomach twist in self-doubt. If she'd only been able to get closer to Mama Mistry, maybe things would have turned out better.

Ravi had told Christabel his mother would adjust to the idea of their marriage in time—but he'd been incorrect. Mama Mistry continued to insist that Ravi had made a crucial life error.

Nonetheless, in the early days, Christabel tried with all her might to win her mother-in-law's approval.

"Ravi, she hates my guts," Christabel said, holding out a tin of homemade jeera biscuits.

She'd asked Nashila in the Principal's office for the recipe and had stuck precisely to the directions. To Christabel, they tasted heavenly: sweet and salty, with the right amount of cumin. Perfect for dunking in chai.

Ravi took a cookie and nibbled its edge. His eyes lit up and he stuffed the rest of it in his mouth.

"They're fantastic, Christa. Don't worry, they won't go to waste." He patted his washboard belly.

"I know. That's the point. I made them for her and she acted as if they tasted like elephant poo."

Three years later, when Sam made her world debut, Mama Mistry stuck to her story that things were only unfolding toward a cataclysmic event.

But she hadn't bargained on losing touch with her beloved son. Ravi was so busy with work and co-parenting that he rarely visited his mother. Christabel was exhausted in her role as a new mom. She didn't miss the in-law strife but she knew Ravi felt guilty.

"Darling, I have a proposition," he said one night, when Christabel had finally rocked Sam to sleep. They lay in bed, shoulder to shoulder in the dark. Ravi stroked the back of Christabel's hand, his touch tender.

"I'm too tired, Ravi," Christabel said.

"Not that kind of proposition. You want to get back to work in a month, and we haven't been able to find a reliable nanny."

"Don't remind me."

"Well, I may have a solution."

Christabel sat up and switched on a bedside lamp. "I'm all ears. What do you have in mind?"

"OK, this is going to sound weird, but my mother's been calling me, begging me to let her take care of Sam."

"Our cursed child? The devil's spawn?" Christabel reached out, snapped the light back off, and flung herself onto her back again, feeling Ravi's body rebound from the impact.

In the end, though, that is exactly what happened. Christabel was never sure what had made Mama Mistry change her mind, but she had. And while the older woman never warmed up to her daughter-in-law, she seemed to fawn over tiny Sam, not to mention be thrilled that she was now in close, daily contact with her son. Christabel was more than happy to let Ravi do the pick-ups and drop-offs and for a while, the arrangement worked.

But Sam was a fussy baby. She cried excessively and was late to start rolling over and sitting up. By the time she could toddle, Mama Mistry had had enough, and when a spot came open in a reputable city-run daycare, Christabel and Ravi transferred Sam there. The staff was patient, but the little girl continued to lag behind the other kids, and Mama Mistry went back to blaming all of her son's problems on having married the wrong woman.

Then came the awful day.

"Mrs. Mistry." The silver-haired pediatrician tugged his earlobe. "If I can have your attention."

"I'm trying," Christabel said, attempting to get hold of her grunting, squirming three-year-old.

Why was Ravi always at the office when she needed him? She had a job, too, but their daughter's well-being was supposed to be their top priority.

"I have some challenging news to share. Perhaps we could ask Ms. Perry to take Samantha aside for a few minutes."

He went to the door and beckoned. A young nurse's aide appeared. She sized up the situation, clamped Sam's arms to her sides, and whisked her away. The consulting room door closed on the little girl's shrieks. Christabel flinched but didn't intercede. Much as she dreaded it, she needed to sit still and listen.

"Mrs. Mistry, I know this is difficult, but we don't have a neat and tidy term to sum up your daughter's condition."

"At least tell me you can help her. Us, too."

He ran a hand over his forehead and studied his notes. "While Samantha's language comprehension skills appear to be gradually developing, her reasoning skills are well below the norm, and she has certain behaviors that are atypical. Her unexplained rages, for example, and her struggles in social settings. Her repetitive movements, too."

Christabel stared into the man's kind, blue eyes and wondered how this had happened to her own sweet child. Who'd been so wanted by both parents. Who should have been leading a charmed life, full of learning and music and joy.

"She's going to need support," he added. "The combined forces of her parents, the medical experts and the educational system."

"What should I tell her caregivers? And my husband?"

"For now, we'll apply the general term of PDD-NOS: Pervasive Developmental Disorder - Not Otherwise Specified."

"Oh, God."

At the time everything had seemed overwhelming. But as a family they should have been able to cope—shouldn't they?

Instead, they fell apart. Ravi left first. Then, all these years later, Sam was taken away.

And now, Christabel was living in exile, courtesy of Ravi's mom. Mama Mistry was probably spinning in her grave.

Christabel turned down the corner of the sheets and sat on the edge of the mattress, brushing her hair. Tears began to roll down her cheeks.

The bitch.

No, admit it. The son-of-a-bitch.

Instead of being there for his family, Ravi had fallen to bits. Mama Mistry had shunned both child and mother, but she hadn't promised to be there in sickness and in health. It had been Ravi's inability to cope with the demands of a special needs child—his own daughter—that had shocked Christabel. Broken her heart. Made her resolve that she'd be there for Sam—no matter what. She'd be her daughter's rock—the opposite of what her own parents had been.

When Ravi eventually left, dispensing his thirty pieces of silver with guilty generosity, Christabel made the toughest decision of her life: she gave up the teaching job she treasured, and threw heart and soul into the challenge of parenting Sam by herself, determined to be her champion.

Some champion. She had failed Sam, utterly.

In the distance, Christabel's cellphone rang. She traced the sound to the kitchen, wiping her eyes with the back of her hand.

"Hello?" Her voice shook.

"Christa? It's Ravi." His baritone was deep and warm. "Are you settling in okay?"

"Yes, thanks. Grace helped, and I've unpacked most of my things. The condo's ideal."

"Glad you like it, darling."

Darling. Even after all their tribulations. She hated herself for responding with a feeling of lightness as the knot in her shoulders loosened.

"How's Sam?" he asked, in a tone that begged for a positive answer.

"She's improving," she said. "Today, Grace almost—"

"That's such good news. You must be thrilled."

Surely, they both should be thrilled. She let it go.

"Are you planning to visit soon? Dr. Cheung wants to see us together to discuss Sam's progress."

"Very soon. Once the current blip has corrected. I've been moving holdings around, trying to avoid the worst of the downturn."

Money first. His daughter's well-being way, way behind. Nothing had changed.

"Sam needs to see you. You're her *dad.*"

"Absolutely, darling. I want to see her, too, of course. And, *you.* Maybe we can have lunch? Graysville has some fantastic wineries."

Christabel let her breath out slowly.

"Darling?"

"Good-bye."

She put the phone down and walked away.

Chapter 7; June 18

From the official records of the late Mrs. Audrey McKay (MSW), formerly of Treffian House

Transcribed from recorded session with Samantha Mistry. Handwritten notes indicated in italics

McKay: Good evening. May I join you, Samantha? It's lovely here on the sun porch, isn't it?

Mistry: Mmmmmm

McKay: This is my favorite spot in all of Treffian House. [Aside to an orderly: Thank you, Robert. I'll take it from here.]

Mistry: [No response]

McKay: You have fewer dolls with you than usual. I see your blond one is all dressed up, ready to go to the ball again.

Mistry: Mmmmmm

McKay: Has the wee Barbie that looks like you gone to bed early? You usually have her with you.

Mistry: [Says nothing but stops fussing with blond Barbie's faux-fur stole. The girl lifts her head and, although it's problematic to tell because the lenses of her glasses need a good wiping, meets my gaze. After more than a month of residency, this is an important development. I must admit to a moment of exhilaration.

I restrain myself from saying anything or moving. Within seconds, Samantha's focal point drops to the floor in front of her]

Mistry: Baaaa

McKay: Pardon me, Samantha?

Mistry: Baaaa [She is becoming agitated. She shakes her head back and forth and drops her blond doll]

McKay: Please, Samantha, take a few deep breaths. In slowly, out slowly.

Mistry: BAAAA! [I confess that I have played the recording several times. While I can't be positive, it may in fact be closer to "bad"]

McKay: Samantha, are you—[At this point, Samantha reaches down and pulls out the darker-skinned Barbie she'd apparently been sitting on. She begins to shake the doll violently. She hammers the doll's head onto the wooden floor of the sunporch]

Mistry: [She screams, her words garbled]

McKay: Samantha, please stop what you are doing. Calm down!

Mistry: [More screaming; she begins to beat the doll against her own head]

McKay: Robert! Robert!

* * *

Observations: I began this session with professional optimism but had to cut it short due to Samantha's extreme agitation which required intervention—a very disappointing outcome. I thought we had achieved a breakthrough.

This is not the first time she has mistreated her Hawaiian Barbie; yet she keeps it with her at all times.

Did she really say the word "bad?" I cannot be sure; maybe it is wishful thinking on my part that she verbalized anything.

Samantha had to be physically subdued. She was sedated and put in soft restraints in her bedroom until she fell asleep.

I fear this brief outburst may influence Dr. Cheung in reinstating Samantha's Rohibital prescription.

I shall have a word with him at the first opportunity.

Chapter 8; June 19

Mama Mistry's coal black eyes bored into hers. The old woman's thoughts scratched their way into Christabel's consciousness.

You ruined my son's life. I curse you.

Mama Mistry stretched out a liver-splotched hand and seized Christabel's chin. Her eyes were merciless. She tightened her grip, and there was a red haze of agony and the sound of teeth grinding together. Or was it bracelets clanking?

Or perhaps it was knocking. On the door.

Christabel sat bolt upright. Sunlight was streaming through a chink in the curtains. Her hands went to her chin. *Thank God.* Still, her whole body shook as she swung her legs out of bed.

Another volley of rapping. Throwing on a robe, she ran to the front door, dragging a hand through sleep-tousled hair.

A stout woman was limping away along the sidewalk. She was dressed head to heel in burgundy: baggy shorts, golf shirt and runners.

"Hello," Christabel called. She clutched her thick, terry housecoat to her neck, partly for decency's sake and partly because the morning air had an un-summery snap to it.

The woman turned around in an ungainly way, favoring her left leg. She had hair that had once been blond, now faded to a yellowy gray. Her wideset blue eyes gave her an air of childlike innocence, and they crinkled at the corners, deepening the network of fine lines that traversed her face. She limped forward, holding a plastic container in both hands.

"You *are* home. Oh dear, did I wake you?" She spoke like a chickadee in springtime, in rapid-fire spurts. "My husband always told me I was more early bird than human."

"No, no—I'm awake." Christabel fought the urge to yawn.

"Aren't you sweet to lie so politely. Now, first things first. My name is Amanda Browning—call me Mandy, everyone does—I'm your closest neighbor."

Mandy pointed her nose at the next bungalow, partially obscured by a stand of lilac bushes festooned with fading blooms. Their overblown scent smelled like cologne sprayed on something dead. Christabel took an involuntary step back.

"Oh, and I've brought you a little housewarming something-something," Mandy continued. "Brownies with walnuts. Baked fresh this morning."

Mandy shut her mouth with a pop. For a second there was welcome silence, before she rattled on. "Dear, dear. I'm doing it again, aren't I? Martin always told me to when to stop."

Christabel cinched the belt on her robe before taking the Tupperware from Mandy's hands. "It's lovely to meet you, Mandy." She put on a warm smile. "I'm Christabel. Please come in for coffee—and a couple of these yummy-looking brownies." She ushered Mandy over the threshold.

"Yes, well, I'm over the moon to have a new neighbor. In the summer everyone around here goes to the cottage. In the winter they head for Florida. That leaves me and Martin—only of course he passed two years ago."

"I'm so sorry," Christabel said.

Mandy let out a tremulous breath and nodded. "The old Indian lady who used to live in this unit was a real meanie. We were so happy when they carted her away, kicking and screaming. There's Alzheimer's and then there's Alzheimer's—the raving, spitting kind. Treated me and Martin like dirt."

Christabel laughed. "Me, too. And I was her daughter-in-law."

Mandy's jaw dropped. "Tell me you're joking!"

"It's okay: I agree with you. She was nasty to just about everyone, except her son. My ex."

She walked the short hallway to the kitchen, Mandy bumping along close behind.

"I'm sorry to be staggering like a drunk hobo. I'm on the list for hip replacement surgery. Can't wait to start walking normally, maybe even jogging."

Mandy attempted a one-two caper. Her breasts heaved under her golf shirt, making the alligator logo dance. She stopped and clapped a hand to her hip.

"It's depressing how much weight I've put on, what with this arthritic joint of mine. And of course, Martin's passing." Her face crumpled.

"It must be very difficult." Christabel waved her new neighbor to a stool at the breakfast bar and held out a box of tissues.

Mandy gave her nose a honk. To allow her some privacy, Christabel found the coffee, and started to figure out her new brewing machine. Within minutes, the aroma of French roast filled the room.

"You mustn't think I'm always bawling." Mandy accepted a steaming mug, but raised a hand like a traffic cop, refusing the brownies. "Yes, cream, please, and sugar, too. We must have our little treats. But some days are harder than others. And I know I've let myself go. I've had to buy bigger clothes, two sizes up! Martin wouldn't mind; he was always partial to a curvy woman." She began to well up again.

Christabel hastily bit into a brownie. "He sounds like a wonderful man. A lucky one, too, especially if you baked for him like this."

Mandy's round cheeks turned pink. "I do *so* love making brownies for folks, and you can certainly use a few calories. I shouldn't, but it's not every day I get to meet a new neighbor, is it?" She chose the biggest brownie in the container and began munching.

Christabel glanced at the kitchen clock. Eight fifteen. Mandy really had been up early to bake these brownies. They were still warm, densely chewy in the middle, and without doubt the most delicious thing Christabel had tasted in weeks. Maybe the *first* thing she'd tasted in weeks.

Mandy finished her coffee. She smacked her lips and gave Christabel a chocolatey smile. "I'd better let you get ready for work."

"I don't work. Yet. But I hope to get a job soon."

"The wineries are often hiring. You know, for people to pour for tastings. Or just walk around town and look for Help Wanted signs. As long as you're okay with making minimum wage."

"Good idea. I'll think about it."

Christabel followed the track of Mandy's gaze. *Damn.* She'd left the folder for Treffian House on the end of the kitchen counter. Mandy's eyes sparkled with curiosity.

"Are you seeing Dr. Cheung, dear? For his special services?"

"I'm not sure what you mean." Christabel swept the brochure into a drawer.

"He does cosmetic touch-ups. On top of being our best GP and taking care of all those unfortunate souls at Treffian House."

Christabel hesitated. Mandy seemed understanding. But how would she react to hearing that Christabel had locked her only child away?

"I have a daughter there. Samantha is sixteen and has special needs."

Saying the words out loud caused a wave of sorrow to climb Christabel's spine. She sank onto her stool, face in hands. Pain zinged through her head.

"You poor thing." Mandy got up awkwardly and put her arms around Christabel's shoulders. "She's in excellent hands at Treffian."

Christabel eased herself out of Mandy's embrace and rubbed her forehead with her fingertips. This was no time to break down. Mandy seemed like a kind woman, but she was a stranger.

Mandy sat back down. "I'm sure you didn't move her into Treffian House without good reason, my dear. And you're nearby. Try to see the bright side."

Christabel blinked. "I'll do my best."

"Dr. Cheung is excellent."

"He's been elusive. I must admit I've had my doubts."

"Nonsense; he's just busy. One day we'll eat a whole pan of brownies and you can tell me the full story. But Martin would say, there I go again. Like Mrs. Kravitz on an old Bewitched re-run."

Christabel gave a shaky laugh.

Mandy beamed at her. "I must admit I'm a naturally curious person."

"Fair warning. Thank you."

Christabel stood and watched as Mandy walked with uneven steps the short distance home, before going back inside to get dressed. She hoped sharing the story would get easier with repetition.

Anyway, it was reassuring to have Mandy next door. Someone solid and ordinary.

Chapter 9: June 20

Christabel stared at her reflection in the bathroom mirror. Interesting how she could look this composed. Apart from the shadows beneath her warm brown eyes, her face was smooth and serene.

She applied her cover-up stick, gently blending the color with her right index finger, erasing the under-eye circles. Passable. But she was too pale. She dabbed china doll circles of liquid blush on her cheekbones, massaging them until she achieved a natural-looking glow.

Good enough. Ravi was coming to see Sam, not her.

She closed her eyes and gripped her ring finger. God, the helpless, tumbling feelings only he could bring out in her. Ravi, who made the tiny hairs on Christabel's arms rise when he smiled at her from across the kitchen table. Ravi, who smelled of cloves and leather, with a hint of mown grass.

But he had moved out. He'd left her to manage alone.

It hadn't been a single event; it had been one too many meltdowns the year Sam turned twelve. Up until that evening Ravi had coped, hanging in, grim-faced, doing what he could. But this time he'd snapped.

"I can't do this anymore," he said when they'd finally calmed Sam down and tucked her into bed. "And you shouldn't have to, either."

Christabel looked up from where she squatted with the dust pan and whiskbroom, sweeping up shards of inexpensive dinnerware. Their original, more elegant set had been smashed, piece by piece, months earlier.

"She's our daughter."

"I know. But, one of these days we'll lose control completely. She needs to be in a safer setting."

Christabel dropped the dust pan on the tiles. Slowly, she rose to her full height, just reaching the level of his chin.

"We've talked about this so many times. *This* is her home."

Within days, he packed his bags and left. In an instant, she became a single mother.

Much, much worse, her daughter lost the father she adored.

Sam had taken out her anger and grief on her mom. Even now, years later, Christabel often sensed resentment in Sam's gaze.

She wandered into her bedroom and began gathering up the clothes she'd tried on earlier that morning. Shaking her head at her own idiocy, she found hangers and put things away. She looked down at herself and evaluated her denim skirt and cream-colored T-shirt. On her feet, sensible flat sandals. A perfect, I'm-not-trying-too-hard outfit.

Even after all the pain he'd caused her, she still felt drawn to him. She'd loved the man so much.

The doorbell rang, and an involuntary smile lifted the corners of her mouth as she hurried to the front hall. When she saw Ravi on the porch, as ruggedly appealing as he'd been the first time she'd caught sight of him, she wanted to pitch herself into his arms.

"Hi." She stood back to allow him to enter.

"Christa, darling."

He moved toward her, arms open, but she offered her hand instead. Recovering his poise, he wrapped her slim hand in his strong, broad one, sending an electrical charge racing throughout her nervous system.

She forced a remote smile onto her face, withdrew from Ravi's clasp, and ushered him into his mother's old home. Once he was seated at the breakfast bar, she poured coffee into two mugs and settled herself in a spot two stools over.

"Looks like you've lived here for years." He took a sip.

He'd always taken his coffee black with sugar. She'd made it for him every morning, and afterward his kisses would taste dark-roasted and sweet.

Enough of that.

"Thanks for having the condo cleaned."

"My pleasure. Feel free to add your own personal touches. Whatever it takes to make it your home."

"I doubt I'll be staying for more than a few months."

Ravi put his mug down. "What do you mean?"

"Well, I hope to find a place of my own—"

"Why would you do that? You know what's mine is yours."

His baritone resonated from the crown of her head, down the nape of her neck. She had no bones, but way too many quivering nerve endings.

"No, Ravi. Once the deal closes on the house, I'll look for an apartment in Graysville with a room for Sam."

His gaze was steady. He stretched out an arm, and before Christabel could pull back, he took her hand.

"Sam will never be able to live in the outside world."

Christabel snatched her hand away. "How can you say that?"

His face was impassive. "You know it's true. You've done more than what's humanly possible, but Sam's dangerous. Just look what she did to you, her own mother."

Christabel covered her ears. After a moment she dropped her hands.

"She can't be locked up forever. I can't bear the thought."

Ravi rose from his stool. He seemed suddenly much older.

"Christa, we signed the papers. It's not up to us anymore."

"But when she gets better—"

"*If* she improves, the decision will be made by someone else. Meanwhile, she has access to top-quality therapy. And *you* are safe, which makes it possible for me to sleep at night."

Christabel stood facing Ravi in the kitchen, arms at her sides. She could feel the weight of sorrow on her shoulders and when she looked at her ex-husband, she knew, by his uncharacteristic slump, that he felt it, too.

"I just love her so much," she said.

"I know, Christa. I know."

The room was quiet. Christabel became aware of the clock's slight electronic tick. Outside in the yard, birds were singing, without a care in the world.

* * *

"Welcome to the Graysville Diner. May I take your order?"

The words could have been spoken by a robot.

Christabel looked up from her menu. Bunny was puffy-faced and disheveled. Not sloppy, precisely, but not fresh from the ironing board, either.

"Thank you, Bunny. I've just been describing your tasty coleslaw to my friend." She noted Ravi's flinch. "But, hey, are you okay?"

"I'm sorry, dear." Bunny shifted from one foot to the other and back, wincing. "I shouldn't have agreed to work a double shift yesterday." She continued to wait, face drawn, pen poised above her order pad.

"All right, then, I'm going to have the grilled cheese sandwich, along with the slaw, please. And Ravi?"

"I'll take the three-egg omelet with fries." He waited until Bunny had trundled off before adding, "Not exactly service with a smile."

"It's odd. When I was here last week, she was all charm and personality."

"Told you we should have tried a winery."

Christabel twisted her hands together in her lap.

"Darling, we need to live our lives," Ravi said, his voice low.

Christabel met his gaze and, like always, felt the tug of his dark eyes.

She had to focus on the upcoming visit with Sam. She needed to think of ways to make it positive. Ravi hadn't been comfortable around their daughter for years, but at least the last time he'd seen her, she'd been able to talk. Maybe only in short phrases, but intelligibly.

Under the tabletop, Christabel began to shred a paper napkin into ribbons.

* * *

"The smell leaves something to be desired," Ravi said, as they were buzzed through.

"You'll get used to it." Christabel scanned the room for Sam.

"I doubt that."

Never adjust to the odor, or not come often enough to have the chance? Likely the latter.

"Where's Sam?" he said, managing to sound both bored and irritated.

"Probably on her way." Christabel walked over to the rug where she usually spent time with Sam, along with her trusty watchdog, Mrs. McKay.

The room was crowded today. Several white-haired women dressed in mint pastel housecoats were parked in front of the big-screen TV, gazing blearily at a close-captioned sit-com. An aide hovered nearby—the guy with the slicked-back hair. Good, he hadn't quit yet. In another corner, three teens around Sam's age were playing a raucous card game meant for younger children. They were overseen by two young, benevolent-looking women Christabel hadn't met yet.

Ravi jolted every time one of the card-playing kids yelled. He'd always hated disruption. His eyelids used to flicker when a younger Sam screamed.

Mrs. McKay strode toward them, Sam trailing behind, wearing a flamingo-pink summer dress—one of the outfits she'd bought on her last shopping spree with Grace, perhaps? Sam was carrying two of her dolls, and her hair was tied up neatly in a ponytail. She'd never sat still long enough to let Christabel style it like that.

Christabel's eyes welled up. Sam looked so much like her dad—shiny black hair, honey-hued skin. Glasses. The erect way she moved when she was happy, as if she were attached to marionette strings. God, those ballet lessons of long ago—Sam doing her utmost to keep pace with the other little girls, her face aglow and her body moving awkwardly to the piano accompaniment.

"Here we are, then, Samantha." Mrs. McKay pointed to a spot on the rug. "And, it appears we have a special visitor for you today. It's a pleasure to meet you at last, Mr. Mistry."

"Hi, Sam." Ravi didn't spare Mrs. McKay as much as a glance. He sat stone-like in his chair, hands on knees.

Sam didn't acknowledge him. She arranged her legs to one side, as though she were riding side-saddle. The effect was ruined when she took her dark-haired doll, gave it a rattling shake that messed up its hair, and crammed it under her skirt.

"Now, Samantha, we've talked about this," Mrs. McKay said.

Sam picked up blond Barbie. She began to stroke its gleaming hair. Christabel detected humming.

"Hello, Sam. It's Mom," she said and grimaced at herself. *You're not calling her on the phone.*

"Samantha has made some progress lately, Mr. Mistry," Mrs. McKay said, raising her gaze. "Apart from one rather severe anxiety attack within the past week, she is learning the routines here. She has been granted more privileges. We are proud of her, as Dr. Cheung will share with you momentarily."

"That's good to hear," Ravi said—flatly.

"Best of all, there are signs that she is beginning to speak again."

Christabel almost jumped up from her chair.

"Really?"

"It may still take time. But my prediction is that we may get a word or two from her in the next week or so."

Ravi stared at Sam, as she continued to stroke her blond doll's hair. His lack of animation was troubling. Yet, when he looked over at Christabel, there was a sudden lightening of his expression.

Minutes passed—Sam preoccupied with her Barbie. The three adults watched her in silence. Christabel's mind wandered, remembering evenings spent playing dolls with eight-year-old Sam, the two of them cozy in front of the fireplace, Ravi sitting nearby in the wingchair.

Sam looked up, as if aware of her mother's thoughts. Was that a beam of recognition in her daughter's eyes?

Mrs. McKay said, "I believe our visiting time is over, Samantha."

Christabel turned toward Ravi, but he was gazing expectantly at Mrs. McKay, like a pupil eager for dismissal.

"If you'll be so good as to wait in the reception area after Samantha and I leave, a nurse will take you to meet with Dr. Cheung," Mrs. McKay said.

"Finally," Christabel murmured.

Mrs. McKay raised disapproving eyebrows. "He is a very busy man, Mrs. Mistry, and he prefers to meet with the father and mother at the same time. It minimizes miscommunication."

"Point taken," Ravi said, heading off Christabel's retort. "My fault entirely."

Mrs. McKay nodded and beckoned to Sam, who rose, holding both dolls. With hesitant steps, and not looking back, Sam followed behind the woman's solid, tweedy back.

As the mismatched pair reached the security door, Christabel could have sworn she heard her daughter utter a single word. *Daddy.* By the slight hitch in Mrs. McKay's tread, she could tell the other woman had heard it, too.

But when Christabel turned to grab Ravi's arm, he was already halfway to the door.

* * *

Dr. Cheung rose from his ergonomic chair, a spiky piece of furniture with levers and knobs jutting out on both sides. Its techno gimmickry provided a stark contrast to the dark woods and upholstery in the rest of the office. A bay window behind him threw golden light on his head and shoulders, casting his features into shadow.

He moved out from behind the bulwark of his desk, and waved them forward. As Christabel sank into a visitor's chair, she was able to study the man who had total control over her daughter's well-being.

Dr. Cheung was youthful, possibly too young to be the person in charge here. She was surprised he didn't wear a white coat; he was dressed in a buttoned-down blue shirt and knife-edged dark trousers. He was good-looking in a cherubic, round-faced way, accentuated by his circular, wire-framed glasses. His black hair was as thick as a teenager's and his straight eyebrows rode high above his dark gray eyes, endowing him with a pleased, inquisitive expression.

"Mr. and Mrs. Mistry, it's a pleasure to meet you both." He had an almost indiscernible accent, Mandarin perhaps. Christabel stared at the diplomas and certificates hanging on the wall behind his desk. There were an impressive number of them, all from Ivy League universities. She was startled to see he had acquired his medical accreditation so long ago—before she had even started university.

"Yes, I am older than I look," he said with a mischievous smile.

"If only all of us were as fortunate," Ravi said.

"Good, strong genes," Dr. Cheung replied. "A squeaky-clean lifestyle, too, but I always think that makes me sound boring."

Christabel leaned forward in her chair. "We'd like to hear your impressions of Sam."

"An interesting case, your daughter," Dr. Cheung said, sitting back down and maneuvering his mouse to refresh his computer screen. "As you know, when she arrived, several weeks ago now, she was in a psychotic state. Screaming, biting, striking out. When she failed to calm down, we had no choice but to sedate her with strong inhibitors."

"Rohibital." Christabel said, and experienced a familiar pang.

"Yes. And also, in the early days, Anxidor, an effective anti-hallucinatory remedy. We had to use a pharmaceutical spectrum approach at first in order to bring Samantha to a point where she was of no danger to herself or to other residents and staff."

"I saw her two weeks later," Christabel said. "She was still right out of it," She lifted a hand to her forehead and rubbed it.

"I know how upsetting it can be to witness a loved one in such a condition. It takes time to refine and pinpoint the exact dosage. She is no longer on Anxidor. We are introducing an SSRI instead. Gradually, of course, so that her system can adjust."

"Could you please keep us up to date on her prescriptions?"

"Darling, Dr. Cheung and his people are experts." Ravi patted Christabel's hand.

She glared at him. "I just want the information. That's okay, isn't it, Dr. Cheung?"

"Of course. A nurse will keep you informed."

Christabel bit her tongue. For now, this would have to do.

"Now, as to Samantha's diagnosis, we agree with her previous panel of doctors—no firm label beyond profound developmental delay. We may refine this as she adjusts to her new surroundings. Hormonal fluctuations may precipitate outbursts or at least influence their severity. We'll keep strict records to see if there is indeed a correlation."

"I believe there is. She was never violent when she was smaller," Christabel said, looking to Ravi. He stared at his hands.

"We also have observed that Samantha suffers from high levels of anxiety and depression," Dr. Cheung said.

"Who wouldn't," Christabel whispered.

Dr. Cheung smiled, his round face angelic. "I sympathize. With both of you, and with Samantha, too, of course. But from a clinical point of view, her rages are significant–including the final incident that involved you, Mrs. Mistry."

There was an interval of silence. Christabel felt Ravi's concern as tangibly as if he were holding her hand. Her spine straightened.

"What's the long-term prognosis, Dr. Cheung? Will Sam be released? I'm not talking tomorrow, or even a month from now. I just mean one day, eventually."

The doctor took off his wire-framed glasses and began to polish them with a cloth he withdrew from a case on the desk. He put them back on slowly, wrapping the curved side arms around his ears.

"I make a point of never sugar-coating the truth," he said. "Based on the observations I have made to date, Samantha will need to stay at Treffian House, or another similar group home, for an indeterminate period of time. Perhaps even the rest of her life."

Christabel leaned forward. "But if things change ..."

"There is always a chance. In this case, and I regret having to deliver such unwelcome news, it's a remote one. It is my professional opinion that Samantha will need long-term supervision and professional care."

"Which Treffian House will provide," Ravi said.

"For the time being." Christabel narrowed her eyes at him before turning back to the doctor. "I appreciate everything you and the staff are doing here, Dr. Cheung, but I need to believe she may be well enough one day to come home."

"You have that prerogative," Dr. Cheung said. "And I have ultimate respect for the power of a mother's love."

He stood up and shook Ravi's hand, then turned to Christabel and took hers. She could feel the man's confidence in his grip, and her own resolution rose.

Chapter 10; June 23

Whoever was pounding on Christabel's front door wouldn't give up. It couldn't be Mandy this early in the morning, and Ravi had returned to the city.

She'd been having such a pleasant dream, too. Christabel and an eager, chatting, ten-year-old Sam had been walking along the beach, laughing at the skirling seagulls–

Christabel jolted upright. *Sam.* Whoever was doing the hammering might be bringing urgent news about Sam.

Heart lodged in her throat, Christabel threw back the covers and sprang out of bed. She didn't stop to put on her terry robe but ran to the condo's entranceway and flung open the door.

"Yes–what is it?" she cried.

A vaguely familiar woman stood on the porch, rain soaking her shoulders and flattening her hair.

"You don't recognize me, Mrs. Mistry." The woman's hazel eyes brimmed with despair.

Christabel blinked. "Bunny?"

"I only have a few minutes. You have to listen to me!"

"Why? And how did you get my address?"

Bunny cast a furtive look to both sides and stepped closer. Christabel inched her way backward, behind the protection of the door.

"I need to talk to you. Please!"

Christabel looked past Bunny to the ratty, old Jeep Cherokee in the driveway. It was filled to the roof with suitcases and boxes, the gaping trunk bungee-corded shut. In the front passenger seat there sat a scarecrow of a young man, his head tipped back against the safety rest. He appeared to be fast asleep.

Christabel opened the door wider. "All right. Tell me whatever it is you need to say."

"You have a daughter at Treffian. I've seen you there. You need to know ..." Bunny's face twisted in anguish.

"Take your time." Christabel shivered.

"There *is* no time!" Bunny choked on a sob. She gestured to the Jeep. "My son. Twenty-two years old—the light of my life."

"Bunny—"

"Look at him. He's almost in a coma. He was a healthy young man a year ago. Nobody will help me. The police say I'm crazy. And certainly none of the staff at Treffian House will admit they did anything wrong."

"Oh my God." Christabel beckoned for the woman to enter, but Bunny shook her head.

"I have to go, now that I got my son out of there."

"You didn't sign over your parental rights?"

"What? No, never. I registered him for a limited convalescence. He, well, he agreed to it. It was after his suicide attempt last year." Bunny closed her eyes for an instant. "But listen! There's something wrong with that place. Last month he began to dwindle away. Aftereffects of pneumonia caused by aspiration, they said. Oxygen depletion in his brain, or some such rubbish."

"Bunny, I'm so sorry. But maybe—"

"Yeah, so maybe he aspirated. But he was a strong, young man a few months ago. They did something to him."

Bunny stopped abruptly. Mandy, limping badly, was rushing up the walk to Christabel's condo. She wore rubber boots and a yellow slicker, its hood covering her graying hair.

"Hello, Christabel. And Bunny."

Bunny's gaze panned from Mandy to Christabel, her eyes filled with terror.

"It's very early, dear," Mandy said, catching her breath. "Christabel here is still in her nightie. Why don't you come to my place for a nice cup of coffee and a chat?"

Bunny turned her back on Mandy and grabbed Christabel's bare forearms, pulling her close.

"Get your daughter out of there." She released Christabel and ran back to her vehicle. "And then, get the hell out of Graysville!" She slammed the car door. There was a squeal of spinning tires as she revved the engine and peeled away from the curb.

After a moment, Mandy put a clammy hand on the small of Christabel's back and gently pushed her into the bungalow. "Well, now, that was very sad, wasn't it?"

While Mandy removed her sodden gear in the entranceway, Christabel collapsed onto a couch in the living room. She clutched a cushion and started to shake.

"Can I get your robe for you, dear?"

Christabel pointed down the hall. "On a hook. Inside the bathroom door."

"Back in a jiff."

In spite of having to drag her left leg, Mandy motored down the hall and fetched the bathrobe. She wrapped Christabel in it, as tenderly as if she were swaddling an infant.

"What was that about, anyway?" Christabel's teeth chattered. A pain began to drill inside her forehead.

"Hush." Mandy put her arms around Christabel. "A disturbed woman, that's all. Angry at the universe."

"I met her before, at the diner. She seemed so sane."

"First impressions can deceive. I only know her casually, myself. Obviously, she's not what she appeared to be."

"Her son, though. She said he was at Treffian House."

"I know what you're thinking. But you have to stop. Sometimes people get sicker even if they have the finest healthcare in the world." Mandy eased Christabel back against the sofa cushions. She tilted her head to one side, frowning. "Your daughter is in the top treatment facility in the province."

"How can you be so certain?"

"Because I personally have known many people who have benefitted from being there. Your own mother-in-law, for example. Got A-one, personalized treatment, God rest her soul. You've done your own research on the place, right?"

Christabel nodded.

"Then you know their reputation. Dr. Cheung is the best there is."

"But Bunny said ..."

"I know. She's broken-hearted."

"In her situation, I'd behave exactly the same way."

Mandy assessed her with dispassionate eyes. "Not if I'm any judge of character, dear."

Christabel was silent for a moment. Then she reached out and patted Mandy's hand. "Thank you for coming to my rescue."

"That's what neighbors are for."

At the door, Mandy climbed into her rubber boots and donned her dripping jacket. Christabel watched her hobble home. The early morning rain soaked into the thirsty grass. A robin, delving into the ground with a greedy yellow beak, emerged with a juicy worm.

Christabel's thoughts raced, keeping pace with her galloping heartbeat and making her head ache. She went in search of the iPad Ravi had bought for her. She was online in seconds.

She scrolled past the ads and found the official site for Treffian House. Nothing new. When an extensive search turned up accolade after accolade, she switched over to check out Dr. Paul Cheung.

Dr. Cheung has the patience of Job.

I am not the easiest of clients, but Dr. Cheung counselled me throughout my hip replacement journey with unceasing care and expertise.

Dr. Cheung did what no other doctor could do: he cured my bad back!

My twelve-year-old son, diagnosed with autism spectrum disorder, was helped immensely by Dr. Cheung and his dedicated staff at Treffian House. If only we hadn't had to move away from Graysville!

The rave reviews went on and on. What would Bunny have made of them?

Not every patient was curable, as Mandy had pointed out. The odds were that Sam was in excellent hands.

She ignored the prickly sensation between her shoulder blades—living in Mama Mistry's condo didn't mean she had to adopt her mother-in-law's superstitious ways. Christabel would be calm and rational and work with the well-reviewed professionals at Treffian House. Science and consistency, combined with love, would find a way.

Chapter 11; June 24

From the official records of the late Mrs. Audrey McKay (MSW), formerly of Treffian House

Transcribed from recorded session with Samantha Mistry. Handwritten notes indicated in italics

McKay: Samantha, I think it's time we tidied up your room a little. Let's see; I'll hand you items and you can put them away.

Mistry: [No answer, but she rises from her bed]

McKay: Here is the lovely pink dress that you wore when your parents visited. Dear me, it is all crumpled up. I'll find a hanger, shall I?

Mistry: Mmmmmm [Samantha does as she's asked. This is real progress]

McKay: And here are your sandals. It's nice you're allowed to wear your own shoes now; you've worked hard to earn this privilege.

Mistry: [Sits on the floor and begins arranging shoes, matching them in pairs. This takes several minutes]

McKay: Samantha, you have done a very good job. I'm proud of you.

Mistry: Mmmmmm [She fiddles with the buckle of a sandal]

McKay: Would you like to go outside for a short walk? Everything is fresh and clean after yesterday's rain. You could bring a sunhat.

Mistry: [No response. Continues playing with the sandal]

McKay: I'll get it for you, shall I? And would you like to bring one of your special dolls?

Mistry: [Accepts the sunhat and rises from the floor]

McKay: You keep them all so tidy.

Mistry: [Takes her two usual dolls, dark and blond, off the dresser]

McKay: You've hardly touched some of them. This red-haired one is still in the box.

Mistry: Nnaahh [She moves to block me]

McKay: I won't touch your doll if you don't want me to, Samantha. Please do try to use your words, though. Now then, shall we go?

* * *

Observations: Samantha Mistry is still nonverbal; however, it is clear that she understands everything I say. She is cooperative and willing to do small chores. We had a walk in the fenced-in area of the grounds. Even though she made no attempt to communicate, as long as I didn't get too close, she showed no sign of agitation.

She continues to be obsessed with her doll collection, favoring some over others. Perhaps I will understand more in time.

Chapter 12; June 26

Christabel sat in an old-fashioned porch swing built for two, rocking herself back and forth. Across from her, Mrs. McKay and Sam perched on a matching swing, swaying to a faster rhythm. Sam's sneakered foot was doing the pushing.

"Mrs. McKay?"

The woman looked up, eyebrows raised. Christabel wasn't sure how to proceed. *Have you been poisoning any of your patients recently?*

Sam looked pink-cheeked and content. In fact, every day she improved. According to her keepers, she was on the verge of being able to speak. It was like all those internet reviews said—Treffian House was a marvelous institution with a first-rate staff.

"Never mind."

Mrs. McKay sat back, her eyes half-closed. The lines that bracketed her mouth were less prominent today. She looked like someone who'd once been young.

"Thank goodness for the breeze," Christabel said, to break the silence.

"Yes, it helps. And Samantha loves this porch." Mrs. McKay glanced over. "Naturally, she's always supervised."

"Of course."

Silence again, apart from the occasional snatch of melody, hummed under Sam's breath. For once, she had no doll with her. She held the chair's side support up high, like a lady with a torch, the other hand resting in her lap. She was the image of sanity.

If only she'd speak.

"Hey, Sam, do you like this hot weather?" Inane, but Christabel had to keep trying.

Mrs. McKay nodded approvingly. They waited to see if Sam would respond. Nothing.

Sam pushed off with her foot again. She'd always loved swings. After Ravi assembled the set in their backyard more than a decade ago, they all spent the afternoon outside, Sam shouting with delight as he propelled her higher and higher. It was so hot that day, too. Later, the sweat on Ravi's skin tasted like the sea.

She gave herself a shake. "Well, I'm certainly grateful for the breeze." *Way to repeat yourself, Christabel Mistry.* But what else could she talk about? *Are you enjoying your latest cocktail of medications? Have you pushed anyone down the stairs lately? Do you hate me?*

Christabel's shirt clung to her and Sam's face glistened with perspiration. Even Mrs. McKay—dressed in a high-necked blouse, wool skirt, and, unbelievably, stockings and oxfords—even she raised a hand to push back a damp lock of her hair.

"I'm going to make cold soup for dinner," Christabel heard herself say. "Vichyssoise. I bought potatoes and some gorgeous leeks at the market yesterday."

Sam continued to touch her feet to the porch boards, rocking herself and Mrs. McKay. They looked like two bored adults riding the kiddie rollercoaster.

"Auntie Grace phoned last night. She asked about you."

She'd really called to tell Christabel that the house in Toronto was now officially on the market. Grace expected it would sell quickly, given its prime location near the city's snootiest private schools. The ones that didn't accept kids like Sam. *Yes, sweetie, there goes the only home you've ever known.*

Mrs. McKay whispered something Christabel didn't catch. This was like taking a test, one she hadn't studied for the night before. If only Sam would look at her, she'd deserve at least a C minus.

"I've started to take long walks every morning. Graysville has a pretty fountain and plenty of historic houses. And a beautiful church, with stained-glass windows, like the one—" She snapped her mouth closed.

It was so damn hot. Why hadn't they stayed inside the air-conditioned building? A headache ghosted behind Christabel's right temple. Surely it was almost time to call it a day.

Finally, out of desperation, she said, "I think Daddy's going to try to come for a visit next week."

Sam's foot went flat, halting the swing. Mrs. McKay twisted her neck to look at her sideways.

After a moment, Sam slanted her toes and pushed off.

"Do you look forward to seeing Daddy?" Christabel asked.

Again, Sam applied her foot brake. Christabel glanced at Mrs. McKay, who said, "Keep talking."

"Daddy can't wait to see you."

"Daddy." Soft but distinct.

Christabel forced herself to sit still, squeezing her arms to her sides.

Out of nowhere, a stab of envy. *Daddy.* She banished it. She was thrilled, of course she was. Mrs. McKay beamed at her, and she grinned back.

As if she'd heard a summons, Sam stood. She took two jerky steps toward her mother and then, with the splendor of sunlight breaking through clouds, she smiled, whirled around, and skipped toward the door. Mrs. McKay rose, mimed a volley of applause, and followed her into the building.

Christabel rocked the swing in time with her euphoric pulse rate. The daylilies in the bed across from the porch trumpeted silently to the sky above.

She had to convince Ravi to come again.

* * *

"Grace, it's Chrissie. Could I bounce something off you?" Christabel cradled the phone between ear and shoulder as she pulled the covers around her. Air conditioning was such a blessing.

"I am a concrete floor to your rubber ball."

"I'm thinking of asking Ravi down for several days."

Pause. "And you're calling me because?"

"I'm afraid he may misinterpret the invitation."

"Duh. Why the overnights?"

"Because the only thing I've seen Sam respond to is her father's name."

Grace snorted. "Girl, I hope you're not deluding yourself. He left you in the lurch, remember?"

"I was no angel."

"Chrissie, you deserve sainthood for what you went through. I know I wouldn't have been strong enough."

"You're wrong. You were there for me throughout my childhood and god-awful teen years, all the way, standing in for Mom and Dad. Even meeting with the Principal that time I got suspended."

"You weren't pushing me down flights of stairs and knocking me out."

Christabel closed her eyes. "She only did that once."

"Once is way too often. I'd have registered her in a group home years ago."

Christabel listened to her sister's steady breathing. Finally, she said, in a hushed tone, "Do you think I did more harm than good?"

"Don't be cuckoo. You're a fantastic mom. But you still need to protect yourself from Ravi. He broke your heart."

"Sam needs him."

"So go ahead and ask the man down. Tell him it's for Sam and he can sleep on his batty old mom's fold-out couch."

"Grace—"

"Not finished here. *Don't* let things get hot and heavy. With Ravi, that is. *Do* feel free to find a different playmate, if you can in your geriatric village."

"As if I'm remotely interested!"

"Sorry to shock you. But Ravi's not the only man on earth. Forgive but never forget, and move on with somebody else—horizontally, if at all possible."

Christabel choked on a laugh. "You're outrageous."

"Yes, Chrissie, I am. But at least I'm one hundred percent on your side."

Chapter 13; July 3

Ravi did everything with flair. At the moment, he was merely angling his silver Mercedes sedan into the condo's parking spot, but he made it look smooth and effortless—and somehow sexy. Christabel stood in front of her bungalow and fought to keep a firm grip on the balloon strings of her commonsense. As he looked up and smiled at her, she felt them slipping away.

He remained in the car and said something she couldn't hear, probably over a Bluetooth connection and more than likely to his broker. The Market set the tempo of his life.

Mandy's door opened and she emerged, dressed in her usual ensemble of baggy Bermuda shorts and polo shirt. She carried a lethal-looking pair of secateurs in her gloved hands. Christabel smiled to herself as the older woman began deadheading her faded lilacs with gusto. The condo fees included professional garden maintenance. Mandy was living up to her self-declared reputation as the nosiest person in Graysville.

Christabel went to welcome Ravi. He dropped his luggage on the walkway and opened his arms wide. In an impish desire to give Mandy her money's worth, Christabel didn't sidestep when he swooped her up into a hug that raised her bare feet inches off the ground.

"You look as beautiful as you did the first time I saw you."

"Flatterer. Come on in where it's cooler." Christabel grabbed one of Ravi's bags and began lugging it into the condo. She didn't glance back, not wanting him to see she was flushed.

As she closed the door behind him, she caught a glimpse of Mandy racing lopsidedly back into her bungalow. Doubtless she'd be on the phone within seconds, alerting her cronies that there was scandal afoot in old Mrs. Mistry's place. For some reason, this thought created a ripple of amusement Christabel only just managed to suppress.

"There's something different about you." Ravi took a step back and studied her.

Christabel's hand stole to her hair. "I haven't had a chance to find a decent salon yet."

"No. It's not your hair. And it's not what you're wearing. Obviously."

Christabel put one hand on her hip, striking a pose. She'd deliberately dressed down, in jeans and a T-shirt.

Ravi snapped his fingers. "You're glowing."

"My headaches have stopped, mostly. Plus, Sam is improving. And the icing on the cake is *you've* come to visit her."

The light in his eyes dimmed. "I'm not a miracle worker."

"None of us are. But she loves and misses you. She'll be overjoyed."

His wry expression showed he was getting the message. Maybe she'd convinced him her intentions were pure. It was going to be much more difficult to convince herself.

* * *

"Here we are." Mrs. McKay led Sam out a side door at Treffian House. "Both your father and mother have come to visit you today."

Sam raised her head and stared straight at Ravi. He cleared his throat and looked away.

Ravi and Christabel were seated together on a porch swing. Their hands were riveted to their own knees, a discreet no-man's land of space separating them, as if they'd been told by a stern parent to keep their distance.

"Shall we all take a walk?" Mrs. McKay gestured to the grounds.

"That's a terrific idea," Christabel said, surging to her feet. She needed to move, and Treffian's gardens beckoned, fragrant and vibrant.

Caught off guard, Ravi slid sideways on the swing. His face collided with the support, bumping his eyeglasses askew.

Christabel was stunned to hear her daughter giggle, a sound like small bells ringing. A rush of joy swept through her body.

Sam walked over to her dad and waited while he straightened his glasses and got up. She gazed at his chest, her face once again tranquil.

Mrs. McKay beamed at them. "We're very fortunate; the gardeners keep us immersed in color from early spring to late fall. The lilies are at their peak right now."

Mrs. McKay and Sam led the way to the gravel path. Christabel couldn't help herself; she took Ravi's hand. When he turned to her, smiling, his eyes were filled with warmth. She wondered if he felt the same spark she did. It was getting harder to keep it tamped down.

Five minutes passed. Sam shuffled along the path, Mrs. McKay beside her. The flowerbeds were lush, blossoms cascading over the neatly edged borders, but the prolonged silence felt unnatural. No wonder Ravi found these visits so trying.

Sam paid no attention to the flowers; she appeared to be concentrating on the ground in front of her. Was she even aware of her surroundings? Her expression had begun to lose definition, becoming almost vacant. *Have her medications been adjusted again?*

Sensing impatience reverberating through Ravi's hand, Christabel let go. How much did he expect from his only child, anyway—the beautiful girl with the silvery giggle?

In front of a rosebush that was one part peach-colored blooms to three parts vicious thorns, Sam began to hum. Ravi pulled his cellphone out and started checking his messages. His face was shadowed. Christabel coughed and rolled her eyes sideways at him.

Mrs. McKay took the hint. "Samantha, I think your father would like you to say hello."

The humming stopped. Christabel held her breath.

"Hello, Sam," Ravi said at last.

Sam dipped her head into a blown rose. She seemed entranced until, without warning, she reached out and poked at a hooked thorn. A bead of crimson formed on her finger. She stuffed it into her mouth and sucked away, her eyes tracking the flight of a fat bumblebee.

Christabel started forward, but Mrs. McKay held up a cautionary hand, shifting her body to block Sam from touching the rosebush again.

"Mr. Mistry, please say something more," Mrs. McKay murmured.

"Sam. Hi. How are you?"

Once again, Christabel took his hand and gave it a reassuring squeeze.

"Sam. Please," Ravi said. "Your mother and I want to know how you are doing."

Sam took her finger out of her mouth.

"Daddy." She pronounced the word clearly. Blood glistened on her lower lip.

As Mrs. McKay walked forward with a hankie at the ready, Sam dived, throwing her chest to the ground and flinging her arms around her father's ankles. Ravi staggered. His eyes widened with shock–and something else, too. Disgust?

"Come on, Ravi. Keep talking," Christabel whispered, keeping a firm grasp on his hand. It was starting to feel slick with sweat.

"I'll try," he muttered. "Sam, we're happy you're healthy."

Still firmly attached to his ankles, Sam wriggled. Christabel gave Ravi's hand a shake.

"Mrs. McKay tells us you're adjusting well to your new home." Ravi turned to look at Christabel, the lines deepening in his face.

"Home," Sam said.

Christabel dropped Ravi's hand and reached both of hers toward her daughter, stopping short of making contact. Sam ignored her, gazing up at her father.

Again, she said, "Home."

"Do you like your new home here?" Christabel asked.

Sam began to breathe heavily. She threw herself face down again. Ravi flinched as she tightened her grip.

"Daddy, home, Daddy, home, Daddy, home," Sam chanted, each word louder and shriller than the one before.

"Daddy, home, Daddy, home, Daddy, home." Her voice climbed a scale in the key of madness.

Ravi tensed, trying to pull free. Christabel felt panic rise in her chest. She stood still, wanting to touch Sam but knowing it would make things worse.

Mrs. McKay had moved swiftly, racing to the intercom on the wall of the house. "Orderlies! Assistance! The rose garden—now!"

In less than a minute, two male aides arrived, surprisingly light on their feet, making hardly any noise despite their muscled bulkiness. They untwined Sam's clutching hands and sandwiched the girl between themselves. Her toes barely brushed the ground as they lugged her away.

"Daddy, home, Daddy, home, Daddy, home ..."

The eerie sound of her screeching receded before cutting off abruptly as the interior security doors closed behind her.

A dull silence fell over the three of them. Mrs. McKay's normally controlled hair was in disarray. Christabel avoided Ravi's eyes. To have been so close, and then to have it come crashing down.

At last, Mrs. McKay said, "Well, then."

"Will they sedate her?" Christabel shook her head at her own stupidity.

Ravi's face was beaded with sweat. "That was gruesome." His dark eyes were empty.

"Yes, highly disturbing," Mrs. McKay said. "But it was also a step forward. Please plan to be a regular visitor, Mr. Mistry. Your daughter needs you."

Apart from the sound of pebbles crunching underfoot, there was no noise as they walked back up the path. When they reached the building, Mrs. McKay patted her hair into place, smiled a tight goodbye and disappeared inside. For a long time, Christabel and Ravi sat on a swing, gently rocking.

Christabel broke the silence. "Thank you."

"For what?"

"Not freaking out."

"I wasn't exactly the Rock of Gibraltar."

"You won't leave, right? You'll stay a few days like we agreed?"

He sighed. "I'll try to hang in."

"Ravi, Sam actually laughed out loud. And she said two words. *Two.*"

"And maybe tomorrow we'll get to three, or four. But do me a favor, please, Christa?"

"I'll try."

"Let's never say the word 'home' around her again."

"It breaks my heart. But I agree."

She looked away. Sam's real home back in the city was on the market. In fact, maybe it was even sold by now.

Chapter 14; July 8

"I wish you could stay," Christabel said, twiddling her fork in her salad.

Ravi shifted his weight, focusing his attention on his appetizer. "Ever since Sam's breakdown, she's more or less ignored me."

"Mrs. McKay says it's a steady stream of 'Daddy, Daddy' every day before we arrive for visitors' hours."

"I do have to get back to Toronto for a few days." He still didn't look up from his lunch. "After that I'll clear my schedule, if you think it'll help."

"Of course it will."

Ravi lowered his cutlery. "But I'm ordering a better sofa bed. My back will never be the same." He smiled at Christabel. "That is, unless you'd like to try a different sleeping arrangement."

She faked renewed interest in her salad. "Go ahead and buy a couch."

Ravi had managed to get them the best table on the covered patio, overlooking long rows of vines that sloped up toward the dramatic backdrop of the escarpment. The sun was playing hide and seek behind cotton batting clouds, throwing flattering shadows on Ravi's symmetrical features. It could have been a magazine ad: an impossibly good-looking, racially ambiguous man in a gloriously picturesque Canadian setting.

Christabel felt a frisson of lust creep up her bare arms.

"Chilly, darling?" Ravi asked.

"Not at all. Ghost walking on my grave. Really, I'm warm and happy."

"But not in love? Not even the least bit?" He widened his eyes as if in jest, but there was an underlying seriousness in his expression.

"Ravi, we've been divorced for almost three years."

"So you keep reminding me. But tell me the truth. Has there been anyone else?"

She sipped her Riesling. She'd never confess to him that he was the only man she'd ever loved. That she lay awake night after night remembering his touch.

"I'm going to plead the Fifth."

"You're not American."

"Doesn't matter. I'm not discussing this. Our marriage is over and done with."

Ravi reached across the table and wound a lock of Christabel's hair behind her ear. His glancing touch made her shiver again.

"It's not a ghost walking on your grave, is it?" He took her hand. "I feel it, too."

Christabel half-heartedly tried to pull away but he pressed her hand to the tablecloth.

"May I remove your salads?" The waiter whisked the plates away without waiting for a response.

Christabel sat back in her chair, attempting to breathe normally.

A college-aged female server with heavily tattooed arms appeared. She placed their entrees on the table with reverence.

"For each of you today we have pan-seared Arctic char, with a swirl of browned butter sauce, accented with a puree of cauliflower and garnished with three local squashes and vine-ripened grape tomatoes." With the mention of each item, she stabbed a blue-inked finger over the food, almost connecting with it.

When she was gone, Christabel leaned toward Ravi. "Why do they always have to do that? I thought she was actually going to poke my food."

"The only thing that annoys *me* is her timing. Just as I was making headway." Ravi reached out a hand.

Christabel picked up her knife and fork. "Let's eat before it gets cold."

* * *

When her cellphone rang at ten o'clock that evening, Christabel almost didn't answer it. She had just climbed under the duvet and picked up the Romance bestseller that had been lying open face down on her bedside table. She'd left off last night, just after the steamy first sexual encounter between the macho hero and the brave, now bodice-less, heroine.

But there might have been an emergency at Treffian House. Or it could be Ravi, calling to say goodnight. Christabel grabbed for the phone.

"Chrissie!" Grace sounded jubilant. "It's done!"

"Really? You've sold it?"

"Told you it wouldn't take long. You'll have to sign the papers but it's a done deal. Solid financing. Large down payment."

"Fantastic! Who bought it?"

"Parents who want to pop their kids into Upper Canada College this fall, so the closing's soon. End of July. And you're getting slightly over your asking price!"

"You're an angel."

"Want me to email everything to you? Or fax it, which is what the old-fashioned broker recommends?"

"Any chance you can visit?" Christabel smoothed a wrinkle on the duvet.

"What, has Ravi left the building?"

"This afternoon just after lunch."

"You were able to resist his manly charms?" Grace sounded stern, but also like she'd burst with curiosity if Christabel didn't spill, juicy bits and all.

"It was such a good thing he came. We had some bumpy moments at Treffian House, but overall he had a positive effect on her." Christabel spoke slowly, deliberately baiting Grace.

"Of course that's awesome news but you know that's *not* what I was asking. Tell me about your close encounters."

Christabel rolled her eyes. "There was nothing of the kind. If it's any of your business."

"Everything about you is my business, kiddo. Speaking of, back to the sale of your house."

"I'll talk to my bank tomorrow and email you the info. And, Grace, wow! I'm very grateful."

"You're welcome, Chrissie. You'll need to empty out the house quickly, but you'll be set financially—for years."

"An independent woman."

"Seriously, Chrissie. Time to move the hell on."

Christabel didn't have the heart to reply. Grace had a terrible track record with romance. But Christabel had experienced true love, once—and maybe it was time for it to bloom again.

She snuggled back into bed and picked up her novel. The hero was tireless, a steam hammer of a lover. Wouldn't it be divine to have a flesh and blood Ravi here with her, under this fluffy duvet?

She groaned with self-disgust, flung the book onto the floor, and switched off the light.

Chapter 15; July 10

From the official records of the late Mrs. Audrey McKay (MSW), formerly of Treffian House

Transcribed from recorded session with Samantha Mistry. Handwritten notes indicated in italics

McKay: Samantha, it's not like you to miss breakfast. Why don't you get up off that bed, and we'll go downstairs together?

Mistry: [No response]

McKay: You've been doing so well lately. We're all very proud of you.

Mistry: [Says nothing, but pokes a hand out from beneath a pillow. In it she is holding the Hawaiian Barbie she almost always carries. Its eyes have been blacked out, and some of the hair has been hacked off]

McKay: Dear me. Barbie has had a rough time of it. Why don't you get up, and we'll take her to the infirmary?

Mistry: [Sits up slowly; doesn't look at me. Her posture suggests regret, but no agitation. Holds out the Barbie]

McKay: We'll tidy her up.

Mistry: Daddy? [She rises from the bed and moves toward the door]

McKay: Not today, Samantha, dear. But your mother says he'll be visiting very soon. He's planning to stay a whole week, too.

Mistry: Daddy.

* * *

Observations: Initially I was worried about Samantha's depressed state, but she perked up appreciably once I mentioned her father's planned visit.

The defacement of the doll is disturbing. If we accept that she sees herself reflected in that particular Barbie, it may follow that she may be prone to self-mutilation. Or could it be she interprets her father's absence as rejection? Is she punishing herself symbolically?

Scissors? Investigate at once! How on earth did she get hold of those? Or did she chew off the Barbie's hair?

I'll have to report this incident to Dr. Cheung. It's beyond my scope. I will try to keep him from increasing the current mix of SSRIs and re-administering anti-psychotics. I fear any heavy-handedness will cause a setback in Samantha's recovery.

Sometimes the easy route involving drugs is chosen over the harder, but ultimately more beneficial, route of behavior modification therapy. I must continue to be vigilant.

Chapter 16; July 11

Grace had done a good job of staging the house, even removing furniture to make the place seem airier. Neon Kalanchoes bloomed in the windows, and a mass of white carnations spilled out of a crystal vase on the dining room table. It was lovely but odd to see flowers here; Christabel had given up on decorative touches a few years ago, after Sam had started smashing stuff.

She glanced around the central hall. This was where Ravi had stood that final evening, suitcase in hand, finished—with fathering, with this house, and with her. Sam screamed and clung to him. And when at last he was able to detach himself, Christabel fended off her hysterical daughter, running away from her and sheltering behind a locked bedroom door, waiting for the storm to pass. She wept while she disinfected the scratches from Sam's nails. Later, she found Sam collapsed in the hallway, fury spent for the moment, but grief still raw.

Grace set a stack of empty boxes on the living room floor and put her hands on her hips. *Why does she always look so much trendier?* Christabel gazed down at herself. *Jeans are jeans, aren't they?*

"You okay?" Grace asked.

Christabel joined her sister and picked up a cream-colored accent cushion. "Just admiring your Martha Stewart touches."

"Tricks of the trade."

"What should I do with the rest of this junk?" Christabel kicked at a beige couch with her sneakered foot, launching a small plume of dust into the air.

"The Sally Ann will pick it up." Grace yawned, showing off her expensive cosmetic dental work.

"I don't want to keep much, beyond Sam's old art folders." Crayoned self-portraits of young Samantha, holding hands with her two parents. Her family, together.

"Let's go room by room. We'll put sticky notes on things: keep, donate, or junk—just like that woman on TV."

Christabel made a face, and Grace quickly added, "Not that you're a hoarder."

"No." She was many things, but not that.

Grace looked at her watch. "If you're going to make the last bus to Boringville, we need to get cracking."

As they climbed the stairs, Christabel touched the newel post that had knocked her unconscious.

No. It hadn't been the post's fault—the culprit had been Sam. Still, Christabel gave it an admonishing rap with her knuckles. For a moment she felt the pang of a headache. Sharp, cruel. Then it was gone.

She took a deep breath and continued into her daughter's bedroom. The bed at Treffian was better, and free of bite marks, too.

"We don't need anything in here."

She placed her fingertips on the wallpaper border. Pink unicorns, chosen by Sam, when she was ten. Back when Mom had been up on that pedestal, almost equal with Dad.

Grace took Christabel by the elbow and tugged her out of Sam's room. In the hallway, they embraced.

"You okay?" Grace wiped a tear from Christabel's cheek.

"Let's move on." Christabel walked resolutely into her old bedroom. "I'll take my books. And maybe the bedside lamp. You gave it to us when we bought the house."

To shine a light on your epic lovemaking, Grace had said. Christabel was mortified but Ravi promised to deliver—and did.

"You sure that's all?"

They went methodically through the rest of the house. The kitchen proved to be the most time-consuming. The Mixmaster, coffee maker, kettle and most of the pots and pans were keepers; the chipped dishes were not.

"Do you remember this?" Christabel held up an ivory china teapot with a leafy pattern.

"Ah, a remnant of our youth." Grace turned and looked out the window.

"Wasn't this part of Mom and Dad's set? I'm not sure how it ended up with me."

"I certainly didn't want it. I'm surprised you did. But then, you were younger. You wouldn't remember ..." Grace walked away before Christabel was able to read the expression on her face.

She shrugged and continued to work unassisted for the next hour. When Grace eventually reappeared in the kitchen doorway, she surveyed the tidy room and gave Christabel a silent round of applause. Christabel bowed, tossed her Sharpie onto the counter, and stretched.

Grace picked up her purse. "Just enough time for pizza and beer at Antonio's. You in?"

"You bet."

As they left the house, Christabel handed the keys to Grace. Neither sister looked back as they walked, arm in arm, down the front steps and away.

Chapter 17; July 12

"What's going on? Everything okay?" Mandy's graying hair looked damp, as if she'd rushed over straight from showering.

"Yes, fine. These men have brought the stuff from my old house, that's all."

"Oh, good. Of course, I do try to allow you your privacy—like I did when that handsome gentleman visited you. And stayed for *days.*" Mandy pinned a smile reminiscent of a Raphael Madonna on her face. It didn't match the greedy look in her eyes.

Christabel hesitated. Maybe she should just take pity on the woman and ask her in, but at that moment a second truck arrived. A dark, well-muscled woman with a clipboard and an albino-pale, reedy man climbed out. They smelled like they'd been smoking—*please, not near the new furniture.*

"Sofa bed for Mrs. Mistry?" the man asked.

"Yes, it goes in the living room. You're going to haul away the old one?"

The woman consulted her paperwork. "Right you are, ma'am."

Christabel pointed. "Just through there."

In the doorway, the two delivery people slipped cloth booties over their work shoes and went inside. Meanwhile, the original movers were tramping back and forth along the sidewalk, carting boxes and depositing them in the locker.

"Oh my. It's like being at the racetrack." Mandy's head swiveled from side to side, following the action. "Fill me in!"

Christabel sighed, trying to keep a watch on both parties of workers. "The man who was staying here was my ex."

"Ohhh." Mandy drew out the word, savoring it like a butterscotch candy.

Christabel gave her a stern look. "He owns this place. From time to time, he may spend the night—in the *living* room—so he can visit Sam. The old sofa bed made his back ache."

Mandy looked crestfallen for a moment, but perked up almost instantly. "Well, he's certainly a very good-looking man. A South Asian George Clooney. I *always* try not to speculate, of course, but I thought he might be a new beau."

"Mandy!" Christabel said, a hand to her mouth. "As if I'd ask a new man to spend the night."

After a few more minutes of watching the workers, Mandy gave her a scrunch of a hug before retreating awkwardly down the sidewalk. Christabel estimated it would take less than ten seconds before her neighbor would be on the phone, updating her Graysville network as to the latest goings-on at the Mistry condo.

When the movers drove off, Christabel left the door ajar for the breeze and sat on the new sofa bed. She gave it a trial bounce. Comfy. She closed her eyes and inhaled. Good, no trace of tobacco, and the crew's slightly sweaty odor was gone, too.

The room suddenly seemed darker, as if the shades had been drawn. Her eyelids flew open. Someone stood in the doorway, silhouetted against the sun. Surely all the men had left.

"Is that what I think it is?" Ravi moved into the light and stood in front of her, a grin on his face. His skin gleamed and his hair looked like he'd just stepped out of the stylist's chair.

She put a hand over her heart. "You startled me!"

"Apparently. The front door wasn't shut. Which isn't smart, even here in sleepy Graysville."

"The delivery guys just left."

"No harm done, but be more cautious."

She felt a flash of irritation but nodded. He was just concerned about her safety, and it was impossible not to respond to his smile. It filled her, warming a spot deep inside. Of its own accord, her hand began to pat the armrest. Ravi reached out and stilled it.

"I never thought I'd be jealous of a piece of furniture." His eyes danced.

"Don't be silly." She rose quickly, pulling her hand away. "Bring your bags in, and get settled while I throw some lunch together. Sandwiches and Perrier?"

"Perfect. And after we visit Sam, we can check out the new mattress—to make sure it has proper lumbar support."

Christabel walked into the kitchen, heat suffusing her skin. She opened the fridge door and stood in the cool air. Without turning around, she sensed Ravi, close behind her.

"I like mayo," he said. "And dill pickles."

"Lettuce and Dijon, too, if your tastes haven't changed. Egg salad or roast beef?"

"You tell me. If you can recall."

"Beef it is."

She grabbed the ingredients and carried them to the counter, while Ravi poured Perrier into two glasses.

"Christa, darling ..."

She put her knife down. "We need to talk—about how we're going to manage our living arrangements. As Sam's parents, not as a couple."

Ravi moved nearer, shoulder to shoulder, a fraction of an inch separating their bodies. There it was, his divine scent—spicy, clean-edged and dead sexy.

She angled away. "See? Like that, just now. You're way too close."

He took a small step backward. "You don't want us to be closer?"

Christabel couldn't moderate her breathing. "I do want that." She met his eyes. Mistake. The man was so magnetic. "But I *need* you to keep your distance."

"Whatever makes you happy." He held her gaze, and backed farther away, leaning his broad shoulders against the opposite wall. Immediately, she felt the room temperature—and her spirits—drop.

"Thank you." Christabel turned to the counter. She continued to assemble the roast beef sandwiches as if they were the most important task she'd ever been assigned.

"Knock, knock!" The sing-song words accompanied two smart raps on the front door.

"For heaven's sake," Christabel said, dropping the waxy bag of sliced meat onto the cutting board and wiping her hands. "It must be Mandy." In a whisper she added, "The town gossip."

"I'll take over the sandwiches."

Christabel handed him the breadknife and made her way to the door.

"Not an awkward moment, I hope?" Mandy's eyes went right to the sofa bed, closed up as tight as an uncooked clam. She scoped out the rest of the room.

Christabel wouldn't put it past Mandy to invent a reason to visit the bedroom in order to check the state of the king-sized bed, too. In fact, it might be wise to let her. That way, she'd report back to all of Graysville that no hanky-panky was happening at the Mistry condo.

"Come on in. We're fixing lunch." Christabel beckoned.

"Dear me, I'm sorry to intrude." Mandy walked past Christabel and smiled broadly at Ravi.

He waved a lettuce leaf in a friendly fashion at her. "I take it you're Mandy. I'm Ravi. May I offer you a sandwich?"

Christabel tried to catch his eye. It was almost as if he enjoyed making her squirm—her punishment for being stand-offish.

"I don't want to be any trouble." Mandy plopped herself down on a kitchen stool and looked at him with spaniel eyes.

"Roast beef okay?"

"As long as it's lean and red as a baboon's butt." Mandy slapped the counter and laughed.

* * *

Later, when they were alone, Ravi asked, "Aren't you going to thank me?"

"For what?"

"Treating you like a distant acquaintance. She'll send out an APB that we're ancient history."

"And that you're available. You flirted outrageously. We'll never get rid of her now."

"I've already warned you about unwanted intruders." He winked at her. "Close the curtains. Bolt the doors."

"Be careful." She moved swiftly away, glad he was unaware of how rapidly her heart was pumping. "I may just change the locks before *your* next visit."

<u>Chapter 18; July 12, Evening</u>

From the official records of the late Mrs. Audrey McKay (MSW), formerly of Treffian House

Transcribed from recorded session with Samantha Mistry. Handwritten notes indicated in italics

Mistry: Daddy. [long pause]

McKay: It was lovely to see your father today, Samantha. You behaved very nicely; I was proud of you.

Mistry: Nice. [She moves to the dresser and picks up the dark Barbie with the uneven hair, putting it on her pillow before sitting down on her bed]

McKay: Yes, it is getting close to bedtime.

Mistry: Where's Daddy?

McKay: He will visit again tomorrow. With your mother, who is always here for you.

Mistry: Want Daddy. [She takes the red-haired Barbie, still in its box, and turns it to face the wall, then gets into bed, shifting Hawaiian Barbie over on the pillow]

McKay: Your parents are so happy you're using more of your words. As am I.

Mistry: [She is still smiling but she closes her eyes]

McKay: Well, there we go. Another day, and such a pleasant one it was, too. I'll wish you sweet dreams now, Samantha.

Mistry: Good night.

McKay: Sleep tight.

Mistry: Give Mommy a great big bite. [Grinds teeth and laughs]

* * *

Observations: Until bedtime, this was a positive day for Samantha. I noted more focus. She was calmer in the presence of her parents than on past visits. She showed animation when her father appeared and stayed close by his side throughout the session. Afterward, she was composed and cooperative. She took her meds, which I believe are finally at an optimal dosage, without her usual fuss.

She continues to add words to her vocabulary. While it appears to be a matter of time before she begins to talk with as much fluency as she did before moving to Treffian House, I wonder about the animosity she appears to have toward her mother.

I shall give Dr. Cheung a full report tomorrow.

Chapter 19; July 22

It was only ten in the morning, but as Christabel walked down Graysville's main street she wilted in the heat. The air, thick with humidity, sat in her lungs.

Even the fountain square, normally thronged with tourists, was abandoned. Christabel approached, wrists outstretched, but at the last minute she drew back. In the glaring sunlight, the lady's tears had taken on a reddish hue. The metallic burbling was mournful, and the water reeked of something murky and organic.

Shuddering, she walked onward. Everyone else had the sense to stay inside. In slow motion, she went store to store, looking for *Help Wanted* signs. She crossed at the corner, a bead of sweat tickling its way down her spine, and started back the other way. When a pebble infiltrated her sandal, she leaned against a crumbly stone building to remove it, sandpapering her fingertips in the process.

By now, her feet had swollen half a size and her hair had lost its bounce. Christabel was on the verge of trudging home to face Ravi's magnanimous I-told-you-so's when she caught sight of a sign in the window of Grandsmith's Books. The store looked like it was ten years overdue for a refurbishing, but at least it wasn't a trashy trinket place or yet another of Graysville's many wine shops.

She pulled open the door, and an attached rope of bells clanged the sound of a caravan crossing the desert. Moving from bright sunshine into relative gloom, she paused, waiting for shadowy forms to take shape.

It was blessedly cooler in here. She took a grateful breath. The room smelled deliciously of old books, unsmoked pipe tobacco, and licorice allsorts–like a reclusive, elderly scholar's apartment. And something else–faint–and not nearly as pleasant. Sharp-edged.

A man sat behind a long, wooden counter covered in haphazard stacks of books, old and new. His face was only partially illuminated by light cast from upside-down tulip lamps that hung from the ceiling on long wires.

"Who are *you*?" He sounded like the Caterpillar in *Alice in Wonderland*, Christabel's favorite childhood novel.

She smiled. Two could play this game.

"I hardly know, sir."

Dead silence. Maybe she shouldn't have been so glib. She was looking for a job, not auditioning for a role in community theatre.

The man rose from his perch and edged around the counter, studying Christabel, who stared back at him.

He laughed. "Yes, I have a touch of the Caterpillar about me, it's true."

The proprietor was long-bodied, with a stoop to his narrow shoulders. His green velvet fez made him appear older, but he was probably around Christabel's age. His long nose slanted down toward a prominent chin. A keen intelligence shone from his tan-gray eyes.

"Permit me to start afresh." He extended a long-fingered hand. "Doby Grandsmith, Esquire, at your service."

Shaking Doby's hand was like trying to grasp an overboiled lasagna noodle. Christabel dropped it as quickly as she could without causing offence. She peered up at him. Well over six feet, and so thin.

"Christabel Mistry," she said.

Doby's odd, taupe-colored eyes registered increased interest. "Any relation to Rohinton?"

"Afraid not."

"Pity. Well, then, what may I show you in the way of a book? No, let me guess." He put his index fingers to his temples and paused. "Ah, I see it all; you're a closet Romance reader."

At this, Christabel felt herself blush. She kept her mouth firmly closed.

"Throwaway fiction is not what you need." Doby dropped his hands and walked a few steps to study her from another angle. "I believe you are navigating difficult times. Hmmm, what to suggest, what to suggest."

"Sir. Mr. Grandsmith—"

"Do not interrupt me, Christabel. And please call me Doby."

"Doby—"

"Now then, I carry no self-help tripe, so don't bother scanning the shelves for that. Proper writing will do you good. Something literary but borderline pornographic." He rifled through a teetering mound of used books. "Ah, DHL to the rescue, again!" He proffered a well-used copy of *Lady Chatterley's Lover.*

"I'm afraid you've got my situation all wrong."

"Impossible. I am a doctor of literature. *Lady Chatterley* is my prescription." He pulled off his ridiculous fez, unleashing exuberant, carrot-colored curls. They clustered around his face, softening his strong features.

"I'm here about your Help Wanted sign."

"Really?" He shook his head, causing his orange ringlets to dance. "The requirements are stiff. Not one candidate has passed my inspection in over a year."

Christabel twisted her fingers together. "Then I guess I won't, either. I have next to no retail experience. But I used to be a teacher, and I do love books. Kids' books, especially," she said, her eye falling on a pile of illustrated novels.

He moved a step closer and scrutinized her, more like she was a mannequin in a shop window than a real-life woman. She could smell his shampoo—citrus laced with peppercorn.

"Yes, your *Alice* reference was a good indicator. And a teacher, eh?" He leaned forward until he was six inches from her face.

Christabel took a step backward. The man was a maniac, and she was alone with him in this high-ceilinged, likely soundproof room.

"You're hired." Doby clapped his hands together. "That is, if you agree to help take care of my ferals. At last count, five." He looked around vaguely.

"I'm fine with cats, but–"

"You may start tomorrow."

"Mr. Grandsmith–Doby, I mean. You haven't even looked at my resume." She reached into her purse for a copy of her unimpressive CV.

He flapped it away. "Unnecessary."

"And we haven't discussed hours."

"Flexible. I'm here all the time, flying solo, like de Saint-Exupéry minus the crash. I could use some relief."

"Would ten until one, five days a week, be possible?"

He beamed at her as if she'd brought him a first edition of *Ulysses* in immaculate condition. The tip of his long nose turned pink.

"Not only possible, but ideal. The wage is penurious, I'm afraid. There's no money in books, you know; merely knowledge–and sometimes a touch of magic."

At that, Doby turned and scribbled a few figures on a yellowed slip of foolscap. He handed it to Christabel, who scanned it, thrilled to see he had offered a much higher wage than the legal minimum.

"And I can start tomorrow?"

He nodded, an errant curl popping him in the eye.

"I accept. Thank you very much."

"My pleasure entirely, Miss Christabel Mistry." He held out the copy of *Lady Chatterley's Lover* and winked. "Don't forget this."

Christabel inclined her head, accepting the gift. Her feet no longer felt sore. She walked swiftly to the doorway, but hesitated under the jangling camel bells.

"And, Doby, I really will have to leave punctually every day." She swallowed and took a shaky breath. "My daughter is–unwell. I visit her every afternoon."

At that, Doby Grandsmith, without appearing to take a single step, materialized directly in front of her. "I solemnly swear to release you every day on time. Your scheduled visits with your daughter shall be sacrosanct."

Out on the sidewalk, she smiled at him through the store's window, and pantomimed a high five when she saw him cast aside the *Help Wanted* sign. He looked down, picked up a tortoiseshell cat, and waved one of its front paws at her.

On the way home she didn't think once about the heat. The creepy dribbling of the town's fountain barely made her footsteps falter. Her mind was on books and her new job.

Doby's eccentricity was likely just quirkiness. Time would tell. For now, she couldn't wait to let Ravi know she was a working woman again. She clasped the novel to her chest and quickened her pace.

Chapter 20; July 23

"Welcome to Grandsmith's Books," Christabel said. "How may I help you?"

"Just browsing, thanks." The well-preserved man began to root through piles of used books on a table in the middle of the store.

Christabel drew a breath of relief. After an hour on the job, she'd already realized there was no logic to the way Doby organized his merchandise.

"How do you ever find anything?" she whispered to him, as he brushed by her behind the counter, holding a black cat in one arm and a tabby in the other.

"There's order in what you perceive as chaos." He handed her the black cat, which dangled bonelessly and purred. "Or at least, there's fiction that-a-way," he said, pointing with his prominent chin, "and non-fiction over there. Oh, and children's books yonder."

"Got it. I think."

"Now, if you don't mind, I'll show you where the litterbox is."

Cuddling the cat, Christabel trailed behind Doby to a back room. She didn't need to be led. She could have found her way blindfolded by following the smell.

"Doby! It reeks back here."

"Alas, I know. I function better as a cat rescuer than a cat maintainer."

"Don't worry. I'll help you get this whole store cleaned up."

She didn't mind. With Sam's behavioral issues, they'd never owned a pet, but she was fond of animals—and, fortunately, not squeamish.

"Excuse me?" the customer called. "Could someone assist me out here?"

"Tallyho, Christabel. You'll be fine."

As she rang through a thick non-fiction tome about household implements in the nineteenth century, Christabel felt absurdly proud of herself. She glanced at the purchaser, who held his hand out for his change. He looked like many other Graysville residents she'd encountered—older and affluent, with artificially smooth skin. She touched her cheek, wondering if weeks of neglect had affected her own appearance—and if he'd been anointing himself with water from the town's fountain. Was there something to the legend, after all?

Her first ever customer departed, and Christabel felt a whoosh of hot July air before the door eased shut, leaving her alone in the front room. She chose a random stack of books to sort. It didn't matter what Doby said; there was zero method to the madness in this place. She'd fix that, even if it took weeks.

The bells jangled again. Christabel looked up, only to be swept into a hearty hug by her Chanel-scented sister.

"Chrissie! I drove all the way to tell you: the deal's done, the new owners have the keys, and your cash is in the bank." Grace grabbed Christabel's hands and danced her in a circle.

"That's fantastic." She smiled, but, for some reason, her feet felt heavy. She stumbled and tried to withdraw, to no avail. Grace intensified her clutch.

"You don't need to depend on That Man anymore. And you certainly don't need this job of yours." At last, Grace relaxed her grip, running her eyes over the shop. "As usual, it's big sister to the rescue."

"But I like it here."

It was a tad too early to be sure. And the lack of cat hygiene was off-putting, but being surrounded by books and having an understanding, intellectual boss had great appeal. Plus, it was liberating to be a working woman again.

"Stinks a bit." Grace wrinkled her nose.

"I'm going to take care of that."

"Take care of what?" Doby entered, wearing rubber gloves and carrying a bulging plastic bag. He stopped in his tracks when he saw Grace.

"'*She walks in beauty* ...'" he said in a reverent tone, raising his gloved hands prayerfully, along with the cat poop bag.

"And you walk with cat shit, apparently." Grace pinched her nose shut.

"Grace, stop it! This is my new boss, Doby Grandsmith. Doby, meet my sister, Grace Newberry." Christabel whipped the bag out of Doby's hand and took it outside.

Re-entering, she bee-lined to the dispenser of antibacterial cleanser and pumped a liberal squirt onto her hands. In the back room, Doby was singing something operatic. *Che gelida manina.* Grace arched an eyebrow at her, but Christabel kept her own face deadpan. So what if her boss was half crazy and she had to deal with cat litter disposal. She didn't need Grace's approval.

"There we are, then. Apologies." Doby strode back into the room, gloves gone and smelling strongly of Palmolive.

"As long as you treat my baby sis right, I'll go easy on you."

Doby appeared to be at a loss for words. His eyes were trained on Grace, drinking her in as if she were a fine Shiraz, from her red, high heeled shoes to her short black skirt and sporty blazer. Christabel shook her head, feeling sorry for him. He was the archetypal class nerd, infatuated with the head cheerleader.

Finally he spoke. "Chemistry."

"Say what?" Grace wasn't even trying to be polite. Christabel shot her a dirty look.

"I prescribe for you a book on chemistry. Linus Pauling. I have it somewhere." Dust flew as he started to dismantle a precarious tower.

"You're kidding, right? I barely passed that subject in Grade Twelve. In fact, maybe I didn't."

"Please, for me. Your sister's new employer." He located the book he was searching for and handed it to a bewildered Grace. "Open it once a day. Any page will do."

She held it gingerly. "Sure, I guess."

"And dine with me. Today. Noon, at the restaurant across the street. Christabel will mind the store."

"I have to get back to the city—" Grace stopped when Christabel glared at her.

"Well. All right." Grace heaved an exaggerated sigh. "If you promise me there's no chemistry test involved."

As Christabel ushered Grace out, she whispered in her sister's ear, "Give him a chance. I think he's a really nice guy—for a change."

"I'll have lunch with the man. For you. After that, all bets are off." Grace whipped off along the hot sidewalk, an aggressively modern woman carrying a musty, old textbook.

Chapter 21; July 25

Christabel zested the rind of a lemon, watching the bright yellow flakes cascade into the bowl. She closed her eyes for a moment and inhaled the essence of sunshine. Tonight's dinner would be simple: lemon chicken with Mediterranean vegetables, served over orzo. A meal she knew Ravi loved.

She glanced at the clock—almost six. He'd arrive any time now. Her hands shook slightly; she steadied them on the cutting board.

She'd encouraged Ravi to visit Sam on his own this afternoon. It was his last day in Graysville, and Sam would be beyond delighted to have him all to herself. Christabel suppressed a twinge of sadness, thinking about her daughter giggling with pleasure at the sight of her dad.

She stirred in chicken stock and tomatoes. Without referring to the open recipe book, she seasoned the poultry, while the oil heated in the skillet. It was good to keep her hands engaged and her mind in neutral. She didn't want to think about this last evening together. The way he'd lift his wineglass, his dark eyes meeting hers, the candlelight glinting on his hair. That devastating smile in his voice. His body generating heat she'd feel clear across the table.

She needed to stop obsessing and concentrate on cooking. And if that didn't distract her enough, she should think about their financial and parental partnership. Banish all memories of their alchemy, like that day, long ago, when they'd made love for the very first time on an escape weekend to ski country, in front of a roaring fire. And afterwards, languorous on the rug, his leg entwined with hers, lost in each other's eyes.

But that had been before he'd let her down.

He'd been so dependable lately, though. She'd forgiven him; was it time to forget?

After visiting Sam this afternoon, Ravi planned to meet with a potential new business partner—someone he'd struck up a relationship with recently. Christabel had been mildly surprised; stodgy Graysville didn't seem like a probable source of high rolling investors. But Ravi had told her not to worry; he'd finish up quickly and be home in time for dinner.

The chicken would take six minutes per side—just enough to kiss the bird, as Grace would say. Then she'd remove it from the pan, add more oil and cook the shallots and garlic. That done, she'd assemble everything and heat the poultry in the broth and voilà: a delectable dinner. Christabel would eat as though taste and smell were the only two senses she knew.

She heard the muted rumble of Ravi's car as it pulled into the driveway. Right on time. She assembled their meal on two warmed plates and lit the candles on the study nook's desk, prettied up with a tablecloth and silverware. For Ravi's last dinner they might as well have a semblance of formality. Besides, sitting across from each other, barricaded by furniture, was better than being side by side at the breakfast counter—less chance of brushing against each other.

"Christa?" Ravi called out as he entered.

"In here."

Christabel laid the plates on the improvised dining surface. He entered the room, bringing energy and purpose, causing everything around him to fade into the background, as if he were illuminated from within.

He inhaled. "Smells fabulous."

She waved a napkin to shoo him over to his side of the table. Before complying, he held her chair and waited until she was seated.

"How was your afternoon?" she asked, cutting her chicken with the single-mindedness of a surgeon.

"Positive. Productive." He tasted his food and closed his eyes, smiling.

"And Sam?"

"Good. Nothing much new to report."

"Having you here has made a huge difference."

"I appreciate your faith in me." The dimple flashed in his left cheek.

Christabel looked away. Her face was scorching, and she fanned herself with her napkin, refusing to meet Ravi's eyes. They ate in silence for a moment.

"And how was your meeting with the new partner?" It was a safe topic.

"Got things sorted."

"Good." She raised a forkful of chicken to her mouth but put it down, untasted, on her plate. Who was she kidding? There was no way she could eat.

The candles flickered, causing shadows to play across Ravi's features. She'd forgotten to put on music and the room was unnaturally quiet, with only the clinking of his cutlery breaking the stillness. He took a few more bites. After what seemed an eternity, he lowered his knife and fork. He stared across the table at Christabel, as if trying to lock her in his memory.

She rose. "If you're finished ..."

"Yes, it was delicious. Here, let me help you."

He stood but didn't pick up his plate. Instead, he caught her by the wrist, taking the dish out of her hand and putting it back on the table. She could feel her pulse fluttering under his touch.

"We were so good together," he said, gently sliding his thumb over her wrist, sending currents of desire racing through her body.

She raised her eyes to his. Nobody else had ever looked at her this way.

"We can't fix the past." Her voice was small. She made no attempt to break free of his grip.

"But we can move forward." He angled closer.

She was aware of his body heat and his spicy fragrance. She couldn't help herself; she took a step nearer. He put his arms around her. Her body fit perfectly against his.

She should move away. It wasn't fair and it wasn't healthy. The man was leaving tomorrow, and she knew better than to stir up old passions.

Christabel slipped her arms around his neck and felt his breath falter, his arms tighten. She lifted her chin and touched her lips to the hot skin of his neck, tasting cinnamon and salt and something dark and sexy.

Then, inevitably, his mouth was on hers; insistent and sure. She responded blindly, demanding more. They moved toward the bedroom, still kissing, shedding articles of clothing along the hallway, bumping into the walls. She felt his hands searching for the clasp of her bra and the miracle of his touch when he freed her breasts, and she pulled him to her so that she could absorb the heat of his skin. When they reached the bed, she took the lead, levering him onto his back, her lips to his.

In the far recesses of her mind, she knew this was it. Her last chance to retreat.

Somehow, using every bit of resolution she still possessed, she slid to one side. They lay facing each other on the pillows, noses touching. He said nothing; stayed where he was, keeping pace with her accelerated breathing.

Her hand moved to touch his cheekbone and finally he kissed her again. She shivered, every nerve craving more, and ran her hands down to his shoulders, pulling him to her. With infinite tenderness, he eased her onto her back, searching her eyes. She nodded tremulously, and he moved to where she wanted him, deep inside.

Chapter 22; July 30

From the official records of the late Mrs. Audrey McKay (MSW), formerly of Treffian House

Transcribed from recorded session with Samantha Mistry, Grant Hilton, and Sophia Liu. Handwritten notes indicated in italics

McKay: Isn't this cozy? Our first group session together. Samantha Mistry, meet Grant Hilton and Sophia Liu.

All: [Silence]

McKay: Perhaps we should start with everyone saying something about themselves. Samantha?

Mistry: I'm Sam. [Looks down at Hawaiian Barbie in her hand]

Hilton: That all you got to say? [Pause] Well, I'm Grant. Sixteen. Can't wait to get out of Treffian but there's this thing I did, back in Etobicoke–

McKay: Not just now, Grant. And Sophia?

Liu: My name is Sophia. I'm fifteen. Way too grown up to play with lame dollies.

McKay: Enough. Respect for each other is critical.

Hilton: Sam, eh? Like Son of Sam. Or something out of Dr. Seuss. [Laughs]

McKay: Not appropriate, Grant.

Mistry: [giggles]. Don't mind.

McKay: Very polite, Samantha, but Grant must work on his manners.

Hilton: Hey, Sam. Do you give a good goddamm? [All three teens giggle]

McKay: Last warning.

Hilton: We'll behave.

Liu: Yes, really.

McKay: Are you sure?

The three teens together: Yeah!

McKay: All right, then. Let's proceed.

Liu: Hey, Sam. I knew an old Mrs. Mistry who used to live here. I watched TV with her sometimes. Judge Judy, mostly.

Mistry: Gramma. [She holds Hawaiian Barbie in her fist, at eye level. They both seem to be looking at Sophia]

Liu: Cool old lady. Used to tell me stories.

McKay: How nice. Can you share one?

Liu: Yeah. There was, like, this one she told me over and over. [Speaks with the quaver of an old woman]: The baby won't stop crying. I go to pick her up. Gently, gently.

Mistry: Baby. Rock-a-bye.

Liu: But she keeps crying.

Mistry: On the tree top.

Liu: And then I can't help it. I shake her and shake her— [Grabs the Barbie from Sam and shakes it]

McKay: Stop that, Sophia! At once!

Liu:—but the brat never shuts up! And—

Mistry: [Screams and tries to take the Barbie back]

McKay: Robert! Remove Sophia. Now.

Liu: [Singing and shouting over Sam's protests, as the orderly pulls her out of the room] Shake, shake, shake ... [Throws doll on floor]

Mistry: [More inarticulate screaming]

Hilton: [Laughing] Fucking-A. Hilarious.

* * *

Observations: Dr. Cheung and I were mistaken. We thought that these three teens, all approximately the same age and all having shown excellent improvement in the past weeks, were ready for a peer meeting.

Not only was it deeply disturbing, in terms of how all three of the teens seemed to regress, but now I am faced with a piece of information which, if true, may put a new slant on Samantha Mistry's underlying condition.

I shall meet with Dr. Cheung at the first opportunity.

The poor child.

Chapter 23; July 31

Christabel whirled through the store, straightening and shelving and singing snatches of pop songs as she worked. Draped over the counter, Doby leafed through a much-thumbed edition of Elizabeth Barrett Browning's poetry. From time to time, he cast a reverent gaze to the rafters, and sighed.

The place could use a good airing. To keep the cats from escaping, Christabel corralled them into the inner room, making sure they were secure, before opening the door to the street. The heat wave had broken and a breeze pirouetted in, carrying with it hints of lavender from the sidewalk planters outside.

"Listen to this." Doby raised an index finger. "'*If thou must love me, let it be for nought except for love's sake only.*'" His English accent was dubious.

"Listen to *this.*" She clapped a couple of clothbound books together, creating a mini-tornado of dust. "It's the sound of me cleaning." But she smiled at Doby. Who was she to even mock-scold the man who paid her well to do a job she enjoyed?

Besides, Elizabeth Barrett Browning's line was thrilling—and so apt. Ravi had left a few days ago but Christabel's skin still felt sweetly sensitive from his touch.

He'd be returning tomorrow for a special team meeting at Treffian House. She dusted off another few textbooks, wondering why Dr. Cheung had insisted they both attend. Whatever the reason, she'd have Ravi by her side. Her sexy, kind ex-husband—maybe not an 'ex' for long—was coming back to Graysville ahead of schedule. And Sam was fine. Mrs. McKay would have told them if there was anything wrong.

"Do you suppose she's even cracked it?" Doby plonked his volume of poetry onto the counter.

"The chemistry book?" Christabel pressed her lips together. Doby was sweet–but what could she say?

"I thought perhaps ..." His voice trailed off.

A mammoth dust bunny that Christabel had somehow missed skittered across the floor. She reached down and grabbed it, grimacing as she tossed it into the bin.

"You never know." She wiped her hand on her jeans. "Although how a textbook can stir up romance, I've no idea."

His eyes regained some of their luster. "Her soul *'hath snatched up mine all faint and weak.'*"

Christabel seized the poetry book. "You've been taking too much of your own medicine." She put it on a shelf beyond his reach.

"So speaks the woman who's obviously been up late reading *Lady Chatterley's Lover*. At the risk of offending, I have noticed a marked change in you, young Christabel. You're vibrant." Doby smirked at her. "See what a little literary titillation can accomplish?"

She bit her tongue. After a moment, Doby shrugged and walked toward the door. Before he reached it, Mandy thumped through the entranceway, almost bowling Doby over in her rush.

"Thank God." Mandy stopped in her tracks when she saw Christabel. "You're still here."

Christabel's knees wobbled. "What's wrong?"

Mandy doubled over at the waist, wheezing. Sweat dripped from her forehead. Doby kicked the door closed, and led her by the arm to the stool.

"Get your breath." He demonstrated, wafting his hand like an orchestra conductor. Mandy straightened up, gasping.

Christabel wanted to smack them both. "Mandy, what's wrong?"

"Accident. At Treffian House."

"Oh, God." Christabel turned toward the door.

"Stop! Samantha's fine. I think." Mandy's face was blotched.

Christabel whipped back around and clutched Mandy's shoulders. "What happened?!"

"A car crashed into the building."

"How do you know Sam's okay?" Christabel couldn't restrain herself from giving Mandy a little shake.

"Happened near Dr. Cheung's office. Nowhere near the patients' rooms. I'll drive you there, to be sure."

Christabel grabbed her purse and ran out the door in the direction Mandy had pointed. She barged through the cluster of tourists surrounding the fountain, Mandy lagging behind, panting heavily. The car was only a short block away. Once they were both inside, Christabel gripped the armrest. *Please God.* She closed her eyes and tried to swallow the panic that was rising in her throat.

Mandy babbled as she drove, her words a muffled blanket of sound. Christabel pressed her foot to the floor, willing the car to get them there more quickly. She should have run all the way—the building wasn't far from the store.

A jumble of parked emergency vehicles came into view, lights flashing. Christabel rolled down her window, flinching at the blare of police radios and voices shouting. Adding to the frenzy, a mobile broadcasting unit passed them, missing Mandy's car by inches, and screeched to a halt. A camera crew jumped out.

"Stop!" Christabel shouted. "Here!"

"There's a spot—" Mandy kept talking but Christabel leapt from the crawling car and sprinted for the front door.

A young policewoman, square-faced and built like a stone cairn, stood in the way. "Ma'am, there's no admittance at the moment." Her gray eyes steady, she frowned at Christabel.

Beyond the cop, the door to the front hall stood open on a turbulent sea of blue uniforms. Christabel turned on her heel and ran to the other side of the building where Dr. Cheung's office was located.

"Ma'am? Ma'am!" she heard as she dashed away, following the tire tracks that ripped across the grass.

She drew up sharply when she saw the utter shambles of the west wall. A vehicle, pleated as though made of origami paper, was lodged in what had been a bay window. Crumpled metal, shards of glass, and chunks of exterior plaster littered the lawn and garden. Under a rosebush, its yellow blooms lush and incongruously joyful, a balding teddy bear sat, close to a single tennis shoe.

"Ma'am, I insist. Stay right where you are." The constable drew up, mousy brown hair unravelling from the knot at the nape of her neck. Her gaze was steely.

Christabel raised her hands together in front of her heart. "My daughter's in there. She's disabled."

The young woman's features softened a fraction.

"Please! I need to know!"

The constable cast a glance over her shoulder. No one was in earshot, but she moved closer to Christabel and spoke at a low volume. "We're not allowed to give details, but I'll say this much: only the driver was hurt. Dead on impact. We can't release the name, you understand."

"Oh, God." Christabel felt tears begin to run down her face. They tasted like an ocean of relief.

She allowed the constable to escort her to the front of the house. Mandy looked up, stuffed her phone in her purse and stumped over. The hug she offered was comforting, but the naked curiosity in her eyes was repellent. Christabel told her she needed time to process what had just happened and walked to the condo, lost in thought.

It made sense that the police couldn't release the name of the driver yet. There were relatives to inform and proper procedures to follow. But Christabel didn't need to speculate. Even in its wrecked state, she had recognized Bunny's old Jeep immediately.

* * *

When she arrived home, she locked the doors and pulled the curtains. In the gloom, she wandered ceaselessly through the condo, wearing off the last of her adrenaline buzz. She didn't dare go outside—Mandy was in the garden, pretending to prune the hedge.

Once her limbs had stopped trembling and her heart had resumed a regular rhythm, Christabel sat down with her iPad and Googled the latest Graysville news. It was disappointingly vague. An unnamed driver had crashed into Treffian House. Police were investigating.

The phone rang.

"Chrissie? What the hell's happening?" Grace's voice shrilled across the miles. "And why haven't you called?"

Christabel winced and held the phone away from her ear. "I'm sorry, but Sam's fine. Or so they tell me."

"You're taking someone else's word?"

"They won't let me in. It's a crime scene. But Mrs. McKay says Sam was in a different part of the building." Christabel lifted her eyes in a silent prayer of thanks.

"What about the doc? It was his office, right?"

"He's fine. Or maybe minor cuts and abrasions. Ravi and I have a meeting there tomorrow—so I guess we'll find out."

"What about the lunatic who did it?"

"Dead." Christabel paused. "You met her the first time you were here—our waitress from the diner."

"What? Why?"

"Her son died. He'd lived at Treffian House for a year or so. They'd moved away but she still blamed them." Christabel shook her head. The woman must have snapped completely.

"Well, I'm just glad you and Sam are okay. But next time anything strange happens in Stepford, call me right away!" There was a severe edge to Grace's tone.

"Okay. And, Grace?"

"Yes?"

"Ravi's staying over tomorrow night. I mean ..."

Silence. Christabel put a hand to her cheek, feeling its warmth.

"I hope you know what you're doing."

Christabel said nothing. Then, "Have you opened Doby's chemistry book yet?"

"Obviously not. Although I must say my lunch with him was surprisingly not horrible."

"Do me a favor—and don't ask why. Could you look at a page or two? For me?"

"Oh, for fuck's sake. Like I'll understand a single word."

"Please?"

"All right. If you swear you'll keep me posted, I'll promise to look at the book from your bat-shit crazy boss. Feel better?"

"Sure do. Love you, big sis."

"Love you, too, brat."

* * *

That night, before Christabel turned off the light, she re-read the sexiest passages in *Lady Chatterley's Lover.* When she fell asleep, dreams of rippling flames melting her body to a state of molten bliss and orgasms filled with wild cries suffused her slumber.

In the wee hours, though, her visions turned to nightmares. Distorted metal. Screams. The town's fountain, running with blood. Sam, half submerged in it, her face deathly white.

Chapter 24; August 1, Afternoon

Twenty-four hours earlier, emergency vehicles had jammed the driveway at Treffian House; now, there were only a few cop cars parked there. Yellow and black crime scene tape cordoned off the crash area, but apart from that, everything seemed tranquil. Birds twittered; a graceful willow trailed its branches across verdant grass.

As Christabel rounded the corner, though, there was an angry thrumming. Grim-faced people mobbed the main entrance, jostling each other as they vied for admittance. Christabel kept her distance.

A deep bass voice cut through the din. "I demand to see my son!" The man puffed out his chest and towered over the trim female constable on duty, but she looked right through him.

"My mother's in there!" a middle-aged woman with heavy black eyebrows yelled.

If only Ravi would get here. For now, Christabel would hover on the fringes. Maybe use the time to try to get a closer peek at the damage from the accident–no, not accident, suicide. And botched murder attempt?

The coast was more or less clear. The only two constables in sight were too busy managing agitated family members to worry about her. Christabel ducked under the police tape and walked swiftly toward Dr. Cheung's office window.

It looked like a construction site, as if the lord of majestic Treffian Manor had commissioned a remodeling of his estate. The path had been raked; no debris remained. A shiny orange tarpaulin was stretched across what yesterday had been a yawning gap.

The gardens, too, were serene. The forlorn teddy bear was no longer sitting sentinel beneath the rose bush. Somehow its absence made her feel bleak, as if the workers had cleaned up not only

Bunny's broken body and Jeep, but also whisked away her son's spirit. Christabel stood for a moment, eyes closed, hoping with little conviction that mother and son were in a better place, reunited.

She checked her phone for the time and made her way back. As she approached the police tape, Ravi waved at her from the crowd, and she felt irresistibly pulled toward him. The Ravi who'd crumbled and left his family those four awful years ago was gone. New, improved Ravi loved her passionately and was committed to being the best father he possibly could be.

He gave her a mock-severe headshake as she dipped under the tape. She couldn't help smiling. She ran and threw her arms around him, and when he kissed her, he lifted her right off the ground.

But she couldn't lose herself in the moment. Not here, with the droning of the crowd in their ears, wasplike and hostile.

"I've been so worried." Ravi set her lightly back down on the grass but kept hold of her shoulders. "How *are* you?"

"Better now you're here. They haven't let me see her."

"Stay right by my side."

He took her hand and led the way, using his broad shoulders to carve a trail to one of the beleaguered cops.

"Excuse me, officer–"

The policeman held up his hand. "We're at full visitor capacity. Check back later." He turned away.

Ravi tapped him on the shoulder. The cop swung back around, eyebrows lowering.

"Officer, we have an appointment with Dr. Cheung. I confirmed it this morning. Mr. and Mrs. Mistry."

The cop surveyed Ravi and Christabel. After a moment, he pushed the intercom button, relaying the information in a monotone. The door clicked open.

"Well, well. OK, Mr. and Mrs. Mistry–proceed. All you other folks, get back. That's right–you there! Get back or you'll lose your place, hear me?"

Protesting voices rose up around them, but Ravi put his arm around Christabel and hustled her inside to safety. Mrs. McKay was waiting in the holding room, as composed as if it were a regular visit.

Christabel rushed to her. "How's Sam?"

"She's fine. Absolutely unaffected by the tragedy. In fact, I believe she remains unaware of it."

"Thank God." Christabel tried to catch Ravi's eye but he stared straight ahead.

Mrs. McKay pressed a buzzer and led them through the next set of security doors. They followed her down some stairs, to a basement hall that was unfamiliar to Christabel.

"Please excuse the Spartan appearance. We've had to move Dr. Cheung's office temporarily." Mrs. McKay walked on, her square heels clacking on the concrete floor.

On each side of the corridor there were numbered wooden doors, with barred windows inset at face level. Christabel peeked inside one as she hurried by, but it was too dark to make anything out.

The hallway itself was spotless but somehow unpleasantly dank. The smell was even worse than it was upstairs—so much so that Christabel's eyes began to sting. Unwashed bodies, perhaps. Could it be that some residents actually lived down here?

As if reading Christabel's mind, Mrs. McKay said, "Nobody lives here—anymore."

"What do you mean?" Christabel held a hand to her nose. "Anymore?"

"Many years ago, the Upper Canada Institute for the Insane was located here. At the time it was considered to be at the leading edge in psychiatric care, but ..." Mrs. McKay gestured vaguely to either side of them. "We're blessed to live in an infinitely more enlightened era."

"I'll say," Ravi said. His skin had taken on a grayish tinge under the harsh lights.

They were moving at a trot, keeping pace with Mrs. McKay. When she suddenly stopped, Christabel stumbled. Ravi caught her arm.

"Here we are," Mrs. McKay said. "And, again, pardon our temporary set-up."

She opened a door and waved them in. The room was painted a gloomy hospital green. It was free of furniture, apart from a circle of metallic folding chairs in the center. The fluorescent strip on the ceiling cast sharp-edged illumination on the three people sitting there.

Sam's seemingly calm gaze fixed on Ravi. She opened her right hand and raggedy-haired Hawaiian Barbie dropped onto the floor beside her.

Dr. Cheung rose from his seat to greet them. He smiled with an unusual air of solemnity. His face, at least, was unmarked by scratches or bruises.

The third person was an attractive woman in her mid-thirties—auburn hair, dark eyes, and creamy skin. She looked like a younger Grace, or maybe even Christabel. Definitely dressed more like Grace, though—in an annoyingly uncrumpled white linen dress.

Christabel bypassed Dr. Cheung's outstretched hand. She knelt by her daughter's chair, careful not to brush up against her.

"Hi, sweetie." Christabel held her breath.

Sam didn't move. Her eyes remained locked on Ravi. After a moment, Christabel stood and went back to shake Dr. Cheung's hand.

"Sorry. I didn't mean to be rude."

"Not at all." He gave her fingers a slight squeeze before releasing them.

Ravi's eyes were trained on the new woman in the room. Christabel's head throbbed. She schooled her features into a neutral expression.

"Hello, Ms.—?"

"I'm Debra Gaston. Nurse and Reiki practitioner. I was assigned to your late mother-in-law's care, Mrs. Mistry. I'll also be working with your daughter."

Debra shook Christabel's hand. Her skin was silk and velvet. Having scrubbed and sorted nonstop for days at Doby's store, Christabel was uncomfortably aware that her own must feel more like steel wool.

"Strange." Ravi tilted his head. "I'm not sure we've ever met."

Christabel almost snorted. *Yes, Ravi, as if you'd forget.*

"Possibly because you visited your late mother on weekends? I usually work Mondays to Fridays." Such a pleasant mezzo.

Thank God for Mrs. McKay, who started rearranging chairs. Hint taken, everyone sat down.

Ravi pulled his eyes away from Debra and fixed them on Dr. Cheung. "We want to express our sympathy to you and your staff. As a member of the Board of Directors, I can assure you we'll be calling an emergency meeting to discuss the approval for funding the repair work."

Christabel gazed at him. *Board member, very impressive.*

"Thank you," Dr. Cheung said, looking down at his hands. "I apologize for not being able to discuss the details. The police are still investigating and there are patient confidentiality issues."

"We understand." Ravi nodded and laced his fingers together on his crossed knee.

Christabel shifted on her metal seat. Her daughter was acting as if she didn't exist, and Debra Gaston was beginning to make her think more and more of herself at a younger age—a significantly younger age. She smoothed her new jeans. They'd looked so trendy in the store.

"Let's start with Samantha's progress." Dr. Cheung picked up the file propped against the leg of his chair. "Mrs. McKay?"

She consulted her notes. "As you can see, Samantha is in good health. We make sure she gets plenty of exercise by walking with her in the garden almost every day. We've had her prescription for eyeglasses updated. A speech pathologist works with her three times a week, and her vocabulary has improved. Generally speaking, she is calm and well-behaved. If things continue in a positive manner, we will enroll her in our in-house education program for our teen residents. It begins after Labor Day. However, there was a recent incident–"

"Leave that for now," Dr. Cheung said.

Mrs. McKay looked down at her notes, her expression unreadable. "As I was saying, she is, for the most part, an exemplary member of this community. Increasingly talkative, too, aren't you, Samantha?"

For a moment, Sam was silent. Then, in a small voice, "Hi, Daddy."

Ravi sat up straighter. "Hi, Sam. Your mom's here, too." He looked around at the others, an embarrassed frown on his face.

Christabel smiled at Sam. "That's okay." She tried to ignore the darts of pain behind her eyes.

"Is it, though?" Ravi looked at the doctor for corroboration. He hadn't as much as glanced at Sam.

"In time, we feel Samantha will show more appropriate social skills." Dr. Cheung bestowed a wise look on each of them through his wire-rimmed glasses.

"If you are satisfied with my report, I shall take Samantha for a walk. Indoors only today, I'm afraid." Mrs. McKay waited for the doctor's nod. "Off we go, Samantha. Say good-bye to your parents."

Mrs. McKay went to the door and held it open. Sam looked mulish for an instant, but then gathered up her doll and walked out of the room. Christabel let out a slow breath as the door clicked shut behind her.

"We are impressed with our daughter's progress." Ravi flashed his most charming smile.

Christabel wanted to give him a sharp pinch. As usual, he'd been visibly uncomfortable near Sam. He was just happy she hadn't made a scene.

No, Christabel, don't. It was a matter of time. He would fall in love with Sam again. She was his one and only child.

"Mrs. Mistry? Are you ready to continue?" Dr. Cheung's urbane tone broke through Christabel's musings.

"Sorry," she muttered, looking down at her entwined fingers.

Dr. Cheung leaned forward, hands on the file folder that rested on his knees. "I must ask both of you to prepare yourselves for what I'm going to share with you today."

"Why?" Christabel and Ravi asked together.

Dr. Cheung hesitated for a moment, fidgeting with the file.

"We have no evidence of any wrongdoing, but–"

"Has someone hurt Sam?" Christabel was halfway out of her chair before Ravi pulled her back.

"Let him finish, Christa."

She brushed off his hand but remained seated. Debra Gaston stared at her with an enigmatic expression on her pretty face.

Dr. Cheung's Adam's apple twitched in his throat. "We have reason to believe Samantha may have suffered head trauma in her early years."

A wave of relief flowed through Christabel's body. She sat further back in in her chair.

"She's never had a concussion," she said. "Not even a bad fall."

She and Ravi had baby-proofed every sharp corner and edge. The house had been a padded refuge.

"There is a possibility–one we will never be able to prove, I caution–that the damage Samantha experienced was not accidental."

There was silence. Long enough for layers of dread to build in Christabel's chest. Much too short to delay what was coming next.

In a smooth murmur, Debra asked, "Are you aware of Shaken Baby Syndrome?"

A kaleidoscope of jumbled thoughts rattled through Christabel's mind—fragments crashing into each other, and falling.

"No way." Ravi crossed his arms. "Christa was a devoted mother."

Dr. Cheung said nothing. His gaze was steady.

Christabel couldn't focus. She felt as if someone had punched her. Her mouth moved but words wouldn't form. She could barely remain upright.

Sam had been a difficult infant, quick to cry. To console her, they logged miles up and down their home's narrow hallway, praying she'd eventually fall asleep. Their nights were wretched, and their mornings were filled with guilty relief, as they dropped her off and headed to work.

Finally, Christabel summoned enough breath to whisper, "What about ..." It was too dreadful. "What about your mom?"

"What?" Ravi whipped off his glasses and glared at her. "*What* did you just say?"

Christabel cringed. "Your mom took care of Sam when she was tiny."

"I can't believe you'd even suggest that." Ravi looked down and fiddled with his glasses.

"Ravi. Look at me."

As if in a trance, he turned toward her. Something about the set of his features was off-kilter. His eyes filled with pleading. And suddenly, Christabel knew.

"I'm afraid I was witness to some of your late mother's outbursts," Debra Gaston said. "On more than one occasion, she alluded to having acted in a way that could be construed as injurious to a small child. At the time, I ascribed her statements to dementia."

"But at that point," Dr. Cheung continued, "we had not yet met Samantha."

"My God." Ravi thrust his hand into the air as if to block the doctor's words.

For a moment, no one spoke. Dr. Cheung stood. "We felt it important to share this information with you. There is at least a possibility that Samantha suffered a traumatic brain injury as an infant which contributed to her developmental delay disorder."

"It's not your fault." Debra's tone was cloying.

In spite of her core-deep anguish, Christabel ached to reach out and punch the woman. Instead, she turned to Ravi.

Shock on his face. Horror. And something else.

"You knew."

He shrank in his chair. "Christa, I–"

"You knew. You picked Sam up every day from your mom's house."

"I didn't know anything for sure–"

"But you kept taking our daughter. Our precious daughter. To that house. Because that's what your mother wanted."

"Christa–"

She knocked his outstretched hand away. "Get away from me."

She wanted to scream. Claw his face.

Even more desperately, she wanted to believe he didn't know.

She turned her back on Ravi. "What can we do now? To help Sam, I mean?"

Dr. Cheung's shoulders rose in a small shrug. "Any damage that might have occurred happened many years ago. This session was for informational purposes only."

Christabel felt ice crystals forming in her veins. She swiveled and glared at Ravi, who gazed back at her, entreaty in his eyes.

Christabel said slowly, "It makes so much sense. I will never forgive your mother. Or you." Choking on a dry sob, she got up and fled the room.

She ran past a startled orderly and through the long corridor–past all the anonymous doors, up the stairs, and out through the police-guarded antechamber, into the daylight. The angry crowd of waiting relatives still milled in front of the entrance. She pushed her way in among the bodies, using her hands like grappling hooks to force her way through.

Chapter 25; August 1, Late Afternoon

Eventually, Christabel stopped running. She wanted to get as far away from Ravi as possible, but she was hit by waves of nausea. Stumbling onward, she managed to make it past the fountain, but when a whiff of its foul-smelling water hit her, she spewed the remnants of her lunch. Every spasm was a reminder of his betrayal.

The acidic tang at the back of her throat tasted of guilt. She'd allowed her infatuation with a man to cloud her judgment. Worse, she'd failed to do a mother's number one job—protect her child.

As she straightened up, wiping her mouth with the back of her hand, a stiff-faced, elderly man approached, walking two long-haired dachshunds.

"Heel, boys." He shortened their leashes and tugged.

They ignored him, straining to get their noses in Christabel's mess. To no one in particular, the man muttered, "Town's going straight to hell," before dragging his dogs away.

She stared after them blankly. *Whatever.* The old guy's opinion didn't matter. Nothing did.

Wearily, she began to walk toward the place she'd been calling home for the last several weeks. She stopped short when it came into view. This wasn't *her* home. It belonged to Ravi and before that, the horrible woman who'd always hated her. The witch who'd hurt Sam.

Drawing closer, she could hear the sound of someone whistling the Disney dwarves' *Heigh-ho* song. Mandy emerged from behind the hedge, carrying a long-handled weed puller in a gloved hand. Her matching khaki shorts and golf shirt were grimy and her hair frizzed out from beneath a man's baseball cap.

"And we're supposed to have first-class gardening service. I ask you." She waved a dandelion with a gnarled tap root, spraying clumps of soil.

"I have a huge favor to ask." It was easier to look at the ball cap than to meet Mandy's gaze. *Grow Young with Us*, the slogan read, below an illustration of Graysville's iconic weeping woman.

"Sure, dear. Anything." Mandy dropped the dandelion and pulled off her work gloves, shoving them into a baggy back pocket. She touched Christabel's shoulder.

A shiver raced the length of Christabel's spine. "Sorry." She stifled a sob. "I've had terrible news. And, I'm wondering–I don't want to sleep in Ravi's condo tonight."

"You must stay with me." Mandy's tone was decisive. "No questions asked." She paused for a moment, and added, "Well, none you have to answer."

"Thanks. I just have to collect a few things." Christabel grasped her key and walked onward with heavy steps. She'd leave it inside for Ravi to pick up, as soon as she could bring herself to remove all her belongings.

The thought of him made her stomach twist. She barely made it to the bathroom before vomiting whatever was left in her system. Once the sensation of vertigo lifted, she washed her face. She reached for one of Mama Mistry's towels but the fabric seemed to burn her skin, and she dropped it onto the tiled floor.

She had to get out of here. From the bedroom closet, she took an overnight bag and threw toiletries into it, adding a change of clothes. That would do for now.

As she turned to wheel her case down the hall, the doorbell rang. She stood still, hoping whoever it was would leave. It rang again, followed by a barrage of knocks. Moments later she heard the scraping of a key in the lock.

"Go away." She sounded so weak. She inhaled and tried again. "Go away!"

"Christa, we need to talk."

She leaned heavily against the dresser. An ornate brass frame toppled, missing her head by a fraction of an inch. It contained a photo of Ravi as a young man. Mama's pet.

"I don't want to talk to you." She gripped the handle of the suitcase. "Get out!"

"I know you're upset." Had his voice always sounded so cold?

"You don't know anything." She let go of the bag and sank into a squat, face in her hands.

Ravi's footsteps drummed along the short hallway. When they stopped, Christabel didn't look up. She sensed him surveying her from a height.

"Christa, please. Stand up." He bent closer. She smelled the spiciness of his skin—something she'd always adored.

Fool me once, shame on you; fool me twice, excruciating shame on me. Her throat constricted.

"Go away. Don't you dare touch me."

"Darling, we can talk this through." Ravi reached down and caressed her hair.

Christabel uncoiled as she struck out at him, aiming for his face. Only her first hit landed, catching him on the jaw. He shielded himself, and she pounded his forearms instead of breaking his nose or blacking his eyes. Primitive sounds of fury accompanied each blow.

Eventually, she leaned her back against the wall and slid down until she was sitting on the bedroom floor.

Ravi dropped his arms and looked at her. "I didn't deserve that."

"Shut up."

"If you'll let me explain—"

"*Shut up*!"

"Christa, I had nothing to do with Sam's condition. And there's no way my mother—"

"Liar."

"You'll see. When you've calmed down—"

"About *this*?"

"Give it a few days. We'll work things out."

"Just go." She pointed to the door, her hand shaking.

"We'll talk soon."

He just had to have the last word. Christabel bit back her response, wanting him gone. She remained silent as his footsteps receded. The door clunked shut behind him.

She looked at her hands. Stupid, puny things. Ravi was uninjured, but she'd managed to bruise every one of her knuckles.

Christabel righted her overnight bag, winced as she took its handle, and wheeled it out of Mama Mistry's condo. She would ask Mandy for some ice for her hands. She'd allow the woman to baby her and she'd accept a jumbo glass of Chardonnay—or maybe two or three—in spite of her queasiness.

Right now, what she needed, more than anything, was to forget.

Chapter 26; August 26

It took Christabel almost a full month to pull herself together. By summer's end, she felt as if she'd been forged in fire.

First, though, had come the meltdown.

Grace had arrived at Mandy's condo, like the cavalry showing up to save the day—only it was much too late for that.

"Oh, my God, Chrissie." She stroked Christabel's hot forehead with a soothing hand. "I'm taking you back to Toronto. No arguments."

Christabel, who'd hardly stirred from Mandy's guest bed for two days, didn't put up a fight. She allowed her sister, assisted by a frantic Mandy, to support her into the passenger seat of a borrowed car. Grace acted as if Christabel didn't smell bad or look like something dragged through hell. She flung her sister's meager overnight bag into the trunk, and they squealed away from the curb as if pursued by demons.

Christabel stayed in Grace's claustrophobic Cabbagetown apartment for three weeks. At first she barely spoke, and she ate next to nothing.

"It's your favorite. Cream of mushroom and a side of buttered toast." Grace pulled her to a sitting position and propped a tray on her lap. She closed Christabel's fingers around the handle of a spoon. "Sweetie, come on now. You need to eat."

"I know. I'll try." Christabel took a small sip. When Grace fed her a sliver of toast, she nibbled it dutifully, and reached for a glass of water. Her throat was so dry.

"You've got to get your strength back." Grace hesitated, then added, "For Sam."

Christabel sat up straighter. She nodded and took another mouthful of soup.

Grace insisted on giving up her bed, but Christabel's sleep, when it came, was full of nightmares. Mama Mistry's eyes glittered, helpless baby Sam screamed for help, and Ravi walked away from them, over and over. Frequently, Christabel thrashed and cried out, and each time Grace was there.

By the second week, Christabel moved beyond shock and distress to a stage of white-hot fury.

"That evil woman!" she raged. "I hope she's rotting in hell!" Christabel stomped back and forth across the miniature living area.

"Shh, Chrissie. I agree. But the neighbors are going to complain again."

"And Ravi? What an absolute bastard! He knew, Grace. He effing knew!"

Even in her overwrought state, Christabel couldn't bring herself to launch the full F-bomb. For some reason, this made her even angrier—at Ravi, but also at herself.

Grace banished her from the apartment for hours at a time, telling Christabel to walk off her wrath in the fresh air. She burned up the miles, arms pumping, winding through complacent Riverdale and hipster Leslieville, muttering under her breath. She might have looked like a lunatic but at least she didn't get Grace evicted.

A few weeks later, the anger was still there, as well as the soul-deep sorrow. Bit by bit, though, coached and cossetted by her sister, Christabel pulled herself together.

She made the rounds of ritzy legal firms in downtown Toronto, investigating how she could remove Sam from Ravi's influence. In total, she spent four thousand dollars of his money on consultations with three top city lawyers. They'd all come highly recommended by Grace's high-flying friends. They all said she had no case.

"Yet another dead end," Christabel reported to Grace, at the end of a vexing afternoon. She paced the room, careful not to make too much noise. "That's it. I'm going back to Graysville."

"Mrs. McKay says Sam's doing fine," Grace said.

"Still. She needs to know someone in her family is there for her. I bet Ravi hasn't bothered to visit."

"You never know."

"And Doby! I've totally let him down, too."

"Nonsense. He lives for that bookstore. And he likes you. He's holding your job for you." Grace looked down at her fresh manicure.

Christabel stopped pacing. "Has that chemistry text given you any ideas?"

"Don't be daft! But he's not just your boss; he's your friend." Grace fidgeted with her glitzy bracelet, and added, "You know there's space above that zany bookstore, right?"

Christabel blinked.

"He says he'll rent it to you if you're one hundred percent determined to go back."

"Are you serious?"

"He used to live there himself. Only moved when he inherited his dad's house. It's probably a disaster zone but you might be able to fix it up."

"Anywhere is better than the Mistry condo." Christabel pulled her sister in for an embrace. She clung to her until Grace began to wriggle.

"I love you." Grace adjusted her mussed clothes. "Try not to scare the shit out of me again."

The next day, they made the trip. Grace drove a rented SUV, her matched set of luggage bumping in the back against Christabel's modest bag. Traffic was light, and they crossed the town line in less than two hours. As they passed each familiar landmark, Christabel felt a growing sense of dread.

"Close your eyes. I'll tell you when you can open them again," Grace commanded. A minute later, she added, "You can look now."

Mama Mistry's condo was behind them, and the eerie fountain, too. Still, Christabel tasted an ashy bitterness on her tongue.

Grace glanced sideways at her. "You okay?"

"I will be." Christabel looked around cautiously. She felt better as they drew nearer to Doby's store. "I have to be."

Grace gave her a staunch nod. "You're not alone. I'm here for now and you have Doby at your beck and call. Your buddy Mandy, too, if you get *really* desperate." She rolled her eyes. "Even after I leave, you can call me any time, and I'll appear like the fabulous big sister I am."

When they entered Grandsmith's Books, Doby sprang up from his stool, causing his green fez to tip crazily to one side.

"Hallelujah and praise the saints! You have returned, my Muses." He wrapped both sisters in a hug.

Grace was the first to break free. "Okay, Professor Wacky, let's get Chrissie settled."

Christabel stared at the two of them. While her sister's tone was bantering, it held an underlying softness. Even more amazing, Grace had laid a gentle hand on Doby's shoulder. It still rested there.

"I'll go get the luggage." Grace turned away and Doby followed.

Christabel wondered what was really developing between the two of them. Something wonderful, she hoped.

"Follow me, my Maidens Two," Doby said, after he and Grace had carried the luggage across the threshold. "This is one of the routes to your new abode. Across the store and through the odiferous cat enclave, I'm afraid. There's also access from the alleyway behind the building." He tromped ahead of them, up some steep wooden stairs.

She was prepared for anything, but much to her surprise, Christabel saw potential in her new apartment. It was half the size of Mama Mistry's place and needed a thorough dusting, but it had a latent shabby-chic charm. The slanting walls and dormer windows made her feel like a college student again. Braided rugs were scattered across the well-worn hardwood and the furniture looked cozy in a broken-in way. Only the kitchenette had been updated, with a sleek two-burner stove and a fridge the width of a shoe box.

"I told Grace it wasn't luxurious." The lines on Doby's forehead deepened. "Does it suffice?"

"It's perfect." Christabel gave him a spontaneous hug that knocked his fez right off. "I can't believe you did this for me."

Doby's face turned pink. "Pleasure's all mine." He patted her awkwardly on the shoulder and quickly put a foot of space between their two bodies.

Christabel picked up his hat and coaxed it back into shape. Doby, his face still flaming, made a fuss of scrutinizing it before replacing it on his head.

"Have you been making out with my sister?" Grace walked through the living room to the kitchen, pausing to fluff up the couch cushions on the way.

"Preposterous suggestion. As you very well know, my affections are otherwise engaged."

Doby had the shining eyes of a man head over heels in love. Grace was impassive.

It would be such a joy if she *did* fall for Doby. Not every man was a cold-hearted sonofabitch.

* * *

According to Doby, Bertram Jonas was the only lawyer worth seeing in Graysville. He'd booked an appointment a week ago, and Christabel headed there as soon as she'd shooed the others out of her apartment. Unpacking would have to wait.

She tapped her fingers on the edge of the lawyer's mahogany desk, studying the man's folksy expression. In return, he beamed wholesome country-boy-turned-lawyer vibes at her. Not for one minute did she buy into the man's aw-shucks sincerity.

Jonas was another of these aging Graysville types, with the smooth, tanned skin of the moneyed class. There was a certain bland look to all of them. Dr. Cheung's skill with fillers and injectables was undeniable, but he was turning high society Graysvillians into clones.

"I'm sorry, ma'am." Jonas crinkled his faded blue eyes. "Short of suing Treffian House for negligence or abuse, and there's no sign of that, there's nothing you can do."

"You're sure?"

He picked up the legal files from his desk and hefted them as if he were doing wrist curls at the gym. "Trust me, ma'am. It's a no-win situation."

She felt her anger rising and tried to breathe more slowly. This whole mess wasn't Jonas's fault, and it wasn't that Sam was getting inferior care at Treffian House. It was that Ravi was on the Board of Directors–and that was loathsome.

"What would *you* do?" she asked, laying both hands flat on Jonas's stack of file folders.

He sat back in his chair. "Eh?"

"If you had a daughter locked up at Treffian House, and an ex-spouse you despised on the Board."

His faded eyes narrowed. "Legally–"

"Forget legally. Give me something human."

He pulled his chair in closer to his desk. "Ma'am–"

"Gut level." She slapped the desktop.

For a moment he sat stiffly. Then, he leaned forward and grinned at her.

"Here it is, then. Accept reality. She's not getting out, which isn't a bad thing. Best facility anywhere. Matter of fact, my grandson once did a spell there."

Christabel frowned. "That all you got?"

"Apart from the obvious–avoid your spouse. Listen, just because he's a Board member doesn't mean he can interfere with her treatment."

"You'd better be right."

"A wise old judge once told me, there is no justice in this profession; there is only the law."

"I've got the picture." Christabel nodded and rose to leave.

He leapt to his feet, hand extended. She shook it briskly, wincing as his sharp-faceted college ring bit into the finger on which she wore her own favorite emerald ring. It was the one she'd always meant to give Sam.

"It has been a pleasure, Mrs. Mistry. The good news is I'm saving you thousands of dollars, which I could actually use to help fund my grandson's college tuition."

As Christabel exited, she glimpsed a reflection of herself in the window. She corrected her posture and walked away with a purposeful stride.

Chapter 27; August 27

Christabel rotated on the spot, her arms outstretched. "I can't believe I've been gone three whole weeks!"

"Almost four, by my calculation." Doby handed her a slim volume with fraying edges. "But I don't believe it's a math primer you need."

"Emily Dickinson. *Poems of Healing*." The words on the cover blurred, and she turned away to gather herself.

"'*If I can stop one heart from breaking, I shall not live in vain.*'" Doby gazed soulfully skyward, then grabbed his fez from the counter and loped toward the store's exit.

"Thank you," she called, after his retreating back. He was all lanky legs and cylindrical head as he disappeared from sight.

She ran a finger along a shelf. There was a fresh layer of dust on every surface. Cat fur tumbleweeded across the floor. She opened the door to the back room and wrinkled her nose.

"Smells like I've got my work cut out for me," she said to a strolling marmalade tom. It stropped against her legs, depositing a trail of orange fluff on her jeans. She reached down to scratch the animal's regal head and smiled. "Thank God I'm back."

Before her shift ended, Christabel took two bulging sacks of garbage to the bin outside, bumping into Doby on re-entry.

He beamed at her. "You bring much-needed sunshine into my studious realm."

"Not really, but I do bring soap and water. And fresh cat litter, which you can reimburse me for." She pulled a receipt from her pocket and handed it to him.

"It shall be added to your next pay. You have my undying gratitude."

"And you, mine. You held my job and rented me an apartment. I'll never be able to quit, right? You know precisely where I live."

He chuckled. "All part of my Machiavellian plan."

Christabel walked to Treffian House, lightly at first and then feeling the full drag of gravity. She'd been telling herself she couldn't wait to see Sam—but was that really true? Even though the last few weeks had been traumatic, she hadn't had to cope with Sam's indifference. Or worse, deal with her slavish love for Ravi.

She detoured to the building's west side, where a month ago Bunny had used her car as a missile, hurtling through the window to her death. Today, all was peaceful. The panes and brickwork had been restored, the churned-up grass re-sodded. Brilliant zinnias and early chrysanthemums nodded in the late summer breeze.

A tapping noise drew her attention. Dr. Cheung beckoned to her from inside his office window. She gave him the thumbs up sign and walked toward the entrance.

At Security, she told a middle-aged aide with a Friar Tuck horseshoe of hair that Dr. Cheung wanted to meet with her. As the man buzzed her through, she wondered again about the personnel turnover. How long would this guy last?

The doctor rose from his ergonomic chair. Somehow it had survived Bunny's assault, but his old desk hadn't. Even though it had been wooden and built like a small citadel, it must have been destroyed in the crash. The new desk was all chrome and glass. Clearly, he wasn't expecting any more grief-maddened parents to drop by unannounced.

He smiled serenely at her. His black hair was neatly parted, and his glasses were smudge-free. The frames looked empty, as if he were wearing fake ones to make himself seem more intelligent. Behind him, several certificates were missing from their former positions on the newly plastered wall. Christabel wondered whether they'd been destroyed and how a doctor went about getting documents replaced.

Never mind that—how can he even sit with his back to the window after all that's happened here?

Dr. Cheung pulled out a chair for her and returned to his seat behind the desk. "We have missed you."

"I'm sorry, but I find that hard to believe." She said the words without thinking, and for an instant she felt ashamed.

But really. As if anyone here had missed her. Probably not her daughter, and even less so the staff. Christabel was always underfoot, keeping an eye on things. Plus, that last scene with Ravi couldn't have enhanced her status.

"You are upset—understandably." Dr. Cheung rolled his chair closer. "But I have always been impressed by your commitment. Too many parents virtually abandon their children once they've been admitted."

Christabel looked up sharply. "But after Bunny's accident, this place was mobbed."

"People are drawn to tragic situations, especially those that hit the news." He smiled sadly and leaned back. His high-tech chair made a hydraulic, whining sound.

"I still can't believe people would walk away from their kids." Christabel passed a hand over her eyes; the light from the window was too bright.

From out of nowhere a memory flashed—a fragment from a day when she was ten. Grace held her tight. Their dad dragged a suitcase down the stairs of their semi. The front door slammed behind him, and his Chevy pulled away from the driveway for the last time.

"It's more common than you'd think. Parents may soothe their consciences with the fact that Treffian House has such a good reputation and relatively luxurious facilities."

"Then they disappear? That's awful."

Again she felt an inner twinge. Awful, yes, but understandable.

"Putting all that aside, we are very glad you're back. It will do Samantha good."

"Has Ravi visited her?" The words flew out of her mouth.

Dr. Cheung studied the far wall of his office. He pursed his lips in a silent whistle.

"I'm sorry. That was inappropriate." Christabel kept her eyes on him.

The doctor looked down at his knuckles as if they were going to give him some much-needed advice. Eventually, he gazed back at Christabel and nodded. "We've convinced him to visit Samantha weekly. His usual day is Sunday."

Christabel's feelings for the doctor melted a few degrees. "Then I'll make sure I don't come that day. Anyway, my sister tells me I need to give Sam more space."

Dr. Cheung turned to his computer screen. "Actually, I have a question to ask you." He cleared his throat. "Would you consider a part-time volunteer position here?"

Christabel's mouth dropped open. "As what?"

"Teacher's assistant. Labor Day is this Monday. After that, we reintroduce schoolwork into our teenage residents' lives—those who can handle it. I understand you're certified—"

"Only as a junior or middle school teacher. And not for years and years."

Her own negativity rang in her ears. Hadn't she recently been thinking of getting back into teaching?

Dr. Cheung gave Christabel an assessing look. "You have more than enough experience to be a teacher's aide here. Mr. Dodd could use the help. Just for an hour or two a week, working with a bright, I'd even say gifted, young man. And it would be an excellent way to interact with Samantha."

She pressed a hand to her stomach to stop the fluttering sensation. It might actually be an interesting challenge. And she could see Sam regularly without being clingy. Let her daughter know she was there for her, in the background.

"May I think about it?"

"Would meeting Mr. Dodd help you decide?" Dr. Cheung asked. "I believe he's here today, working on lesson plans."

Christabel gulped and nodded. Dr. Cheung picked up the phone and made the arrangements. He handed her a scribbled note, and she left the office, escorted by the same aide who had brought her there. As she glanced back through the small window in the doctor's door she saw him, still sitting at his shiny new desk, twirling a pen this way and that. A smile played on his face.

She hadn't agreed to anything, at least not yet. Why was he so pleased with himself?

* * *

Christabel had never visited the east wing before. She was relieved that her Friar Tuck guide, who walked stolidly in front of her the whole way, never saying a word, didn't take her to the nightmarish basement. That people had once lived in its cell-like rooms appalled her.

They went through the common area and continued on past a cheery dining room. It was empty at the moment, but in the adjoining kitchen, crockery rattled and people called to each other. The aroma of baking bread wafted through the double doorway. There'd be fresh rolls for dinner tonight. All the comforts of home for these modern-day inmates—minus the home itself.

Christabel looked down at the paper in her hand. Room 106. Just as she was about to ask the aide how much farther it was, he pointed and she saw they had arrived. Before she could thank him, he lumbered off in the direction of the common room.

She rapped on the door. It swung open, revealing an owlish man in his mid-twenties. He was short, about the same height as Christabel. A lock of blond hair dangled across his forehead, almost obscuring his eyes. He swept it back before ushering Christabel inside the classroom.

It was spacious, containing only a few student desks, positioned well apart. Unlike other rooms at Treffian, this one had a large window that let in some natural light, even though protective iron mesh obscured the lower half. There was a single whiteboard and a waist-high shelf of books but no other schoolroom furnishings. It probably wouldn't be wise to have a bulletin board in a place like this.

"You must be Mrs. Mistry." He sounded as if he'd recently recovered from a bout of laryngitis.

Christabel made a snap decision. "Let's make that Ms. Newberry. Christabel. And you are Mr. Dodd." She smiled politely at him.

"Only to my students. Call me Steve."

"Happy to."

"Good, we've got the introductory crap out of the way."

His wheeze of laughter gave way to a paroxysm of coughing. He pulled an inhaler out of his pocket and took a forceful puff. His wide blue eyes teared up, making them appear even larger.

"It's a god-awful year for ragweed. Sucks to be me," he said, holding his L-shaped inhaler to his forehead.

After a few jagged breaths, he put it back in his pocket and gestured toward a large desk at the front of the room. It was covered with sheaves of paper, neatly organized under speckled fieldstones that served as paperweights.

"I'm sure you're wondering what your Assistant's role here might be," he said, quickly adding, "And please don't take that as an insult. I know you have more actual classroom experience than I do." He walked over and picked up a stone, rolling it between his palms.

Christabel smiled at him. "In another lifetime, maybe." She took the only visitor's chair, next to the bookshelf. "I'm more than a little rusty, and I never taught high school or Special Ed. So tell me: what would my role be?"

Steve's brow smoothed. "Well, there's a kid named Grant Hilton. Sixteen years old." He perched on the edge of his desk. "Grant's at grade level or above academically, so he doesn't have the same needs as some of the other students, who keep me more than fully occupied. I tend to leave him to his own devices. He requires attention, though, and I simply don't have the time."

"Why is he here?" Christabel picked up a book. *Catcher in the Rye. Seriously? For these kids?*

"He's got a history of self-mutilation and at least four suicide attempts."

Christabel gasped. "Listen, I'm no therapist."

"Yeah, I made that sound awfully melodramatic. Good way to lose my only qualified candidate."

"I haven't left—yet."

"You don't need to worry. Grant's been more or less stable for months. His parents still never visit, though."

Christabel bit her lower lip and glanced at the window. Outside, clouds were forming. Not that the weather made much of a difference to Treffian's residents.

She met Steve's eyes. "Maybe I could give it a try. What would I be teaching?"

"Creative Writing. You wouldn't have to do much except provide feedback. Even an hour a week would be an improvement over what he got from me last year."

"And if he doesn't respond? Or I find it isn't for me?" Christabel picked up another book, this one from the Harry Potter series. *That's more like it.*

"You can quit at any time—unlike me. No hard feelings." Steve raised a hand in a Boy Scout salute.

Christabel laughed. "Sign me up. How about two afternoons a week, an hour at a time, to start?"

"Mondays and Thursdays at one o'clock work for you?' he asked, and waited for her nod. "Which means your first session will be Thursday, what with Labor Day coming up."

"Where will my daughter be?"

"Right here. As long as she can adapt. I haven't met her yet."

Christabel hesitated. She needed to tell him, but the words never formed easily. "Her reading skills are almost non-existent."

Steve sighed. "See, that's my problem. I've got some students with challenges like Samantha's, and then there's Grant, who's got a whole other set of problems. One teacher can't do it all."

"I'll give it a try. I'm sure I can switch up my hours at the store. But tell me, Steve–what brought you to Treffian House in the first place?"

He coughed into the crook of his elbow. "Fulltime teaching gigs are hard to get."

"If you got an offer at a regular high school, would you take it?"

Steve gazed around the room and eventually looked back at Christabel. "Truthfully? In a flash."

Christabel nodded and gave him a firm good-bye handshake. At least Steve was honest. When it came to dealing with all the other professionals at Treffian, she was never entirely sure.

Chapter 28; August 28

From the official records of the late Mrs. Audrey McKay (MSW), formerly of Treffian House

Transcribed from recorded session with Samantha Mistry. Handwritten notes indicated in italics.

McKay: Samantha, stay back from that tree. See? There's a wasps' nest. I shall have a word with the gardeners.

Mistry: Beware my sting.

McKay: *What* did you say? [Did Samantha actually just quote Shakespeare? Her words were garbled. I can't be sure]

Mistry: [She makes a buzzing sound]

McKay: Let's practice our conversational skills. School begins next week, and Mr. Dodd will want to hear your speaking voice. I'll start. How are you, Samantha?

Mistry: Fine.

McKay: I'm glad to hear that. And if you can say, 'Fine, thanks' next time—well, that would be even better. How was your visit with your mother yesterday?

Mistry: Fine. Thanks. [She smiles at me]

McKay: Well done! Did you know she used to be a teacher?

Mistry: Nope.

McKay: Yes, indeed, and she may help Mr. Dodd this fall. Won't that be nice?

Mistry: Guess so. [She begins to make the buzzing sound again]

McKay: Of course, it will be!

Mistry: Daddy?

McKay: He's been a regular visitor, hasn't he? I believe he plans to keep coming on Sundays.

Mistry: Today?

McKay: No, we will have to wait four more days. But your mother will visit.

Mistry: Want Daddy. [She scowls]

McKay: Not today, but soon.

Mistry: [Raises her arms and runs around the tree, making an angry buzzing sound. Fortunately, she stops of her own accord, before I have to call for assistance]

* * *

Observations: It is encouraging to see Samantha cooperating and improving her language skills. I believe she is ready to begin a limited schedule of classes next week.

She is also managing to control her anger. Although clearly frustrated that her father won't be visiting until the weekend, she accepted the news without putting up too much of a fuss.

As usual, she seems ambivalent about her mother. Yet—I was pleased Samantha indicated their visit yesterday was positive. It was the first they'd had in weeks.

So many parents are negligent—even totally absent. It must break Mrs. Mistry's heart to be taken for granted.

Chapter 29; September 26

Grant had used a pen for his wrinkled assignment, pressing so hard he'd poked a starburst of tiny holes through the paper. Christabel could feel him hovering over her as she finished writing her final comment.

"Fantastic potential in this story." She glanced up. "Awfully gritty, though."

His gray eyes narrowed. "That's a whole new level of what the fuck."

She'd have to ask Steve about Treffian's academic policy regarding four-letter words.

Except for his language, everything about Grant was pristine—from his brushed, wheat-colored hair to his close-clipped fingernails. He looked like a clean-cut all-star who would never dream of uttering an off-color word.

Christabel did a final flip through the pages, made one correction, and held the story out. As Grant moved to take it, his cuff rode up, exposing perfectly parallel, white scars that climbed his inner arm, like rungs on a ladder. He glowered at Christabel. She didn't blink.

"It's a promising first draft. Now lose the attitude and re-write it." She softened her voice. "And this is for a Grade Twelve Creative Writing credit so edit out at least some of the C- and F-words, okay?"

Without thinking, she reached up to pat him on the shoulder. He flinched and threw his work into the air, collapsing to the ground. He lay rigid, eyes screwed shut. The closely-written pages fell all around him, like autumn leaves tossed in a windstorm.

The best thing to do was ignore him.

Across the room, Steve was attempting to keep four other teens occupied. They were seated on wooden chairs behind individual, matching desks, well separated from each other. Sam was humming, making a sound like a contented bee in hot sunshine. Christabel smiled.

She moved closer, her sneakers making no sound on the hardwood. Steve's job was fascinating, but so tough. Every kid had specific academic abilities and emotional challenges. Up to this point Christabel hadn't witnessed a meltdown, but she'd been warned it could happen at any time.

She reached into her pocket and touched her panic button. Steve had given it to her when she'd started helping in the classroom.

"Always have this on you." He'd dangled it by its keychain attachment. "Most days go off without a hitch, but you never know."

"Do you feel safe here?" She'd tucked the gadget away without looking at it.

He hadn't responded.

Still on the floor, Grant heaved a theatrical sigh, and Christabel jumped and spun around. He grinned at her and gathered his scattered sheets, before taking a seat back at his desk. Without further ado, he began his second draft, writing with manic fury. He shunned the class computer. The machine leeched away his imagination, he'd told Christabel, and she'd nodded, unsure if he was serious. In any case, he'd be fully occupied for the next half hour.

She edged next to Sam's desk and peeked over her shoulder. Her assignment looked like a simple puzzle of some kind with lots of colors and hardly any words. Sam ignored it. In front of her, sitting straight-legged on the desk and also staring wide-eyed at Steve, Hawaiian Barbie was auditing the lesson.

Steve pointed at something on Sam's page, and handed her a colored pencil. He waited until she was fully engaged before waving Christabel to the back of the room.

"I must say, I like Thursdays," he said.

"Why?"

"The kids are always quieter." He took his puffer out of his pocket and gave himself a shot, blinking. "Fridays they're hyped up about the weekend, and Mondays can be tricky, but on Thursdays everyone mellows out."

"I wonder why." Christabel hadn't spotted any trends, but then she'd only been volunteering for less than a month. Besides, she was only here twice a week.

"Debra's Reiki sessions are on Wednesdays," Steve said. "All five of these kids go. Calms them right down."

A guaranteed quiet day wasn't anything to sneer at. Still, Christabel frowned. No one had informed her that Sam had started Reiki treatments. At the first chance, she'd ask Mrs. McKay for an update.

After her hour in the classroom was up, she buzzed Security for an escort. She'd just gathered her belongings and was saying good-bye to Steve when there was a knock on the door. Christabel opened it, expecting an orderly, and was surprised to see Dr. Cheung. For the first time since she'd met him, he was wearing a white lab coat. It made him appear older, more official.

"Let's grab a coffee," he said. "The cafeteria will be empty–lunch ended a while ago."

"Lovely to have a bit of your time, Dr. Cheung."

"I'm never too busy for you."

"Excuse me?"

"And please call me Paul. We're co-workers now." He revealed his teeth in a boyish smile.

"All right. Paul."

It felt awkward, like she'd been given a shot of Novocain in her tongue. Even so, it was about time they lost the formality. They were bumping into each other a lot these days, in the corridors and on the grounds, even once or twice at the Valu-Mart in town. They might as well be collegial.

Inside the cafeteria, no servers were in sight. Without hesitating, Paul lifted a hinged section of counter and walked behind it to an industrial, stainless-steel urn. He poured two steaming mugs of coffee. Behind the swinging door leading to the kitchen, a radio was blasting out a Justin Bieber song. Christa could hear a man and woman singing along, one flat and the other sharp. She winced.

Paul chuckled and handed her a mug as they sat down at a table. "Not a Belieber, I take it?"

"Not particularly. But I'm all for the staff enjoying themselves while they work."

He nodded and emptied a creamer into his mug. As he stirred his coffee, the aroma of hazelnut floated on the air. "We haven't had a chance to chat recently. I hope you're enjoying your new teaching role."

There was a glimmer in his eyes that Christabel had never picked up on before. She paused. Was he merely being friendly, or was it something more?

"So far, so good." She took a cautious sip of coffee. "I need to ask you something. Is it true Sam sees Debra Gaston on Wednesdays?"

Paul's smile flickered. "Yes, as we discussed back in the summer, Sam's therapy has been expanded to include Reiki." He raised his mug to his lips and swallowed a mouthful. He grimaced. "Flavored coffee. If I didn't need the caffeine, I'd give it a pass." He made a toasting gesture with the mug and drank some more.

Christabel searched Paul's face. "Don't worry, I'm not anti-Reiki. I just want to know what's being done and why."

A harp-like tone interrupted them. He reached inside his white coat, checked his phone, and tucked it back into his pocket. His face impassive, he rose and walked swiftly to a bin of dirty dishes, placing his half-full mug in it with a clink.

"My apologies. I'm needed elsewhere. Please set up an appointment via my secretary, and we can discuss Sam's therapy soon." He glanced at his watch and left.

Christabel sat unmoving. *Set up an appointment via my secretary?* Had she just been given the brush-off?

She sipped the hot, nutty coffee. It actually tasted quite decent, and school was over for the day. She could have a one-on-one visit with Sam. Better yet, she could go back to her cozy apartment and immerse herself in Emily Dickinson.

She gazed at the high, escape-proof window. Rain was running down the glass in streams. She sighed. Until the weather cleared, a refill might be a wise call.

Self-service was probably against the rules, but the songbirds in the kitchen were too busy murdering Adele to care. Nevertheless, she threw a guilty look over her shoulder as she lifted the drawbridge-like section of the counter and entered the staff-only area.

The coffee sputtered out in gouts, making rude gassy noises before drying up completely. She was about to take her half-filled mug back to the table when she heard voices approaching from the hallway. Feeling absurdly guilty, she froze like a naughty child caught in the act of going through her mother's makeup.

"Right this way, Mr. Mistry," a woman said.

Before Christabel could stop herself, she dropped to a crouch behind the counter. The door to the hallway thunked closed. Ravi and whoever he was with didn't say anything for several seconds. As long as they weren't on a quest for coffee, her hiding place was safe—for now.

She hadn't seen Ravi in weeks, since the confrontation at the condo. Christabel gritted her teeth to keep them from chattering. Who was he with? And what was he doing here on a Thursday, anyway?

"You're a naughty one." The woman's voice was a purr.

Christabel caught her breath.

"Blame the treatments. They make me frisky." His words were muffled.

He was speaking into the woman's hair, perhaps—like he'd often done with Christabel, tickling her ear with his hot, eager breath.

She felt nausea rising and swallowed, hard. Ravi was an asshole and she'd renounced him forever. Still, it hurt like hell. No matter what had happened in the past, Ravi had never been unfaithful—that she knew of. And even if they were divorced and she hated him to his weak, dishonest core, this was torture. Her nerves felt flayed and raw.

Christabel remained motionless, focusing on not barfing up hazelnut-flavored coffee. She would bet whatever was left of her sanity the woman was Debra Gaston. Unimaginative man, to go from an ex-wife that rejected him to a similar make in a newer model. God, what if there'd been a whole parade of auburn-haired women in his life over the years?

Apart from the mindless music drifting in from the kitchen, the only sound was a series of muted moans. Christabel scrunched her eyes closed, even though there was no way she could see anything from her hiding spot.

An eternity of a minute passed. The workers in the next room started belting out an Ed Sheeran song. Someone was banging a metal pot with a wooden spoon, keeping ragged time. Anything was far better than listening to her ex-husband make out.

"I've got to go, Debra darling."

And there it was—*darling*. Not even two months had elapsed since their final break-up, and Christabel had been replaced.

"Come back soon. And Ravi?"

"Yes, babe?"

Babe?

"Stay with me on your next visit."

"Of course."

"My place—or yours, if you'd rather."

My God, the woman's voice was so throaty. She must have taken a course—How to Talk like a Sex Goddess.

The cafeteria door clicked twice—open, shut. Very slowly, Christabel stood up, knees popping as she straightened. In the distorted reflection of the stainless-steel urn, she saw an Edvard Munch *Scream* of a face, framed by wild wisps of auburn hair.

Really, Ravi? So soon? He'd evidently taken Christabel at her word and moved the hell on.

What did it matter? She already despised him.

From a rack of clean dishware, Christabel selected an empty mug. She weighed it in her hand. At the last second, she stopped herself from hurling it across the room.

She carefully put it back in the rack, tweaked her hair into place, lifted her chin, and marched out of the cafeteria. When a passing aide ran after her, protesting that she couldn't walk unescorted through the hallways, Christabel held her head high and kept going. She was the embodiment of composure and determination—on the outside, anyway.

Chapter 30; October 9

If only Christabel could escape from the tiny treatment room. Surely there wasn't enough oxygen for the four people crowded inside, but she'd demanded this demonstration, and now she'd just have to try to get through it.

Paul cleared his throat. "Reiki therapy is simple, effective and non-invasive. The benefits can be quite astonishing. Your family members are fortunate to have an expert like Debra Gaston working here." He bowed his head graciously at Debra, who stood beside him.

Christabel looked sideways at the only other observer in the small space—a hoary oldster, seated next to her. He must be someone's grandfather, if not great-grandfather. Still, she couldn't bear the ogling smirk he was leveling at Debra, who was dressed in workaday J.Crew clothes, shirt high to the neck.

"Thank you for your kind introduction, Dr. Cheung," Debra said in a professional tone. She leaned against the treatment table, which took up most of the room. "Now, before I give the two of you a short demonstration, do you have any questions?"

"If it's so damn effective, why haven't medical research studies proven it?" The old guy poked his bony elbow into Christabel's side.

She shifted her chair farther away.

"Perhaps Dr. Cheung is ahead of his time." Debra aimed a megawatt smile at the geezer. "Certainly, he's more open-minded to alternative therapies than is the scientific community as a whole."

The old man sat back, outwardly satisfied. Christabel was bursting with questions but didn't trust herself to ask them. Although she'd had two weeks to process the scene in the cafeteria, being in this confined zone with Debra was making her queasy.

"If there are no more questions, let's proceed." Debra enunciated precisely, as if addressing a class of slow learners.

She turned on a small lamp before killing the harsh fluorescent overhead lighting. Unhurriedly, she rolled up the cuffs on her shirt sleeves and applied some antibacterial gel to her hands. Christabel caught a glimpse of a tattoo on Debra's inner wrist. It was an infinity symbol. *Meaning what—Ravi's never-ending love?*

Paul nodded good-bye and slipped out, pausing to hold the door open for Grant Hilton, who entered from the hallway. The boy wore crisp jeans and a Blood Incantation T-shirt, his golden hair as tidy as always. His air of studied nonchalance changed abruptly when he saw the old man.

"Gramps? What the hell?"

"Delighted to see you, too." The man remained seated, fingers interlaced on his lap, back stiff.

"For a Reiki demo? Are you kidding me? Why not on any other of the hundreds of days since I've been stuck in the middle of fuckin' nowhere?" Grant's voice shook. He clamped his mouth shut and looked away.

Christabel gripped the arms of her chair. Beside her, Gramps studied his cuticles.

"I'm sorry, Grant," Debra said, honey-smooth. "I was unaware that you hadn't been informed of your grandfather's arrival."

She pulled Grant gently by the arm. He put up no resistance, dutifully shuffling the short distance to the treatment table, gaze lowered. He sat on its edge, feet dangling. Christabel shrank back, feeling like an interloper, but Gramps sat up straighter, ready for the show.

"For the purpose of this demonstration, I'll condense what is typically a forty-five-minute session into ten minutes or so." Debra stroked Grant's shoulder as he lay down on his back. "Don't worry, Grant, you won't be shortchanged. We'll do your full treatment after these folks have left."

"Can't be too fucking soon." Grant propped himself on his elbows, glaring at his grandfather.

"Relax. That's right; put your head on the pillow. Close your eyes." Using her left hand, palm down, Debra began to move it in an aerial overview, starting at Grant's head and traveling gradually lower. "What I am doing is scanning Grant's body, checking for any areas that might need special help."

"And you're able to determine that–how, exactly?" Gramps didn't seem to be buying into the whole Reiki thing.

In spite of not liking the guy, Christabel was grateful he was asking questions. She still wasn't sure her own vocal cords would work.

"It's all energy flow, sir. Life force." Debra's hand never faltered. Her movements through the air above Grant's body were elegant and confident.

"Horse crap." Gramps shifted in his chair, releasing an odor of mothballs with a sour undertone. Christabel held a finger under her nostrils and glanced sideways again. He looked even more ancient than before in the room's muted lighting.

"That's what I thought," Grant said, sounding much more relaxed. "Thing is, this shit works." Almost light-hearted, in fact. He yawned, showing plenty of orthodontically perfected teeth.

"After the initial scan, I place my hands on my patient, fully clothed, as you can see, following the chakra sequence from the crown, downward. The patient then turns over and I continue. Usually this takes up most of the session, but I am condensing it for you."

"Not by nearly enough," Gramps snorted.

Poor Grant. Why was the old bugger even here?

As Debra moved her hands on the boy's body, chakra by chakra, Grant seemed to grow increasingly composed. Even though it pained Christabel to admit it to herself, the woman might be competent, maybe even gifted.

With Grant once again lying on his back, Debra announced, "And now for the final cleansing." She began to stroke her arms in the air over his body, from head to feet.

"I am sweeping the auras," she said, continuing her graceful but bizarre ballet, shaking her hands at the end of each pass.

"When this is over, someone's going to have to shovel up the bullshit." Somehow, though, Gramps sounded a little less skeptical. Had a note of enthusiasm actually crept into his voice?

If so, Christabel understood why. Grant was in a state of bliss, on the verge of sleep. His hands trailed limply on each side of the treatment table, and his head lolled. The corners of his lips curved upward in uncomplicated contentment.

"And finally, I'm going to try to feel his healing," Debra said, laying one hand on Grant's forehead and the other on his chest. A few seconds passed before she added, "You know, even in this brief session, I believe we've achieved some excellent results."

Christabel made herself speak up. "Does Sam—" She looked at Debra's exquisitely arched eyebrows, not wanting to meet her eyes. "Does Sam like Reiki?"

Lifting her hands, Debra smiled at Christabel, no subtext apparent. "All the kids find it therapeutic. One look at Grant here will tell you everything you need to know. Whether or not you believe it has healing abilities, it's clear it relaxes them. Samantha loves it."

Christabel took a moment to process this. She nodded and rose from her chair without making another comment.

As she waited for an escort to open the door, she was startled to see an expression of naked desire on Grant's grandfather's face. She followed his gaze.

It wasn't Debra the man was leering at. His whole attention was laser-focused on a very drowsy Grant.

Chapter 31; December 3, morning

It was amazing how a routine helped make the days pass. With the steadiness of her morning store hours and her afternoon teaching gig, Christabel's days rippled by. Sam might not be any more affectionate, but at least she was calm and stable, and that was reason enough for optimism.

Christabel felt she was emerging, bit by bit, from the bleakest year of her life. In fact, as winter approached, she actually felt a spark of Christmas spirit begin to glow in her heart, much to her own surprise.

The merchants of Graysville seemed to be in a festive mood, too. Shopfronts all down the street were festooned with glittering ornaments and garlands, as if each business owner was trying to outdo the next. Only the woe-begotten woman of the fountain lacked adornment—her brass hands still clasped the fateful letter and her head was bare. The water had been turned off for the winter, but somehow icicles hung from the hem of her dress, and occasionally elderly tourists would secretively snap them off and suck on them, much to the townspeople's amusement.

Christabel turned away from the window. "Doby, do we have any decorations?"

"Nary a bauble." Doby sat on the stool behind the counter, his face buried in a glossy paperback, a far cry from his usual moldering hardcover.

"Grace could help us decorate," Christabel said. "She should be here any minute. In fact, that could be her rent-a-car pulling up now."

Doby's head pivoted so quickly she almost laughed.

"Alas, no." His shoulders slumped.

"When she does arrive, would you mind watching the store—that is, if I can get her to drive me to the garden center? I'll make swags for the window. Maybe cedar, if we can get our hands on any."

Doby shut his book with a snap. Christabel caught a glimpse of the title—*The Nerd's Guide to Getting the Girl.* She suppressed a smile.

"Or *you* can mind the store," he said, a gleam in his eyes. "Come to think of it, a touch of seasonal cheer would not go amiss around here. Within moderation, of course, and nothing too tinselly that my ferals might swallow."

"Agreed. Cat safety must be our highest priority." Christabel paused. "By the way, I'm glad you've changed your opinion about self-help books."

"Bah, humbug," Doby said, stuffing *The Nerd's Guide* under the counter.

He walked to the coatrack, grabbed his jacket and fez, and kept watch at the window. Within moments, and without uttering another word, he zipped out of the store and hopped into a white Ford Escape, Grace at the wheel. After a moment's apparent convincing, Grace shrugged and drove off, a beaming Doby sitting smugly beside her.

Christabel picked up the fluffy, orange cat and sat on the stool Doby had just vacated. She settled there, quietly singing *The First Noel,* accompanied by the cat's unabated motorboat purring.

"You're a smelly old guy," Christabel said, rubbing the cat's ears. "But you've become more lap cat than alley cat. It's about time we gave you a name."

She turned the cat to face her, nose to nose. "Noel, maybe."

It emitted a low growl.

"Maybe not *quite* a pet yet," she said, putting it down. "But you've come a long way."

Apart from the steady ticking of the Seth Thomas clock, the store was quiet. She loved it here, in this room of fact and fantasy, with its high ceilings and antique veneers and the shifting population of grateful felines. It was a haven. More, it was *home*.

Christabel was proud of her work over the past few months. Doby had allowed her to completely re-organize the collection, shelving all of the books in a customer-friendly fashion. Although sales had been less than brisk lately, she'd kept herself busy. She might still be a mess on the inside, but she was able to get through her days without crumbling, even when she occasionally bumped into Ravi and Debra together.

* * *

"Please don't ignore me, Christa."

It had been early November when Ravi had followed Christabel through the common room at Treffian House. She'd hurried ahead, dodging dozing old folks in wheelchairs in a vain attempt to evade him.

She stopped, only because she had to wait for an attendant to buzz her out. Cornered, she turned to confront her ex-husband.

She hoped he'd look haggard. Instead, he was more handsome than ever. The lines of his face were smoother, his eyes calm. His hair was styled in a younger cut—Debra's influence, no doubt.

Christabel stood her ground, trying to compose herself. Sooner or later, she'd have to talk to Ravi. He *was* Sam's other parent.

Lately, he seemed to be doing a better job of that. He visited Treffian House regularly—probably as an excuse to see Debra—but, either way, Sam benefitted.

Christabel's chin began to shake. Irked with herself, she elbowed her way past him and out into the reception area.

"All right. What is it you want to say?" She chose a chair and sat, twining her fingers together on her lap.

He waited for the orderly to leave. Then he pulled up a chair across from her, clasping his hands lightly on a crossed knee. Everything about him looked rich, from his camel coat to his tasseled

Italian loafers. Emotions waged war in her gut—regret and rage, and, in spite of herself, one or two surviving love butterflies.

He put a hand over his heart. "First of all, you need to know that I never lied when I told you I loved you."

It was such a cheesy gesture—yet, she felt a stinging behind her eyes.

"And we'll never know for certain that my mother didn't take good care of Sam," he added.

"Good *care*? She was abusing Sam. More than likely causing permanent brain damage."

"We'll never know for sure. But you've made it plain that you want nothing to do with me. For the record, this time, *I* never would have left *you*. You hurt me; very, very much."

She studied his pained expression. It had always been about Ravi and what worked for him—not for her, and definitely not for Sam.

"One other thing." He paused. "After you broke off our relationship, things were tough. Much more than tough, actually. I was a mess. And, well, Debra helped." Ravi looked away. "I guess you could say I'm seeing her these days."

"I'm aware."

Ravi's eyebrows shot up, but no way would she say another word on this topic. Seconds passed.

"I'll let you go, then." He paused, his eyes filled with sad-clown concern. "I only wanted to clear the air—reassure you I'll always be there for you, financially. But like you, I'm moving on."

He rose and touched Christabel's head before leaving, sending a wave of revulsion throughout her body. She counted to ten, slowly, and then willed her tensed muscles to relax. Her temples pounded but she remained in control, until she'd walked home. Only then, in the privacy of her apartment, did she cry—but Ravi would never know.

* * *

The camel bells jangled, startling her. A tall man entered Grandsmith's Books, bringing with him a gust of crisp, icy air. He wore a charcoal overcoat and a matching wedge-shaped driving cap. A bohemian, knitted red scarf covered the lower half of his face.

"Getting wintry out there, isn't it?" Christabel asked, putting down her book of William Blake's poems and rising from her stool.

The man stamped his feet on the mat. There was very little snow as yet and she wondered why he was being so dramatic.

"I'd forgotten how cold it is in this part of the world." A low, gravelly drawl. He stuffed his leather gloves into his pockets and began to unwind the scarf. Unfurled, it hung to his knees, making him look like an elderly schoolboy.

He dangled the ends. "I just bought this at the crafts store down the street, to keep my face from freezing off."

Underneath his cap, his hair was steel gray, matching his dark, piercing eyes. He was likely in his late seventies, quite dashing for an older gent. Familiar, somehow. Maybe because he reminded her a bit of the late Leonard Cohen, all strong lines and sharp angles—charisma in spades.

At least she had a client. She'd see what she could sell him and regale Doby later with a success story when he returned to the store with Grace.

"What may I help you find today, sir?" she asked, moving out from behind the counter. "We have an excellent assortment of rare, out of print novels. All the top bestsellers, too."

The man walked forward until he was so close that she was forced to look up into his face. For a second, she felt panicky, but she collected herself and walked past him to the shelves. He followed, again too closely.

"Non-fiction—biographies over here." She swept a hand across the dust-free shelf, but the man still seemed to be studying her.

"Something to read in my hotel room would be good," he said finally. "Possibly a thriller." He strolled away from her, toward the bestseller shelf. "Have you read this one?" He picked up a paperback with a garish collage of assault weapons on its cover, black on red.

"No, but I hear great things. Non-stop action." She went behind the counter and felt her pulse start to steady.

"I'll take it."

Christabel was handing the man his receipt when the bells on the door jangled. Grace and Doby entered, carrying bulging sacks.

Grace was bright-cheeked from the cold. "Wait until you see what we've bought ..."

The color drained from her face. Her knees wobbled, and she dropped her bags. There was a tinkling sound of breaking glass as Christabel raced out from behind the counter, catching her sister in mid-collapse.

"Doby! Give me a hand!"

He dropped his parcels and sprang forward to prop up Grace's other side. Together, he and Christabel maneuvered her across the floor and onto the stool. They bracketed Grace as she sat there in her puffy winter jacket, a look of horror in her eyes.

"What is *he* doing here?"

"He just bought a book." Christabel squeezed Grace's fingers and smiled an apology at the customer.

Grace dropped her chin to her chest. "Get him out of here." She started to sob.

As she took her sister in her arms, Christabel caught sight of Doby's expression, matching her own feelings of shock. Grace was the strong one; the sister who never cried. Christabel tightened the hug.

Doby stretched himself to his full, ungainly height. "Sir, I must ask you to leave."

Over the ridiculous homemade scarf, the man's penetrating eyes raked him up and down. "No need for violence. I'll take my book and leave peacefully."

He walked to the door and opened it. Cold air poured in, as the man turned to look straight at Christabel.

"Goodbye for now. And don't feel bad. I'm gratified that at least *one* of my daughters recognizes her loving father."

Chapter 32; December 3, afternoon

The afternoon was a write-off. Doby turned out the lights and closed the store. Grace sobbed, as he and Christabel supported her upstairs to the couch. The two of them took sentry posts at either end. Christabel's arms ached to reach out and hug Grace, but the distant look in her sister's eyes stopped her.

From time to time, Doby silently held out a box of Kleenex. Grace grabbed handfuls, mopping her face and tossing the used tissues on the floor. No one made a move to clean up the mess.

Christabel's throat was tight. That man had been her father–her *dad.* Emotions churned inside her–anger, sadness, confusion–alarming her with their intensity.

He'd always been a lousy parent. Christabel's hazy memories were of an imposing figure that appeared at erratic intervals. Between their mom's alcoholic rages and his shouting, the house was a battlefield–until she died and he left.

There was that one night, though, just before his final departure. Christabel was asleep, snuggled up with Bear. She squeezed Bear tightly, the way Grace always hugged her, with fierce possessiveness. Now that Mom was gone, Grace's hugs came even more often. It was wonderful to be loved so deeply.

Her dreams were of fields of clover, with fat, puffy blossoms. When she pulled out each spiky clover petal and sucked the bottom of it, the sweetness on her tongue was heavenly. She looked over at the next clump, and saw Grace, in the form of a blue butterfly, perched on another bloom. The world was fragrant and still.

A glancing touch woke her up. She smiled, and peered through the darkness for Grace, who often fell asleep beside her these days.

But it was someone else—someone larger. How strange—her father had paid her a midnight visit.

"Daddy?"

"Shhh. Quiet, now." He stroked her arm.

She turned over and lay on her back, reaching her arms up for a hug. It was nice her dad was showing her some attention. He was hardly ever home.

The door flew open and Grace appeared, pajamaed and frantic. "What the hell?"

"Language, dear child." Their dad's voice was charming—lazy and full of humor.

"What are you doing in here?" Why was Grace being so snappy?

"My younger daughter needed me. Nightmares." And why was Dad lying? He didn't have to. Christabel was so happy he was here.

"I'll stay with her. You can go." Grace pushed him away and flounced onto the bed, making Christabel's body bounce.

Their dad moved toward the door. "If you need me, Christabel, I'll be just down the hall."

"Promise?"

"Always," he said, and left.

Three days later, he was gone for good.

After that, Grace was mom, dad, and big sister, wrapped up in one stable, protective package. She bestowed a constant stream of love on Christabel, and, when pushed too far, an occasional well-deserved kick in the ass.

Christabel never needed or wanted anyone else. Still, she would love to talk to her father—put the bastard under klieg lights and interrogate him.

"Dad, you left us. Why?" She closed her eyes, imagining the scene. She, leaning across a wooden table; her father, lounging in his chair, one arm thrown over its back. In her fantasy, he was wearing black and white striped prisoner's clothes, a matching bellhop-style hat on his silvery head.

"Why do you ask?" There it was—his amused tone, like he was trying to suppress a chuckle.

"You owe me an explanation. Now, talk."

"It seemed the right thing to do at the time." Fantasy Dad was being as cryptic as Real Dad had always been. It was maddening.

"You never sent me a single birthday card. Why not?"

"Must have slipped my mind, my dear. Although you were never completely out of my thoughts. A father's love is forever." He yawned.

She bridled. "Why didn't you come to my high school graduation? Or college? What about when I got married? Had my daughter—*your* granddaughter? How could you abandon us so completely?"

But her imaginary dad was just like her real dad. He simply vanished.

Christabel clenched her fists.

Grace was silent now, apart from the occasional wrenching hiccup. Doby got up and moved restlessly around the room. After a while he went to the kitchen and brought back unwanted tea and cookies.

"There, there," he said over and over, like an obsessive parrot. His eyes were red-rimmed and frantic.

Grace looked through him. Christabel shrugged at Doby, resigning herself to a longer wait. When the town clock struck four, she rose and walked to the window, looking out at the peaceful Graysville afternoon. The sun was getting low on the horizon, casting ruddy beams that glinted off the Christmas decorations of the main street shops. The woman of the fountain hid in the shadows, except for a halo atop her head, created by the oblique rays.

"Chrissie?"

"I'm right here." Christabel rushed over and sat on the couch next to her sister.

"That man." Grace took a breath. "He ruined my life."

Christabel felt her heart constrict. Grace had been stuck parenting when she should have been partying and traveling and maybe even marrying.

"It must have been a nightmare for you, Gracie." Christabel hoped her words wouldn't set off a whole new frenzy of tears.

Grace stared into the distance, her face a mask of despair.

"I hate to think what a burden I was." Christabel shifted her weight, but Grace pulled her closer.

"*What*?"

"You were almost a kid yourself." Christabel's chin quivered.

She'd stolen her sister's youth. What advantage was Grace ever given?

"Listen. You—" Grace hiccupped, a strangely lonely sound.

"You were too young. You had to deal with my teenage years, all alone."

"It wasn't your fault."

"Still." Christabel hung her head.

She'd been oblivious to Grace's emotional turmoil all those years—selfishly happy to have her sister all to herself.

"Listen to me," Grace's eyes were haunted. "I'm only going to say this once." She lifted her hands to her mouth, as if to stifle something terrible.

Christabel forced herself to sit still. "Go on."

Grace lowered her hands slightly. "He was a shitty father—we both know that. But what I've never told you is that when I was nine, he started to ... Christ, help me." Again, Grace shielded her mouth.

Christabel felt cold to her core. "Oh, my God."

Doby leaned in as if to put an arm around Grace's shoulders. He backed off when Christabel shook her head fiercely at him.

"I had no one to turn to." Grace hugged a cushion to her chest. "It went on for years."

No sound in the room. Christabel gripped her sister's hand. How could she not have known?

Grace spoke again, rushing her words. "I was so thankful when he'd go away, often for weeks on end. Then, that night, I saw him with you."

"Oh, Grace." Christabel's eyes filled with angry tears.

"I told him I'd report him if he didn't leave. Told him to get the fuck out of our lives." She gasped for breath. "And he did. Left us for good this time, except for sending his pay-off money."

Christabel pulled Grace in for a gentle hug. "We should call the police. It's not too late."

"No." Grace pushed her away. "We made a deal. He sent his payments until you were through university. Anyway, I don't want to relive it."

Doby stood up and walked toward the kitchen. "'*There is a pain so utter—it swallows substance up ...*'"

Grace's bloodshot eyes followed him. "What is he going on about?"

"Emily Dickinson. His way of expressing solidarity. Oh, Gracie, what you must have suffered—"

"Enough. I would do it all over. But I never want to see that man again—*ever.* That's it. I'm done talking."

Grace sprawled full length on the couch, turning her head toward the backrest. Christabel fetched a blanket from the bed and tucked her sister in, before joining Doby in the kitchen.

As the kettle began to shriek on the tiny stovetop, he switched the burner off. She opened the cabinet beneath the sink and pulled out a bottle of Johnny Walker Blue. Doby turned his back on the box of tea and held out his mug. She cracked the seal and poured a shot for both of them. They stared solemnly at each other before downing them.

Ravi had bought the scotch for his visits. She'd never liked the taste but it was so expensive, she'd balked at pouring it down the drain when she'd moved here.

The thought of her ex made her shudder. What were the odds of having not just one, but *two* appallingly deficient men in her life?

Doby waggled the bottle at her. She held out her mug and accepted a generous refill. When she gulped it, the whiskey burned a righteous path all the way down.

She turned to Doby. "You'll never hurt my sister, will you?"

He laid his hand on his heart. "I vow to be a force of goodness, the breaking sun on a troubled landscape."

"Where's that from?" Christabel studied Doby's expression.

"Pure Doby doggerel, I'm afraid."

When he hoisted the whiskey bottle again, Christabel shook her head. She put her cup in the sink and walked back into the living room, her eyes on Grace. Doby joined her, and they stood shoulder to shoulder. After a moment he settled on the floor next to the couch and closed his eyes.

When Sam had been diagnosed, Christabel had more or less given up on God. She hadn't prayed seriously in years. But now, watching Grace's chest rise and fall in the twilit apartment room, Christabel sent a message heavenward.

"Please bless my sister, Grace. Send her strength and help her heal." She thought for a few seconds, and added, "And don't waste your time worrying about me, God. I'm going to be just fine. Amen."

She turned and went downstairs, flicked on the lights and fed the ferals. Tomorrow she'd bundle Grace out of town, far away from their father's influence. Then, she'd try to figure out what the hell he was doing in Graysville.

Chapter 33: December 5

It was just before five o'clock. The sky was darkening, leaden clouds overlaid on a slate sky, and no stars shone. Christabel glanced over her shoulder, speeding up as she passed the statue. She told herself it was only her imagination that the lady had raised her eyes from the letter and was watching her as she walked beyond the Victorian primness of Graysville, toward its seedy town line.

It was time to meet her father, face to face. She knew where he was staying, having called every hotel, motel, and inn in the area, until she'd hit pay dirt. Before the clerk in Reception had connected her call, she'd hung up.

She picked up her pace, the echoes of her footsteps growing louder, as the shadows merged with the oncoming night. Traffic was sporadic. A large SUV flanked her for a short distance, the driver's face obscured in the dim light. Christabel kept her eyes focused straight ahead and strode on.

A group of tacky, two-story motels came into sight. She scanned the blinking neon signs for the Le Roi, pronounced 'Lee Roy' by the locals–disdainfully, as if it were some unwelcome yokel's name.

It was the last in the sorry row. Its aluminum siding was battered from drunk drivers' late-night mishaps, and some of the shutters were missing. At least half the bulbs in the exterior door-side lamps were dead. The sound of claws skittering behind industrial garbage bins startled her, and Christabel found herself jogging toward the entrance. Why would her prosperous-looking father stay in such a dump?

The lobby was a '70s throwback, all fake teak and faded orange corduroy. Behind the counter, a middle-aged man wearing demi-moon glasses was tapping away on a computer keyboard, playing computer solitaire, perhaps. His greasy black comb-over revealed flaky patches of scalp.

Christabel cleared her throat. "I'm here to see Mr. Newberry. Could you tell me his room number?"

He peered at her blearily. "No can do. Policy."

"Could you let him know his daughter is here?"

With an exasperated sigh, the clerk let go of his mouse and picked up the receiver. He ran a tobacco-stained finger down a column in a ledger filled with handwritten scrawls and put the phone back in its cradle.

"Gone."

Christabel gripped the edge of the sticky countertop. "But he was here as of four o'clock today."

She'd been dreading the confrontation. Now she realized that not seeing him would be much worse. She leaned across the counter, trying to decipher the wildly slanting scribbles in the ledger.

"Take a good long look, why don'tcha. Room 136. Checked out before my shift."

"Do you have a contact number or address for him?"

"Nah. Paid cash." He shifted his attention to the computer screen.

After a moment, she pulled her hood up and left, feeling her adrenaline level plummet. Once again, the bastard had ghosted her.

She might as well double-check his room before making the long walk home. Number 136 fronted on the parking lot, the outside lamp barely illuminating its crooked numerals. Christabel leaned against the window, nose pressed to the glass. The television was still on, tuned to CNN, bathing the shabby room in blue, flickering light. The bed was rumpled, and a few beverage cans were strewn on the dresser. Why had her father left in such a rush?

It had grown darker. She shivered and turned toward home. A breeze whisked dead leaves across the asphalt, making the sound of small bones rattling. She began to walk down the sidewalk, but stopped when she heard the thunk of a car door.

She swung around, in time to see a tall figure get into a battered-looking sedan. It couldn't be, but it was—an older man, swathed in a long wool scarf. She sprinted back and pounded on the hood just as the car began to pull forward.

The tires kept rolling. Christabel dropped her hands and stood her ground. Surely her father would stop.

He blasted the horn, braking at the last second. The window opened a crack. "Are you too stupid to get out of the way of a moving vehicle?"

Christabel banged her fist one last time on the car's hood. "You almost killed me!" She marched to the driver's-side door, blinking as she left the headlights' glare.

He didn't turn off the engine, nor did he open the window any further. "A drama queen like your mother, I see."

"You know nothing about me!" She tried to open his door. It was locked. "Get out. We have to talk."

He put the car in gear. "Not interested."

"Wait—"

He shook his head, abruptly reversed over the small walkway in front of the motel, and pulled away, tires squealing.

Christabel stood alone in the parking lot, hands clenched by her sides, staring after him. There was nothing to do but walk home. For the time being, her questions would have to wait.

Chapter 34; December 9

Christabel gave the store's lock a final jab, and at last it clicked. She stuffed the key into her pocket and hurried along the sidewalk, dodging icy patches and clutching the collar of her wool coat to her neck. The weather had turned nastier, sharp-edged snow pellets beginning to fall. Her jog to Treffian House had never felt so long.

"Sorry I'm late," she said *sotto voce* to Steve, who was distributing pieces of construction paper to some of the students.

He'd pre-cut a variety of vaguely Christmassy shapes. Evergreen trees, sleds, stars. No scissors, not even blunt-edged ones, were in sight. Sam reached up and grabbed some paper, after flicking a glance and a half-smile her way. It wasn't much, but it made Christabel's heart lighten.

"I'll dock your pay." Steve winked, adding in an undertone, "But do me a favor. See what's bugging Grant."

The boy sat slumped over his desk at the back of the room. Christabel took off her damp coat and hung it on a hook before taking slow steps to his side. No quick movements. No raised voices. She felt in her pocket to make sure her panic button was there.

"Hi, Grant. Are you feeling all right?"

The top of his blond hair was tousled. Strange. Grant was an obsessively tidy teenager.

"I'm fine." His sagging posture didn't change.

"I've been looking forward to the next installment of your novella. May I read it?"

Grant raised his head slightly and peered at her through his thick, straight lashes. His eyes were glassy. His mouth worked, as if he wanted to tell her something but couldn't get the words out.

"Grant, you don't look well. Maybe you should go back to your room and rest. I'll call an attendant for you."

His gray eyes narrowed. "Don't bother." He pulled himself to a more upright position, still leaning heavily on his forearms, head drooping as if too heavy for his neck. "I didn't get my chapter finished. Sorry, Ms. Newberry."

"Oh. Well, that's okay." She resisted the urge to touch his shoulder. "Don't push yourself too hard today."

With a shaking hand, he picked up his pen. After a moment, he put it to one side and laid his head down. His eyelids fluttered closed.

Christabel looked at him in alarm. She forced herself to take smooth, steady steps back to Steve's desk, where he sat, watching his other students fuss with their art projects. Sam wielded a glue stick with gusto, a sparkle in her eye.

"He's not himself, is he?" Steve gazed across the room at Grant.

"No," she said in a low voice. "I don't think he's ill, though. Just exhausted."

Without lifting his head, Grant said in a hollow tone, "I can hear you, you know."

Christabel bent close to Steve's ear. "I'll go see if I can find Mrs. McKay or Dr. Cheung."

Steve nodded and rang for an aide to escort Christabel. Within two minutes, the Friar Tuck guy arrived. This fellow seemed to be becoming a permanent fixture.

"I'm afraid I don't know your name," she said, following him.

"Took you long enough to ask, *Christabel*," he said in a grumpy voice. "It's Jonathan."

He marched ahead in uncompanionable silence, rushing off the moment they arrived at Paul's office, as if he couldn't wait to get away from her. Paul was on the phone, but he signaled for her to enter and take a seat.

"Right, right. Yes, we'll take your request under consideration, Mr. Hilton. Good-bye." He hung up and looked across the desk at

Christabel, his smile of greeting turning to a frown. "Is there something wrong?"

"I'm sorry, but were you talking to Grant's grandfather just now?"

"Why do you ask?" Paul steepled his fingers together on his desktop.

"Just that I actually came here to talk to you about Grant's health. He seems—well, not exactly ill, but not himself. Has anything changed that Steve and I should know?"

Paul hesitated. "No. Same as always. We've been pleased that his grandfather has been visiting him. After Debra's Reiki demonstration Mr. Hilton has become quite a convert himself, and he always makes time to visit his grandson when he has his appointments."

"Do you think that's wise? I mean, Grant didn't seem to get along with him." She snapped her mouth closed, wanting to kick herself. She'd crossed a line. Not only that—if residents had a choice in the matter, would Sam ever let *her* visit?

Paul waited several more seconds before giving her a decisive nod. "I will investigate. Thank you for bringing it to my attention."

He adjusted his tie—a conservative blue with a navy pinstripe that matched his suit jacket precisely. Crisp, businesslike. No doctor's white today.

Christabel rose to leave. She felt guilty, like she was letting Grant down. But what more could she do?

"A minute more of your time, please," Paul said.

"What is it? Sam?"

He blinked. "Oh, no. Nothing like that. It's just ..." Paul reached up to adjust his glasses. "What I would like to suggest is dinner. Perhaps next Saturday?"

Christabel couldn't have been more astonished. She tried to gather her fragmented thoughts.

"That's a tempting offer." She steadied her voice. "And I'm flattered. But I'm afraid I'm still recovering from ... well, you know all about my situation. Maybe one day in the future?"

Paul gave her a considering look. He'd be an excellent poker player.

Finally, he said, "Let's give it some more time, then. But I do want to get to know you better. Let me know when you're ready."

The doctor had chutzpah, she had to give him that. But, even if there weren't ethical concerns, would she ever be interested? Christabel doubted it. She had no time for mind-reading and second-guessing. Still ...

There was a knock on the door. Mrs. McKay poked her head inside. "Dr. Cheung? Ah, Mrs. Mistry, it's a pleasure to see you."

Mrs. McKay smiled tightly and patted her rigorously curled hair. It was shaped like a WWII German helmet. Fleetingly, Christabel wondered whether it would feel as hard to the touch.

"I'm just leaving," Christabel said. "I was here to tell Dr. Cheung that Grant Hilton seems unwell. Oh, and I'm going by Ms. Newberry now."

She'd shed one bastard's name for another's. And how weird that she and Mrs. McKay were still so formal. Everyone else around here had loosened up ages ago.

"I'll walk you back to the classroom then, shall I?" Mrs. McKay didn't give Christabel a chance to demur, but took her firmly by the elbow and led her out of the room.

"Weren't you hoping to have a meeting with Dr. Cheung?" Christabel asked as Mrs. McKay whisked her along.

"It will keep. I'm interested in what you can tell me about Grant." Mrs. McKay's oxfords made clunking sounds as she strode purposefully down the hall, still holding onto Christabel's elbow.

"Maybe I'm overreacting, but he seems strangely lethargic."

Mrs. McKay said nothing. When Christabel looked sideways, the woman's mouth was compressed.

"Have you noticed this before?" Mrs. McKay maintained her trotting pace but released her grip on Christabel.

“No. But I’m only in the classroom twice a week.” Christabel gave her arm a secretive rub, wondering if she’d develop a bruise.

“Hmm.”

When they reached the classroom, Grant appeared to be asleep, his head resting on the desktop. Mrs. McKay took one look at him and turned around sharply, departing without a word. Maybe she was off to have a clinical discussion with Paul about Grant’s condition.

They’d better have one—and soon. This institution didn’t need another tragedy.

Chapter 35; December 11

From the official records of the late Mrs. Audrey McKay (MSW), formerly of Treffian House

Transcribed from recorded session with Samantha Mistry. Handwritten notes indicated in italics

Mistry: Reiki. Yay!

McKay: Yes, you certainly enjoy your sessions with Ms. Gaston. What do you like most about them?

Mistry: Dunno. She's pretty.

McKay: Yes, and?

Mistry: Daddy comes, too. And sometimes Grandpa!

McKay: Dear me, quite a family party. And your mother?

Mistry: Nope.

McKay: Ah, too bad. But you enjoy your sessions, which is the main thing.

Mistry: I get all sleepy. Comfy.

McKay: Really? Maybe I'll observe your next session.

Mistry: Nope.

McKay: Why not?

Mistry: Don't want you. No Mommy. No you.

* * *

Observations: Samantha seems to be enjoying and benefiting from her Reiki sessions with Debra Gaston. But Grant Hilton is faltering. I wonder if Reiki has a cumulative, lethargy-inducing effect the longer the subject engages in it.

Or is it something else that Debra Gaston does during the therapy that enervates him? (Drugs?) I am going to find a way to observe one of his appointments.

Even as I write this, I realize how ridiculous it sounds. Grant may have a virus. Samantha is thriving. For now I will keep my suspicions to myself.

Chapter 36; December 16

Christabel jogged up the stairs to Treffian House, almost bumping into Paul, who was hovering inside the first security door. She seemed to be running into him a lot these days.

"A moment of your time?" His eyes were insistent.

She halted in the entranceway and tried not to tap her foot on the tiled floor. There were only a few minutes to go until she was due in the classroom. Poor Grant needed her, and Steve got anxious when she was late—and then there was Sam, who one of these days might be truly happy to see her.

"I hate to hold you up," Paul said quietly, "but I wanted to let you know that Grant Hilton is on the mend."

"That's excellent." She felt her muscles relax and smiled at him. "I've been worried."

He took her hand and pressed it but let go abruptly when Mrs. McKay arrived to escort Christabel to the classroom. His good-bye nod was professional and cool.

Christabel's hand still tingled as she kept pace with Mrs. McKay. Perhaps it was just a physical reflex—her body craving human contact. She needed more than that in her next relationship.

"I took your words seriously, Ms. Newberry," Mrs. McKay said, breaking the silence, "and can assure you that Grant is going to be fine."

Christabel looked sideways at her. "Yes, well, that's what Dr. Cheung just said." She didn't mean to sound snippy, but she was going to be late for class. She walked faster.

"You may want to know ..." Mrs. McKay paused. "The boy will not be having outside visitors for a while. His grandfather is abroad."

"Pardon me, but I'm not sure why you're telling me this." Christabel unbuttoned her wool coat as they continued down the hallway.

"No reason, no reason," Mrs. McKay said, in an absent voice. "Ah, here we are." Turning on her heel, she left before Christabel could say good-bye.

The classroom buzzed with activity. Sam, her nose close to the whiteboard, traced outlined block letters, humming as she worked. Her long dark hair caught the light, making her look like a short-sighted angel. Steve huddled with three students near the front of the room, playing a Bingo-based numbers game, the kids laughing uproariously. He was fully engaged in the activity and didn't look up.

At a desk in the back, Grant wrote at a furious clip, his forehead furrowed. Pieces of crumpled paper littered his desk and the floor. As Christabel walked over to join him, she noticed a different doll sitting on her daughter's desk. Auburn Barbie—the one that had never been unboxed.

A glow sparked in her heart. Everyone was doing well today, and there was a spirit of optimism in the air. Grant's cheeks were pink, his eyes clear. He was once again his usual, fastidious self.

"Busy here. Genius at work." Still scribbling, Grant waved a curt dismissal.

"Carry on," Christabel said. Why worry about manners when it was such a joy to see the boy was better? "I'll check if Mr. Dodd needs any help."

Just then, she heard a knock. Steve was engrossed in the noisy game, so Christabel went to answer it.

Debra Gaston stood in the hallway, her hand raised to knock again. She wore a figure-accentuating red dress and looked like she'd just walked out of the pages of *Glamor*.

"Hello." She brushed past Christabel. "I'm here to pick up Sam for a Reiki appointment."

"But today's Monday." Christabel spoke through clenched teeth.

Debra waved to get Sam's attention. "Schedules do change."

Christabel's heart dropped as she saw her daughter's face light up. Sam tossed her dry erase marker aside and ran over, throwing her slim arms around Debra. When Debra returned the embrace, her auburn hair mingled with Sam's dark locks.

Christabel couldn't bear it. She couldn't bear being in that room for a minute longer. Grant was oblivious. Steve was immersed in his game. Christabel unhooked her coat and scarf and turned to leave.

"Ms. Newberry!" Debra rushed back and grabbed her by the sleeve. "You aren't authorized to walk unaccompanied."

Christabel pulled her arm away. "Try and stop me." Her pulse rate accelerated.

The two women faced each other. Across the room, Steve watched them but didn't budge.

"It's for your own safety," Debra said. Cool, no-nonsense. "You must allow me to escort you. Sam can come, too. We'll drop you off at the front lobby on our way to her treatment session."

Christabel ignored her and appealed to Steve. "Sorry, I've got to go. I'm not feeling well. But, shouldn't Sam stay in class?"

"Huh?" He seemed mesmerized by the drama.

Debra turned on her most charming smile. "Sam will be gone for less than an hour." She walked to Steve's side and placed her hand on his shoulder.

He nodded–wordlessly. Christabel barely managed to swallow her scream of frustration.

In the corridor, Debra walked hand in hand with Sam. Christabel followed, staring at the shapely back of this woman who had captured her ex-husband's heart–not to mention her daughter's affections, too. Anger clashed with sorrow inside her. Though she hated to admit it, she burned with pure, sizzling jealousy.

"Reiki, Reiki." Sam was practically skipping.

"That's great," Christabel said, more emphatically than necessary in an effort to keep the shakiness out of her voice.

"Samantha is an excellent Reiki client. So receptive." Debra gave Sam a sideways hug.

Christabel didn't bother answering.

But then Sam said, "Daddy, too."

"*What?*" Christabel stopped and stared at the back of her daughter's head.

"I love Reiki. Daddy loves Reiki." Sam giggled and did a little hop.

"Sometimes Mr. Mistry comes to observe." Debra hadn't broken pace, and Christabel was forced to hurry in order to catch up. Sam gamboled along beside them like a puppy.

"Why on earth would Ravi come to Sam's session?" Christabel asked.

Other than the fact that he was sleeping with the therapist.

"Mr. Mistry is extremely interested in his daughter's progress."

"He is? That's so gratifying to hear. It's such a change from—" Christabel barely managed to choke back a snide remark.

They'd reached the inner security door. Debra pressed the button to let Christabel out, but before she could leave, Ravi entered. He wore a long overcoat of fine, gray wool and his cheeks were burnished from the cold. Everything about him was mannequin-ideal, from his styled hair to his white teeth, revealed as he smiled at Debra.

Could this day get any worse? Christabel folded her arms across her chest and glared at her ex-husband.

"Hello, Christa," he said, seemingly unaware of her hostility.

"I hear you're a Reiki convert," she said, tight-lipped.

"Yes, Debra has shown Sam and me a thing or two about that ancient art." His eyes crinkled at the corners as they rested on Debra.

Christabel felt her stomach lurch.

"Hi, Daddy." Sam moved to her father's side and seized his hand.

He winced, the smile erased. "Hi, Sam."

"Let's go, Daddy. Reiki time." Sam tugged her father. "You and me."

"Don't let me hold you up." Christabel walked to the door.

Nobody stopped her. Nobody said good-bye.

As she crossed the entranceway, she heard Ravi say, "Hold on, Sam. We have to wait for Grandpa."

"*Excuse* me?" Christabel slowly turned around.

"I was talking to Sam."

"*Grandpa?*"

"Yes. Your dad. He got in touch with me a while back."

"And you've invited him here, to see Sam? Without even asking me?" Christabel could hear her voice rising.

"He's Sam's grandfather. She has every right to see him." He stared over her head. "As a matter of fact, we're partners on a deal."

Now it made sense. Sam was just the conduit. As always in Ravi's life, business was king.

Debra moved slightly, as if to guard him. Christabel edged past without even glancing at her.

"Listen to me, Ravi. My father is a very bad man."

"I understand your sense of abandonment. But people change."

"You don't know a thing about him!" Her mind raced.

"I got references. Quality ones." He smirked, as if the word of corporate colleagues trumped anything a bitter ex-wife might have to say.

Forgetting all about self-control, Christabel gripped Ravi by his lapels. "You keep that man away from our daughter. Do you hear me?"

"This isn't healthy for Sam," Debra said, smoothing Sam's hair with calm hands. "I assure you, Ms. Newberry, our first commitment is to her well-being."

"I like Grandpa," Sam said, a worried frown darkening her face.

Christabel took a trembling breath. "Keep him the hell away from our daughter, Ravi. Or, so help me God, I'll go to the police."

"Oh, please, you don't need to be so dramatic." Debra's tone was pure saccharine. "Treffian's residents are supervised at all times during visits."

Christabel wanted to punch her.

"Of course you can follow up on your concerns," Debra continued, a placid half-smile on her face. "That's your right. But, I do want to emphasize that Mr. Newberry is welcome here. Sam's father believes it's good for his daughter to have other family members visit."

Christabel felt her fists rise of their own accord. Sam was gaping at her. Taking a shaky breath, Christabel dropped her hands.

"Christa," Ravi said evenly, "do you want me to explain the legalities again?" He exchanged a meaningful glance with Debra.

"The thing is," Debra said, "Treffian House has legal control over Samantha's well-being. She is *our* ward. We decide what's best for her."

"What's *best*? If you think that my father, who abandoned me when I was a kid, and did unspeakable things to my sister—" Christabel stopped herself. "I have to insist. Keep him away from Sam."

Behind Christabel, the door clicked open. Footsteps approached.

"Grandpa's here. Yay!" Sam said, her face lighting up.

Christabel groped for a wall to lean on. Her legs felt useless, rubbery.

"Delightful to see you again," a deep voice said behind her, juicy with amusement. "Such a special family reunion." Christabel's father walked closer and draped one arm over Ravi's shoulder, the other over Debra's. He no longer wore the craft-store scarf—a classic Burberry had taken its place. His cologne held notes of cedar and bergamot. "Are we ready, folks?"

"One second, please." Debra looked directly at Christabel. "This seems as good a time as any to share our news."

"I'll tell her if you like," Ravi said.

"Allow me," Christabel's father said. His dark eyes were piercing. "Surely by now you've noticed the resemblance. If you inherited even an iota of my IQ, you can't have missed it."

Christabel turned to leave but Ravi grabbed her arm. "You need to hear this."

She wrenched herself out of his grip. "Back off."

Ravi held his hands up like a magician with nothing up his sleeves.

Christabel skewered her father with a stare. "Go on, then."

"We'll get the DNA test results soon," her father drawled.

"No." This wasn't happening.

"I must confess I was a bit of a rogue in my younger days–and take a good, hard look at her." He paused, obviously savoring the moment. "It may well turn out that Debra is yet another of my beautiful children."

Christabel heard a roaring in her ears. Her father hadn't just said what she thought he'd said.

He held out his arms as if to embrace them all and flashed Christabel a brilliant smile.

"Which would make us one big, happy family."

* * *

"Doby?" Christabel put her cellphone on speaker, so she'd have both hands free to wring. If she'd been a smoker she would have gone through a pack and a half by now.

"Indeed, it is I."

"How's Grace?"

He was silent, apart from his steady breathing. A moment later, Christabel heard his footsteps, followed by the sound of a door closing.

When he spoke, it was in hushed tones. "She's getting stronger. Still having flashbacks, though. Tomorrow she's going to her first therapist's appointment."

"I can't tell you how relieved I am that you're staying with her."

"As a reed bends in the wind, I bow to Grace's every whim."

"I'm so grateful. And, whatever you do, keep her in Toronto for now."

"You are an enigma shrouded in a mystery."

"I know. And I'll explain everything. Soon." She laid her hands flat on the tabletop and stared at the phone.

"As you wish. I entrust the store and all its contents to you. Provide the ferals with some special Christmas comestibles, and carry on."

"Will do, Doby. Give my love to Grace." She clicked off.

The night loomed ahead, certain to be sleepless. There was no point in going to bed. She had too much information to digest.

She'd done what she could. After the nightmarish encounter with Ravi and her dad, she'd met with Paul and Mrs. McKay. She'd negotiated, hard, citing Treffian House's own rules and they'd eventually agreed. Debra might be Sam's half-aunt, and relatives were never left alone with residents. From now on, until the DNA tests proved negative, her sessions with Sam would be observed by at least one other Treffian House employee.

Having won a reprieve made Christabel feel stronger. For now, Sam was safe. And if the DNA tests showed there was no blood connection—a result devoutly to be wished for—Christabel was confident she'd come up with a Plan B.

She pulled up a chair and looked out her dormer window. Except for the unlit fountain, Graysville was illuminated like Whoville before the Grinch's raid. As the Christmas lights sparkled and snowflakes fell, Christabel felt tears trail down her cheeks. For Sam and Grace, sinned against and forever damaged, and for herself, blinded by love and betrayed.

After a while she sat up straight and wiped her eyes. Screw her father and Ravi, and, while she was at it, screw Debra who may turn out to be a half-sister by blood but wasn't any kind of relative Christabel would ever want in her life.

She couldn't change the past, but she could make sure that the future was as bright as possible for the people who mattered—the ones who needed her.

Chapter 37; December 25

Christabel awoke to semidarkness. She stretched, feeling the Siberian expanse of starchy sheets. No stocking stuffed with treats hung from her bed-knob. No scent of coffee wafted from the kitchen; no child laughed. The silence was profound.

She sat up and swung her feet to the floor. So what if she'd never been all by herself on Christmas morning? She was fine.

She wrapped herself in her plush housecoat. As she began to move around her apartment, a chorus of wails broke out from the floor below. The ferals couldn't care less that it was a holiday. They wanted their breakfast, and they wanted it now.

She clattered downstairs and poured out the usual dry kibble. It looked dreary, but it was nothing that a dollop of canned food couldn't remedy. It *was* Christmas, after all.

As she put the heaping cat dishes on the floor, her phone rang.

"Hello?"

"Merry Ho-ho!"

Christabel held the receiver out from her ear. How had she allowed herself to be roped into spending Christmas Day with Mandy?

"Coming over soon?"

Christabel glanced at the clock. "I thought we said lunchtime."

Mandy had been persistent about the Christmas visit. She claimed the coast was clear; Ravi hadn't shown up at the condo next door for ages.

"I don't know if you're aware of this, Christabel," she'd added with barely muted gusto. "But people are talking. Oh, I'll just say it. Everyone says he's moved in with Debra Gaston."

Christabel was proud of herself when she refrained from reacting.

"Thanks, but I'm going to stay home."

But Mandy refused to take no for an answer. When all else failed, she commented morosely that it was sad for a widow to have to face yet another Christmas on her own. Christabel had caved. And now the day was here.

"All righty. Come on over at 11:30—sharp!"

Christabel hung up and looked down at the cats. They'd gobbled their feast in no time at all. Now they wove in and out between her slippered feet, holding their tails aloft.

"At least you guys don't talk," she said, carefully extricating herself from their midst.

She sighed and climbed the stairs. As she dressed in black jeans and a cable knit turtleneck—the only article of red clothing she owned—she thought about family. Grace was in the city with Doby, a good man who obviously loved her. Sam was at Treffian House, waiting for Ravi, who'd promised to have lunch with her. Whether or not Debra showed up, too, Friar Tuck Jonathan would be there, overseeing everything that transpired.

Treffian House policy. *Take that, Debra.*

God only knew where her father was spending Christmas. Just the thought made her head ache, and she went to the medicine cabinet to get an Advil. Her temples still throbbed when she left her apartment, but they felt a little better after she shut the door with unnecessary emphasis.

* * *

Mandy had prepared enough to feed a family of twelve. Turkey, all the fixings, two fresh-baked loaves of bread, mashed potatoes running with butter, green beans with almonds, and more. With a sheepish shrug, Christabel handed over her contribution of a mixed green salad, white wine, and a box of chocolates.

"You shouldn't have!" Mandy crowed. She wore a pair of baggy green sweatpants and one of the most startlingly ugly Christmas sweaters Christabel had ever seen.

"Wow, Mandy, you've gone overboard." Christabel circumnavigated the feast. Two places had been set opposite each other in the middle of the long table, with a myriad of platters and bowls extending to either side.

"Let's eat before it gets cold. Put some meat on those skinny bones, girl."

Obediently, Christabel sat down. She inhaled deeply, appreciating the savory-sweet scent of a traditional Christmas feast. There was something so comfortingly normal about it. Mandy was still bustling about, waggling her hips to Michael Bublé's *Jingle Bells.* She fired up the candle centerpiece with a long-nosed lighter that made a snapping sound, then laughed when Christabel jumped.

"Now, isn't this lovely? Let's pop our crackers. In my house, Christmas just ain't Christmas without paper crowns!"

Mandy held up her cracker, giving one end to Christabel. They each pulled and there was a modest bang. A pink paper crown cascaded out, along with a tiny deck of cards. Christabel was next. Her crown was blue and she was now the lucky owner of a silver key chain shaped like a heart.

"My, aren't we regal?" Mandy put both hands to her head and preened. "Now let's eat."

There was something different about Mandy tonight. She appeared to be bursting with health.

"Mandy, did you have a facial or something?" Christabel helped herself to a piece of warm bread.

Mandy's hand fluttered to her cheek. "I'll share my little secret, but only with you. Mum's the word!"

"Who would I tell? Doby's cats?"

Mandy leaned forward. "I've had two appointments with the marvelous Dr. Cheung. Injectables. Take a gander at the skin around my lips."

Christabel shifted the candles to one side. Even close up, Mandy's skin looked supple and almost line-free. "He's done an exceptional job."

Mandy wriggled her eyebrows. "And I don't have a frozen forehead, either. Dr. Cheung's an artiste." She gazed appraisingly at Christabel. "There's no shame in spiffing yourself up, you know. You might enjoy a bit of a makeover, after everything you've been through."

"It shows?" Christabel spoke idly as she reached for more stuffing and gravy.

Mandy's silence was eloquent.

"Oh, dear." Christabel put her fork down and touched her index fingers to her eyebrows, pulling them apart. "Would this be better?"

"Don't make fun. And, yes, that does look better. You should set up an appointment. Really."

"Maybe one day."

Surely a few lines here and there could be tolerated. She didn't want to be youth-obsessed like Ravi.

She focused on Mandy again. Something else had changed.

All at once, it hit her. "Hey, you were just rushing around like a star athlete. Don't tell me Dr. Cheung's fillers took away your hip pain."

Mandy's blue eyes took on a dreamy cast. "I've had an awakening."

Christabel suppressed a laugh. She put down her knife and fork. "Tell me more."

"I will, but if it bothers you, I'll stop," Mandy said. She reached over to pat Christabel's hand.

"Sounds mysterious."

"Not really, but it might hurt your feelings. The truth is, dear, I've been visiting Debra Gaston for Reiki treatments."

Christabel slowly slid her hand from under Mandy's. She said nothing for a moment, gauging her own emotions. She didn't feel hurt, exactly. And Mandy really did look much healthier.

"I'm all for you feeling better."

"Oh, that's so kind of you. I may not need an operation after all. Just get a load of this!" Mandy stood up and did a pirouette, her crown tilted at a rakish angle.

Christabel smiled and removed her blue crown, laying it on the table. "Not only nimble, but also as big-hearted as only you can be. Inviting me to such a delicious meal."

"It's not over yet. Let's clear away the dishes and we'll enjoy dessert in the living room. Pecan pie. Or apple—with coffee and brandy!"

An hour later, both women were stretched out on Mandy's matching Naugahyde recliners, watching the first *Home Alone* movie. Macaulay Culkin had been such an adorable kid. Christabel still laughed in all the same old spots—the aftershave scene being her particular favorite. This year, she related to the kid's primal scream more than ever before.

An end table was within easy reach of each woman, well-stocked with a brandy glass, remnants of pie, and coffee. From time to time, one of them gave a contented sigh. When Mandy belched and coughed to cover it up, Christabel grinned but remained tactfully silent.

Macaulay Culkin had outwitted the bandits. The afternoon was winding down. It might be time to go home, feed the cats, and call Grace.

Suddenly, Mandy muted the television and rose from her chair. She pulled the curtain aside and gazed out the window. "Who on earth's that?"

"Where?" Christabel craned her neck, but Mandy was blocking her view.

"There's a man. Not your ex-hubby—an older gent, silver hair. He's knocking on the door of your old condo."

Christabel stood and looked out over the older woman's shoulder. "Oh, for God's sake." She swallowed. "It's my father."

"Goodness! He's a handsome gentleman." Mandy fluffed up her hair.

"He's a ..." Christabel struggled to find words. "Well, I have to warn you. He's *not* a gentleman, Mandy. Really."

Christabel didn't know what else to say. *By the way, my father may also turn out to be your cherished Reiki therapist's long-lost dad. And, incidentally, he touches children.*

"He seems to have a key," Mandy added. "Yes, there he goes. He's inside." A light glowed in the next bungalow. "It appears I may have a new neighbor."

"I don't know what his arrangement with Ravi is, Mandy, but do be careful. He's not a good guy."

It was all she could offer without betraying Grace.

"It isn't like I want to have an affair with him or anything like that," Mandy shimmied away from the window, twitching her hips in a way that would have horrified Michael Bublé, whose caroling could once again be heard from the dining room speakers.

Was she hoping her new neighbor would look across the yard and see her gyrating in the lamplight? Christabel drew back into the shadows.

Abandoning her plans of an early departure, she curled up on her lounger. As Mandy boogied on, Christabel treated herself to a third piece of pie and an extra-large shot of brandy.

Only after the lights went out next door did she say goodnight and begin her trek home. The sickle moon brooded in the sky. When a long-abandoned wooden wind chime clacked in a sudden breeze, she gave a small shriek and ran the rest of the way.

She fed the cats their dinner before double-checking all the locks. Then, leaving her bedside lamp on, she slipped between the sheets and tossed and turned all night.

Chapter 38: December 26

Christabel hurried through the main entrance at Treffian House, stamping her feet to get rid of the snow clinging to her boots. This wasn't a festive place to spend the holidays. Although colored lights shimmered in the wan dusk outside, inside the building there were no decorations or signs of Christmas cheer, and when Jonathan came to collect her, he was even more taciturn than usual.

The old folks watching the inaudible television were lethargic. Christabel shivered as she entered the room, shadowed by Jonathan. It was like being escorted by a zombie through a pack of ghosts.

"Did you have a merry Christmas, Jonathan?" Someone had to make an effort.

No response. Then, "All right, I guess." He didn't look at her.

"I hope Santa was good to you." Christabel rolled her eyes at how ridiculous she sounded.

Again, a pause. Then, "No offence, but I prefer to keep my private life private."

She was relieved when Paul arrived and Jonathan departed in a round-shouldered huff.

"What's up with him?" Christabel asked. "He almost tore my head off when I asked how he was doing."

"Christmas exhaustion, that's all. We're slightly short-staffed until the New Year."

"You're kidding me, right?" It was hard enough to sleep at night, knowing her father might be lurking in the vicinity. Christabel needed to believe Sam was safe.

"Nothing to be concerned about. Everything's covered."

"Meaning people are overworked." She thought quickly. "Maybe there's something I can do."

Paul raised his eyebrows. "I don't see how."

"Sam could spend a few days with me."

He frowned. "Not a good idea. She's less volatile these days, but it's too much of a safety risk—for both of you."

"Even for a couple of days?"

"Not even that." He was silent for a moment. "But don't worry. Samantha and all the other residents are always well supervised."

She placed a hand on his forearm. "Promise me that's true."

"When are you going to start trusting me?" he asked in a low voice.

She felt her cheeks grow warm. "It's not a matter of trust, Paul. It's—"

She stopped, quickly withdrawing her hand as Mrs. McKay entered the room.

"Hello, Ms. Newberry."

Sam trailed behind her, carrying auburn Barbie in one hand. Her expression was blank. As she sank onto the rug in front of Christabel and began playing with her doll, she hummed something. It sounded like *Santa Claus is Coming to Town.*

"Have you informed Ms. Newberry of my vacation schedule?" There was only a suggestion of an upward inflection at the end of the question.

Paul flashed Mrs. McKay an irritated look. "Not yet."

So much for trust.

"What are your plans, Mrs. McKay?" Christabel made herself focus on Sam, who was pretending Barbie could fly. The doll was outfitted in a slinky purple number Christabel had never seen before. Apparently, Daddy had come through with a Christmas gift.

"I shall be visiting my family in Scotland." She hesitated, her eyes flicking in Paul's direction. "I'll only be away a few days. Back first thing in the New Year."

"And while you're gone—"

"Samantha will receive excellent care and attention." Paul took a step toward the exit.

"Wait a minute." Christabel stood in his way. "This is important. Why didn't you tell me?"

He cast an annoyed glance over her shoulder at Mrs. McKay. "I didn't want you to worry unnecessarily. Samantha is always closely tended."

"Right. And as a mere mother with no legal standing, I should just take your word for it." Out of the corner of her eye, she saw Mrs. McKay sit down stiffly in a chair close to Sam's spot on the carpet—avoiding the confrontation she had started, it seemed.

"Samantha will be—"

"Well supervised at all times. Gotcha. Without Mrs. McKay, her primary caregiver."

"It's a matter of a few days. Nothing more."

"A few days without Mrs. McKay is huge. God, Paul, just let me have Sam for those days." She looked away, fighting tears. "I'm her mother. The person who knows her best. I'm asking *you* to trust *me*."

Paul's phone rang. He shifted slightly to one side and answered it. After a couple of monosyllabic responses, he hung up and turned back to Christabel. His eyes were thoughtful.

"I'm sorry. I must go. I do have a proposal, though—a compromise."

"Tell me."

"If you truly feel confident that you can handle Samantha, I'll authorize an offsite pass. One night only."

Mrs. McKay stood and faced them. "I must protest—"

"Yes!" Christabel beamed at him. "When can we arrange it?"

"She's not stable enough," Mrs. McKay said in a hushed but urgent tone, moving closer to Christabel. "Yes, she has come a long way, but she's not ready—and, I'm afraid it might be too much for both of you."

“I’m the best judge of that.” Paul turned his back on her and took Christabel’s hand. “Let’s say, New Year’s Eve. We’ll only be a phone call away if you run into any difficulties.”

“I’m so grateful.” Christabel smiled at him and saw his answering beam. She wasn’t sure if it was Mrs. McKay or Sam who made the “tch” sound, but she didn’t care.

“Trust me now?” His fingers pressed hers.

She squeezed back. “Getting there.”

Chapter 39; December 31

Multicolored lights, strung high above the walkway, threw rainbows across the unsullied whiteness of the bordering snowbanks. As Christabel approached Treffian House, she had to admit the setting was exquisite. Season's Greetings from Paradise.

It might look like a winter wonderland, but she couldn't wait to get Sam out of there, even if it was just for one night. Christabel had been counting down the days. Her boots crunched on the rock-salted walkway as she strode to the doorway.

She rang the buzzer, stepped forward when the door swung open, and stopped abruptly. Debra Gaston stood in the entranceway, her lips parted in a dazzling white-toothed display. As always, she was coordinated and polished, from her gleaming chignon to her sleek, salt stain-free boots.

"Happy New Year's Eve!" she said, as if she were hosting a party.

"Thanks," Christabel said, not even trying to smile in return.

She looked beyond Debra, checking if Ravi was lurking in the background. She'd bet anything he was. And maybe good old Pop Newberry, to complete the joyous family scenario.

"Please come with me." Debra led the way through the security door. "Oh, and I'm sure you're wondering."

"About?"

Debra walked a few steps further. "Our DNA tests." She was silent for a beat, and then said quietly, "Still no results."

"Listen, Debra. I already have a sister. I'm not in the market for another one. But we need to work together, for Sam's sake, so I'm going to try to be civilized." Not quite how she had rehearsed it, but not bad. She'd kept the shaking in her voice under control.

Debra looked away. She took a moment to collect herself.

"Sam's in her room with her dad and Jonathan, packing," Debra said, in her normal, professional tone, picking up her pace.

There were only a few snoring seniors in the common room, watched over by one bored-looking female aide, who looked almost as elderly. Debra tried to make desultory conversation along their path. Christabel was unresponsive—sister or no sister. Please, God, let the latter be true.

"Here we are." Debra said, unnecessarily, when they reached their destination.

Christabel brushed past her. Sam sat on the floor near her dad, an open duffel bag between them.

Ignoring Ravi, Christabel said, "Hi, Sam."

As the official non-family-member observer, Jonathan slouched against the wall, leafing through a magazine. *Canadian Art.* Interesting choice.

Sam stuffed some rolled-up socks into her bag. There were several pairs in there already. Couldn't Ravi even get simple packing right? Or was he too afraid to intervene?

"Look, Sam," Debra said, "your mom's here to pick you up." Her mezzo was sugarplum sweet. Christabel felt the skin on her back prickle.

Sam did glance up—for a fraction of a second. Then she went right back to her packing. Another pair of socks. And another.

Ravi gave Christabel a meaningful look. She was sick and tired of always having to play the heavy. Keeping her lips sealed, she sat on the edge of Sam's bed.

Sam had run out of socks. Now she began to stack pairs of panties into the bag. Hardly any room was left. When she tried to stuff in four pairs of jeans and was unable to close the zipper, she snorted in frustration. Finally, she balled her fists and glared at Christabel.

Christabel forced herself not to move. She kept her hands folded on her lap. For once, Ravi would have to step up.

Several seconds passed before he snapped. "Sam, you've got way too much stuff in there." He took the bag from her and began to take out garments.

"No, Daddy." Sam stood up in front of her father, hands on her hips.

He ignored her and kept removing items.

"I said, NO." Sam grabbed the duffel out of Ravi's hands. She plopped herself back on the floor and started re-stuffing the bag.

"I could use some help here, Christa," Ravi muttered.

"Oh, I think you're managing just fine."

One look at Debra's serene face dispelled any possible guilt. Let the woman observe Ravi in a temper and they'd see how long her infatuation lasted.

"May I help?" Debra sank gracefully onto the rug next to Sam. She held out her palms, near but not touching Sam's possessions.

Sam's eyes, behind her thick lenses, seemed to focus on Debra's hands, then move to her face. When Debra smiled at her, Sam grinned back. Debra upended the bag and began repacking it. Christabel had to hand it to the woman: she definitely knew how to control a difficult teenager, even one as brittle as Sam.

There was a brisk rap on the door. Paul, bundled in a gray cashmere coat, popped his head into the room. "All set for a happy New Year?" The lenses of his glasses were frosted at the edges.

"I didn't know you were coming back this evening." Debra kept her eyes focused on her packing.

"Just a few last-minute things to take care of," he said, unbuttoning his coat. "Mrs. McKay is smart to take an occasional vacation. When she's gone, I notice just how much I rely on her. Can't wait for her to return tomorrow."

"Mm-hm," Debra murmured.

"I always think of Mrs. McKay as Treffian's backbone," Christabel said, glancing at Debra. Was that a twitch?

"I agree," Paul said. "She's one of a kind." Did Christabel imagine it, or did he wink at her?

Without another word, Debra whisked out of the room. Ravi detached Sam's hands from his arm and followed. Paul chuckled and nodded to Jonathan, who tucked his magazine under his arm and lumbered off.

If Christabel hadn't been worried about Sam's reaction to Ravi and Debra's hasty disappearance, she would have shared his amusement. Instead, she held her breath.

Fortunately, Sam was unflustered. She merely looked from the doctor to her mother and picked up her bag. From her collection of Barbie dolls on top of the dresser, she selected her current favorites. Hawaiian Barbie was going to have a night away, along with her blond and auburn sisters.

"Ready."

"Me, too. Here's your coat." Christabel took it from a hanger and laid it on the bed, allowing Sam to put it on unaided. "And wish Dr. Cheung a happy New Year."

"Happy New Year, Dr. Cheung." At least Sam sounded polite.

"Happy New Year to you, too, Samantha. And to you, Christabel. I hope we all find joy and make many new discoveries in the year ahead."

Christabel smiled uncertainly at him. He was always so formal. Was he still trying to get closer to her? If so, his way of speaking sent mixed messages. She was puzzled about her own feelings, too.

She settled for a simple, "Happy New Year, Paul."

She picked up Sam's bag and held out her hand. Sam looked the other way, so Christabel sighed and set off slowly beside Paul, checking frequently to see her daughter trailing a short distance behind. When they reached the security doors and Paul buzzed them out, Sam made a sound like a rooster crowing, and Christabel felt her heart expand.

This was the best thing that had happened to them in months. She waved to Paul as she left with Sam for their first off-site overnight.

* * *

Inside the store, Sam sat, mesmerized, letting the cats dodge and dart around her for an hour. She only allowed Christabel to lead her to the apartment when it was time for dinner. In spite of herself, Christabel felt her pulse accelerate as they climbed the narrow staircase. Of course Sam wouldn't try anything—and she didn't—but it was still a relief to arrive safely on the landing.

Together, they made Kraft Dinner and ketchup with a side of mushy peas, which was Sam's all-time favorite meal and one she never got at Treffian House. They put on their pajamas and sat at either end of the couch to watch *A Charlie Brown Christmas,* Sam stuffing a cushion between their two bodies as a barrier. When Christabel peeked sideways, she saw that Sam was sound asleep. Christabel jettisoned the cushion and tucked blankets around her. Then she gently removed Sam's glasses and kissed her forehead.

"Happy New Year, my sweet daughter," she whispered, looking at Sam's angelic face.

As she crept into bed, she made a resolution. The new year would be better for them both. It had to be.

Chapter 40; January 1, Daytime

"Mommy?"

Christabel rolled over and pushed the hair out of her eyes. Sam's face was inches away. She hadn't yet put on her glasses. With her dark hair and eyes, she looked like a Goya portrait—The Clothed Maja—knowing yet innocent. Wise beyond her years.

"Hey, aren't your toes cold?" Christabel asked, shifting herself to the other side of the bed. She patted the empty spot, but Sam didn't budge.

"Want to see the kitties." Was that a hint of enthusiasm?

"Really? This early? Well, they'll be happy to have their breakfast. I'll tell you what. You can feed them, okay?"

Christabel got up and retrieved Sam's eyeglasses, and Sam shoved them on crookedly. She squirmed with impatience as Christabel helped her into her housecoat. Her sixteen-year-old body jiggled in a womanly way, and Christabel glanced away.

"Kitties. Now!" Sam jerked herself out of her mother's reach and scowled.

"Yes, yes. Let's go. Careful on the stairs." Christabel stuffed the keys into her pocket. She waited until Sam had reached the bottom step before following her to unlock the shop's internal door.

"Kitties!" Sam sank to the floor and laughed as the cats walked back and forth over her lap, wafting their tails in her face. Fiery orange Noel butted the other four out of the way and touched his nose to hers. Sam closed her eyes in bliss.

It was too bad they hadn't had a pet or two in the old days. Maybe Sam would have been happier.

Christabel shook the thought from her head. "Come and help me. They're hungry."

"'kay!" Sam rose and held out her hands for the bowl of kibble. She took precise steps, not spilling a single morsel, and placed it in the middle of the swarming pack.

"Mommy?"

"Yes, Sam?"

"I love this."

Christabel's heart swelled with happiness. She leaned against the wall, reveling in the peace of the moment. If only every day could start like this.

The cats had finished their meal, and Sam was lost in her new world of sensation. Purrs and pounces and whisker flicks seemed to delight her more than anything she'd ever experienced before. She sat cross-legged, a huge grin on her face, and let her private circus play on.

Christabel tiptoed to the door. "Would you like me to bring your breakfast down here? I can make bacon and eggs? And orange juice?"

"Yes, yes, yes!"

"Okay. If you need anything, just call."

Sam was in the same position when Christabel returned with a steaming plate of food. When the pack began to take too much interest in her breakfast, she rose, clutching the dish protectively.

"No, kitty. Bad kitty."

"Sweetie, he's not a bad kitty. Just a fan of bacon. Why not sit over here on the stool?"

Sam nodded. She settled herself and poked at her sunny-side-up eggs with a wedge of toast.

"This is where Mommy works, you know," Christabel said, running her hand along the length of the counter. "It's a bit like the library we used to visit, don't you think?" Not even a glance. "Why don't I get you something to read while you eat?"

Christabel searched the shelves and chose a well-used copy of *Corduroy*, filled with vibrant pictures. It was written for a preschooler. Or for someone like Sam, who found joy in color and didn't care about storyline.

"Happy?" After a moment, Christabel dared tuck a lock of Sam's hair behind her ear.

Sam didn't seem to notice. How long had it been since Christabel had been allowed to touch her daughter this way?

"Mmmmmm." Sam began to hum. It was her old favorite. *Can you ....*

Christabel picked up the empty plate. On her way back upstairs, she sang along to Sam's tune. It was the kind of morning that called for music—for singing just for the heck of it.

This was exactly how things should be on New Year's Day.

They didn't get dressed until almost lunch time. Sam insisted on preparing the meal. She went through the fridge, oohing and aahing. After lengthy consideration, she took two large plates and doled out sliced cheese sandwiches, dill pickles, somewhat squashy pieces of avocado, and ice cream that immediately started to melt all over everything else. Christabel ate every scrap that was put in front of her. She told Sam she'd never enjoyed a lunch more, and meant it.

Cats, books, and a nap rounded out the day. All too soon it was late afternoon. Feeling like the oxygen was being sucked out of the room, Christabel told Sam to pack up her things.

"Can I take orange kitty?"

"No, sweetie, this is Noel's home. But you can come back and visit him. Soon, I hope. And you can take a couple of books." Christabel went to the preschooler section and pulled out two of the most colorful volumes. "How about these?"

Sam held out her hand and accepted them. Her movement was wooden, as if a beautiful nymph was turning back into a tree.

Side by side, they walked the short blocks to Treffian House, Christabel carrying the duffel bag and Sam holding Hawaiian Barbie in her fist like a candle. Fat snowflakes fell on their shoulders, melting on contact, but the lady of the fountain wore a cap of icy white, and, for once, looked jaunty. All the stores were closed and, once they entered the residential streets, they saw no one out and about on the sidewalks. The dusky afternoon wrapped them in tranquil beauty.

Christabel's throat ached with the desire to say something. What kind of comment could she make, anyway? *Sorry you have to go back to the slammer?*

They turned a corner and there it was—Treffian House, a picture-perfect residence in an idyllic town. A place of grace and tranquility. Christabel glanced sideways at Sam, who was shaking the snow off Barbie, and rang Treffian's doorbell with a gloved finger, standing back so that the camera could catch her image. They entered the antechamber, pressed the buzzer for the inner security door, and waited.

Within a minute, Mrs. McKay appeared. She looked as she always did, neat and pressed, and with hair tightly curled—not like someone who had flown in a cramped, tourist-class seat across the Atlantic Ocean that same day. Except, perhaps, her pale blue eyes were even more washed out than usual.

"Welcome home, Samantha," Mrs. McKay said.

Christabel stifled a protest. *Home?*

Sam's glasses were steamy from contact with the warm lobby air. She walked forward a pace, bumped into a chair, and halted, scowling.

"How nice to see you again, Ms. Newberry," Mrs. McKay added softly.

Christabel met her gaze and saw nothing but kindness and concern. Immediately, remorse flooded her body. If anyone had tried to make this a comfortable setting for Sam, it was Mrs. McKay. Christabel should show more gratitude. Sam, too, she thought, as her daughter continued on the way to her bedroom, stiff-shouldered and unresponsive.

"It's great to have you back." Christabel's attention was on her daughter, as they followed her along the hallway. "Good trip to Scotland, I hope?"

Sam's head was down, her hair spiraling out from under her winter hat. Christabel had opted for peace in the apartment over personal neatness. Mrs. McKay would have it untangled in no time.

When they arrived at Sam's room, Christabel wasn't sure what to do next. Was it wiser to leave quickly or stay to get her settled in? Sam was starting to resemble a thunderhead, black brows forming a V. She took off her coat and hat and let them fall to the floor, then kicked off her boots, adding them to the messy pile.

Christabel looked at Mrs. McKay and mouthed, "Should I go?"

Mrs. McKay held up a finger. "Your mother must leave us soon. But first, shall I help you put your clothes away?"

"You do it." Sam sat on the bed and crossed her arms, Hawaiian Barbie clenched in one of her hands. The doll smiled at them, white teeth sparkling.

"Hmm. We moved past this stage a while ago, and you gained privileges. Let's make sure you keep them. I shall hand you a hanger and you may put your coat away properly. Here you are."

Sam glowered at her.

"Sam, please hang up your coat." Christabel tried to take the hanger from Mrs. McKay but the woman resisted.

"Please wait."

It took several anxiety-ridden seconds, but Sam finally stood up and put Barbie face down on her pillow. She grabbed the plastic hanger out of Mrs. McKay's hand, and hung the garment up. Without being told, she also put her hat and mittens on a ledge to dry and placed her boots on a mat beside the door. She returned to the bed and threw herself onto her stomach beside Barbie, glasses askew, dark hair partially obscuring her face.

"Thank you, Samantha," Mrs. McKay said.

God bless this woman. She got results from Sam that Christabel had never been able to achieve. Plus, Mrs. McKay appeared to be entirely unruffled. Christabel, on the other hand, was beginning to perspire.

"Want daddy," Sam said, in a flinty voice.

Christabel flinched and looked away.

Mrs. McKay sat on the bed beside Sam. "He is not here today. He'll visit soon." She had such a soothing Highland burr.

"Want daddy." Sam lifted her face from the pillow. Behind her smudged lenses, her eyes were stones.

Christabel felt ill. She and Sam had celebrated a wonderful New Year's together. Now they were back where they'd started.

Sam raised and lowered her head, slowly at first, then more violently. Her glasses fell to the floor. Mrs. McKay picked them up, checked to see they were unbroken, and put them safely on the dresser.

"Want daddy. Want daddy!" Sam hurled her Barbie across the room. Christabel jumped back. Surely Sam hadn't been aiming for her?

Mrs. McKay gave a miniscule shake of her head, but Christabel couldn't help herself. She squatted beside the bed.

"Sam, honey—"

"Daddy! Now!"

"Why don't—"

"And Debra!"

Christabel stood up with a jerk. She took two steps back, recoiling as if Sam had hit her.

Sam pulled the pillow over her head and lay rigid.

Mrs. McKay slipped across the room to Christabel's side. "She's experiencing transition anxiety. It's very common. Please don't take it personally."

"Thanks. But, to me, it's always personal. I have to keep reminding myself it's not her fault."

Mrs. McKay arched an eyebrow. "Samantha has the capacity to use better social skills. She can be strategic when she speaks. We talk a great deal about the power of her words."

Christabel glanced at Sam, who was peering out from under the pillow. There was a smirk on her face, but when she caught her mother's gaze, she immediately changed it to a scowl. Christabel caught her breath. Was Sam deliberately trying to hurt her feelings?

"Samantha, dear, stand up and say good-bye to your mother."

Sam rose from the bed and unhurriedly approached, until she stood toe-to-toe with Christabel. A faint trace of garlic from lunchtime's dill pickles wafted on Sam's breath, as well as something else, acidic and somehow menacing. Christabel forced herself not to back away, holding her hands at her sides, as if she were in her yoga class back in the city. *Tadasana.* Mountain pose. Conscious breathing, in and out.

"Manners, Samantha." For the first time that evening, Mrs. McKay's voice rose. "Give your mother more space."

Sam dropped her head back, elongating her neck. Her hair spooled down her back. In that instant, Christabel was only peripherally aware of Mrs. McKay, leaping to her feet.

But Mrs. McKay was too late. With the speed of a rattler striking, Sam smashed her forehead into her mother's with a spiteful crack.

Christabel saw brilliant streaks of light behind her closed eyelids. Searing pain. As she sank to her knees, she was vaguely aware of Mrs. McKay yelling for help. Somewhere, far in the background, she heard the silvery tinkle of her daughter's laugh.

Chapter 41; January 1, Evening and January 2, Morning

She lay on something hard and cold—a tiled floor, perhaps. It was important to sit up, but at the moment she could barely even open her eyes against the bright light from the ceiling fixture. The small room was crowded; shoes flashed by, in and out of her range of vision. Someone was screaming. Was it Sam?

Christabel tried to prop herself up on her elbows but collapsed as pain knifed through her temples. All she could do was turn her head to one side and watch as two white-clad orderlies struggled to hold Sam down on the bed. Grim-faced, Mrs. McKay spoke urgently into her phone, her words muffled by Sam's shrieking.

Christabel closed her eyes. Sam was psychotic. The experts had been right—the girl posed a danger to others, including her mother. Maybe especially her mother.

Beneath Christabel's eyelids, tears pricked. She swallowed hard. In spite of the spiking agony in her head, she resisted the urge to break down and sob. She wasn't the ultimate victim here. Sam was going to be locked up for the rest of her life.

Mrs. McKay put her phone away and knelt beside Christabel. "I'm relieved to see you're awake, dearie."

"Oh, God." In spite of Christabel's best efforts, she felt her facial muscles spasm.

"There's no shame in crying." Mrs. McKay's own faded eyes filled with tears. "I've called Dr. Cheung, and he's on his way. We'll have Samantha taken care of in a few minutes, and then we'll pay special attention to your poor wee head."

"Thank you." It was all Christabel could manage.

She closed her eyes again. There was no choice but to remain prone on the floor, listening to her daughter's anguished yelps.

The door flew wide. Christabel managed to force her eyelids open as Paul rushed in. He wore a ski jacket and jeans and must have just pulled off a knit cap because his black hair was alive with static, some of it sticking up wildly. He looked like a frantic schoolboy, late for an exam.

"Christabel?" He sank to the floor beside her and took one of her hands in both of his.

"I'm okay." She pointed weakly at Sam.

"I'll get her settled. Don't try to get up. I'll be right back."

A middle-aged Filipino nurse entered the room, pushing a medical cart almost larger than she was. She and Paul stood near the men holding Sam down, blocking Christabel's view, but she did catch sight of the syringe. Moments later, the slackening of Sam's limbs. The orderlies stood back. At a nod from the doctor, they left the room.

Paul knelt on the floor next to Christabel. "Let's have a look at you."

Mrs. McKay and the nurse crouched on either side of him. All three of their faces were creased with worry.

"Wasn't out for more than a second or two. Horrible headache, that's all."

Gingerly, she put her hand to her head and was surprised to feel the wool of her winter cap. Thank God she'd had it on; it may have saved her.

Paul carefully removed the hat and handed it to Mrs. McKay. Christabel felt the soothing touch of his fingers, cool against her forehead.

"Can you sit up?" He offered a hand and Christabel took it.

She winced as she pulled herself to a seated position. Her vision wavered for a moment, bands of iridescent colors distorting the nearby faces. Across the room, Sam was splayed on the bed, mouth gaping. Her eyes were almost closed, but even through the slits she seemed to be studying her mother. Christabel shuddered.

"I've got to get out of here." She tried to stand.

Paul placed gentle hands on her shoulders. "Not yet." Turning to the nurse, he said, "A wheelchair, please?" And to Mrs. McKay, "Please see to Samantha. I'll take things from here."

Mrs. McKay nodded and crossed to the bed. She began to undress Sam, as if the girl were still a child. Sam growled, but her legs and arms dangled helplessly. Christabel wanted to look away but somehow couldn't.

A male orderly arrived with a wheelchair, and he and the nurse assisted Christabel up into the seat. She had an impression that he was very young and had dark skin, but the aura that surrounded him made it difficult to take in any more. Her headache was overwhelming, and she couldn't summon enough energy to even thank them.

Paul walked alongside the chair, as the aide pushed Christabel through the doorway and down the long hallways. She propped her head in one hand. No one spoke.

At last, they arrived at a room on an unfamiliar corridor. The orderly switched on a light, and Christabel raised a hand to shield her eyes. Halos seemed to strobe around each piece of furniture, but she made out a single bed, a dresser and very little else. Standard Treffian accommodations, like Sam's.

"Why are we here?" she asked, trying to turn her head toward Paul, but dropping it back into her hand.

"I'm admitting you temporarily, for observation," Paul said.

"No! I have to take care of the cats—and the store."

"You can't leave. This is your second concussion. Give us your sister's contact information, and we'll call her."

"Grace is going through a difficult time. I don't want to disturb her." With a mammoth effort, Christabel put both hands on the armrests of the wheelchair and attempted to stand. Her legs had other plans.

Paul's eyes were full of compassion. She dropped her gaze.

"Please. Your sister's number."

She tried to remember it. "Oh God, I know it off by heart, too. But it's in my phone. Please tell her I'm fine."

"You can't return to your apartment alone. At least not for the next forty-eight hours."

"She can send Doby here on his own."

"You're going to need emotional support, too."

"What about Sam?" It wasn't exactly an afterthought, but Christabel heard the hollow note. Even a mother could only hope for so long.

"She'll get the finest treatment." There was a slight edge to Paul's voice. "You do agree that we're capable of giving it to her?"

"More than capable. And, Paul?"

"Yes?"

"Thank you."

"You're welcome. Someone will check in on you every hour while you're sleeping. And we'll get you scanned, too, by early morning." He rolled her wheelchair up to the bed, adding, "I'm afraid this is all we've got." He handed her hospital-issue nightshirt and shrugged apologetically.

She tried to smile at him. With his help, she shifted from the chair to the bed. The softness of the mattress had a magnetic pull. She couldn't wait to put her head on the pillow.

Paul left the room, and Christabel heard a key click in the lock before footsteps echoed down the hallway. If anything, being locked in was reassuring. Now, no one could sneak in during the night and hurt her, intentionally or not.

Within seconds of slipping between the sheets, she was gone. Her sleep was cavernous and dream-free. Occasionally during the night she came to partial consciousness, aware of a person, or possibly two, moving quietly about in the room. Once, when she fluttered her eyes open, she saw Paul. His hand was on her wrist and he was looking at his watch, but when he sensed her gaze he nodded, without saying a word. She drifted back off to sleep, still feeling a throbbing pain in her head, but reassured.

Before dawn, she partially woke again. Someone was standing beside her bed, trickling fingers across her forehead and stirring the air just above her body. She tried to open her eyes but her lids were cemented shut. She could feel herself breathing heavily; in fact, she could *hear* herself wheezing as if someone were inflating her lungs, like the bellows of an old-fashioned pump organ. With every ounce of willpower, she attempted to thrash and wake herself up.

Christabel heard herself moan—loudly, almost like a chanting monk. In the background, someone was whispering, ongoing and sibilant. It wasn't any language Christabel recognized. She shivered, still moaning, her limbs paralyzed, her eyes darting wildly beneath obstinately immovable lids.

The whooshing sensations eventually stopped. Christabel felt herself sliding into deep sleep.

Maybe it was the air circulating in the vents, or the psychedelic aftereffects of the concussion—but before she dropped off, someone seemed to speak, close by.

"I think we're even."

* * *

It was morning when Christabel eventually woke up, for real. She blinked, elated that her eyelids were free. Attendants arrived to wheel her to another part of the building for a series of tests, including a CT scan. When she returned to her room, a cart holding a breakfast tray had been rolled in. The smell of steamy oatmeal and piping hot coffee was tantalizing, and she realized she was ravenous. She sat up and lifted her spoon.

Then she froze, astonished.

Her head didn't hurt. She was still shaken by her troubling pre-dawn experience, yes. Still heartsick about Sam.

But there was no pain—not even a bit. In fact, she hadn't felt this clear-minded in months. Not since back in the springtime, before Sam had yanked her down the stairs.

She put her hands to her temples and squeezed, then nodded vigorously several times. When that failed to make her dizzy or cause any pain, she shook her head from side to side. Nothing. Finally, she pressed her fingertips to the spot on her forehead that Sam had savagely butted.

Last night it had hurt like the blazes. Now it felt just fine.

Chapter 42; January 2

Christabel pulled on her boots and stood up. "I'm leaving."

"No, you're not." Paul tried to tug her back into a seated position. He was wearing his white doctor's jacket today—a man with power, backed by science.

Christabel remained standing, her feet planted firmly. "You've confirmed that my CT scan shows no evidence of damage."

Paul considered her, his head tilted to one side. She smiled, but there was no answering twinkle in his gray eyes. He reached out and held her wrist, dropping his gaze to his watch, and frowning.

"I'm absolutely fine. In fact, I've never felt better." She slipped from Paul's grasp and crossed the room to fetch her coat.

"Impossible. I've never seen a recovery like this."

"But you agree, don't you? I'm healthy enough to go home?"

"Strangely enough, yes, I think I do."

He walked across to her, reached into his breast pocket, and pulled out his ophthalmoscope. Turning its blinding light on, he stared for an overly long time into each of her eyes. Christabel backed away, seeing spots for a moment. Paul slowly replaced the instrument, looking at her with what appeared to be awe.

"Chalk it up to my strong constitution," she said. "And the excellent and prompt care I received." She didn't add anything about any possible supernatural occurrences—not here, where they might lock her up.

"All right," Paul said. "You're free to leave. But stay home for now. Rest and recuperate. And at the first sign of a headache—or blurriness of vision, or anything—return. Got it?"

"Yes, sir!" She saluted, clicking her heels together and marveling that this caused her no pain.

"And keep your sister nearby for a week, minimum. You're not cleared to live on your own."

As if he could stop her. But it was a relief to know that Grace and Doby were in town. She couldn't wait to see them. They were so reassuringly real.

* * *

"What gives?" Grace looked from Christabel to Doby.

"Doby is going to take you for a ride—in the countryside," Christabel said, quickly adding, when she saw Grace was about to argue, "Just for the afternoon."

She'd only been home for a few hours, and already Christabel was sick of being treated like an invalid. Ignoring her protests, Grace had made her recline on the couch and fluffed her pillows at least a dozen times. Doby had brought her way too many cups of chamomile tea.

She begged Doby to get Grace the heck out of there.

"Your limo awaits," he said, making a grand sweeping gesture toward the staircase.

"You'd better still be lying on that couch when we get back," Grace said, shaking a finger at Christabel. Looking at the keys in Doby's hand, she added, as she headed out. "BMW? Don't mind if I do."

Alone in her apartment, Christabel threw back the covers and climbed out of bed. She ran the shower until it filled her small bathroom with steam, then gave herself a prolonged scrub with a loofah until she stung pleasantly all over.

After that, against doctor's orders, she got dressed, put on her coat and hat, and walked to Treffian House.

* * *

"Is Debra Gaston working today?"

"Please wait. I'll check," a tinny voice said, over the intercom.

Minutes passed. Christabel perched on the edge of a chair, her back straight. It was incredible how well she felt, physically. Mentally, though, was a different story. What in the world had happened to her last night?

Paul walked in through the security doors. "Christabel? You're supposed to be resting."

She put a guilty hand over her mouth. "Busted. But, I'm totally fine." She waggled her head.

"Stop that. You won't be fine if you push yourself too hard." He held the door open to the common room and they both went inside.

The place was hopping today. The usual bevy of old folks was hanging out, some of them fast asleep, others staring into space or at the television. There were also three young male patients, one chalky white and the other two much healthier-looking shades of tan. They were engrossed in playing a board game on a fold-out table, under close observation by two female orderlies, one who appeared to be no older than her charges and the other with an I'm-so-over-this air of weariness. At irregular intervals one of the boys would hoot, but whether it was a cry of victory or an involuntary Tourette's tic, Christabel wasn't sure.

"We can go to my office." Paul's expression was solemn.

"I'm actually hoping to see Debra."

He pinched his lips together. "I won't keep you, then." He turned to leave.

She laid a hand on his forearm. "Paul, please. Is there something I should know about her?"

His expression was indecipherable. "What do you mean?"

"I don't really know. Like, have you noticed anything ... strange about her? Does she have any special skills? Some kind of naturopathic power, or something?"

"I have no idea what you're talking about. I'm sorry, but I really must go."

She gave his forearm a last entreating squeeze. "Is there something going on here?"

He met her eyes. It seemed he was about to say something, but his phone rang. He answered it, listened for a moment and said, "I'll be there right away." With a worried half-smile, he pressed Christabel's hand and hurried off.

Before the door closed, Debra whirled through it, looking like a model in a spread for country living. She wore skintight black jeans with just the correct amount of fraying fabric and a shirt that emphasized her curves. Her shiny hair was loose today, framing her face in waves. She didn't look like a sorceress, or even like someone who may have been awake for a good part of the night.

Her smile was neutral. "I'm sorry to keep you waiting. I was in a therapy session."

Christabel gathered her thoughts. Maybe she was way, way off. After all, she'd been conked pretty severely on her head.

"This may sound odd," Christabel began, "but did you happen to drop by my room last night?"

Debra stared at her. "I wasn't at work yesterday."

"Really? I could have sworn I saw you. Or at least heard you. Just before dawn?"

Debra stood very still. Her eyes were unreadable. "Perhaps it was a nightmare, brought on by your injury."

"Which is now all better—in less than twelve hours, incredibly enough. And if you did anything to help me—"

"I was at home all night. As I was until noon today. In bed." She paused. "Ask Ravi, if you don't believe me."

Christabel flinched. She turned to leave, but Debra put a hand out to stop her.

"I spoke without thinking." Debra sighed. "That's no excuse, but it's been a tough time for me."

"How so?" Christabel asked, mechanically.

Debra looked down at the floor. "We just got the test results. It turns out that your father isn't related to me at all. And after everything I've done ..."

"Then we're *not* half-sisters." Christabel erased her involuntary smile, but not swiftly enough.

"I can see you're devastated."

Was Christabel wrong; had Debra's stricken expression been sincere? For a few seconds, the woman—who looked so much like her younger self—stood there, seemingly on the brink of saying something. Then, across the common room, the Tourette's kid whooped and startled them both. Without another word, Debra pushed the security button, ushered Christabel out, and let the door close between them.

* * *

By the time Doby dropped Grace off late that evening, Christabel had donned her pajamas and was sitting up in bed, a book open on her lap. She'd turned on all the lights in the apartment. Somehow, she felt safer that way.

Grace entered, yipped, and ran to flick most of the switches off. She snatched the book out of Christabel's hands and clapped it shut without marking the place.

"What do you think you're doing?"

"Reading."

"Lie the hell back down!" Grace waved a scolding finger at Christabel, who remained seated, bolt upright.

"I got the all-clear from Paul Cheung. You can return to the city. No need to miss a payday for me." Christabel turned the bedside lamp back on.

Grace's features seemed to shift, morphing from shock to something approaching embarrassment. "I have something to tell you." She sounded almost shy.

Shyness was so un-Grace-like. She was obviously stalling for time, removing her coat and boots as slowly as she possibly could. Fiddling with a hanger. Checking herself in a mirror and re-arranging her hat-flattened hair.

"What's up, Grace?"

"Don't laugh." Grace sat down on the bed but didn't meet her sister's gaze. "I've actually grown very close to Doby." She fidgeted with the corner of the comforter. "Romantically, I mean."

Christabel felt her eyebrows rise. "And?"

"He asked me to marry him today." Grace took a tremulous breath. "I accepted. We're going to start planning our wedding, for springtime or sooner."

Christabel opened her mouth and closed it. Finally, she summoned up the wits to say, "Whatever makes you happy, makes me happy. And I think Doby's the sweetest guy ever. But ..."

"He's not my type?" Grace twiddled a lock of auburn hair. It showed a touch of gray at the roots.

"Definitely not. I've been secretly cheering for him, but I never really thought you'd be seriously interested." Christabel tried to read Grace's expression, but her sister turned her face away.

"He's been nothing but kindness, making me tea and driving me to therapy appointments."

"So he's a great aide de camp and chauffeur. But where's the passion?" Christabel took Grace's hand. The tendons stood out.

"We visited his home today," Grace said, nonchalantly. "Have you ever been there?"

"No. What's it like?" Christabel let go and sat back, studying her sister's face.

"Impressive. In the family for years. Lots of property." Grace's eyes shone.

Christabel tried to maintain her composure as she digested this. Doby, rich?

It was true he never seemed to be worried about the store's poor sales. He paid her generously and drove a sleek, late model BMW. Apparently, he was also the sole owner of an estate.

It all added up. Grace had found her Pemberley at last.

She felt a rush of happiness. Grace deserved the best, and so did Doby. This could be a great match—Grace bringing savvy and courage and Doby, wealth and sensitivity. They were both smart and kind and funny. Lasting marriages had been established on much less.

"Congratulations." She pulled Grace in for a lengthy hug.

"And the most fabulous thing," Grace said, as she untangled herself. "I'm quitting my job and moving to Graysville. You and I are going to be neighbors!"

Chapter 43; January 6

From the official records of the late Mrs. Audrey McKay (MSW), formerly of Treffian House

Transcribed from recorded session with Samantha Mistry. Handwritten notes indicated in italics

McKay: You're looking better, Samantha. I'm glad you're out of bed. How are you feeling?

Mistry: Baaa.

McKay: Try again. Use your words.

Mistry: Baaaa. [She flaps her hands up and down, and tries again]. Baaad.

McKay: Thank you. But I'm sorry that you aren't feeling well.

Mistry: Debra?

McKay: Ms. Gaston isn't here at the moment. She and your father are away for a few days.

Mistry: Mmmmm. [She gets up from the bed and walks to her dresser. From the Barbie collection she takes her favorite Hawaiian model and returns to the bed]. Mmmmm.

McKay: Shall we go downstairs to the cafeteria?

Mistry: Nope.

McKay: I saw Grant and Sophia there earlier. They may still be eating their breakfast. Do you want to go see?

Mistry: Nope.

McKay: Dr. Cheung says you should get back to your normal routine. That means no meals in your room. And school starts next week. Won't that be nice?

Mistry: Nope. Go 'way.

McKay: I can see you're having a tough day.

Mistry: [flops face-down on her bed; drops Barbie on the floor]

* * *

Observations: Samantha has regressed. The change in her prescriptions, precipitated by the attack on her mother, may be the cause. While I am sorry to see Samantha struggling as she adjusts to the new meds, I am in full agreement with Dr. Cheung that the safety of others is paramount.

We were all so shocked by the girl's vicious behavior. We must never allow ourselves to become complacent. I was guilty of this, and poor Ms. Newberry suffered the consequences. Samantha, too. If only I'd spotted the signs.

Chapter 44; January 13 - 2:00pm

A whiteboard eraser flew by Christabel, barely missing her ear. Wordlessly, she stooped to pick it up. As she did, a marker whistled over her head.

School was back in session. After the extended Christmas vacation, some of the Treffian House students weren't just restless; they were bouncing off the walls. At the front of the room, three teens were engaged in a mock battle. Steve hadn't intervened; his eyes were cast up at the ceiling as if he were praying for divine intervention.

Christabel positioned herself near Grant's desk. The boy, seemingly unaffected by the mounting chaos, scrawled words into a notebook. They flowed from his pen like water from a hose. The kid was a force of nature–talented and driven. She wished with all her heart that he'd graduate–from high school and from Treffian House, too.

There were no other students in the room today. Sam's desk was bare, and no Barbie sat surveying the classroom in overly made-up judgment. Earlier, Christabel had tried to drop by her daughter's room, but Sam hadn't yet stirred from her bed. Christabel had felt both relieved and guilty, and had left quickly.

The battling kids were really going at it now. The thwack of a hand connecting with a cheek resounded, along with a startled yelp. While Steve rushed in to break things up, Christabel reached into her jeans pocket and pushed the panic alarm–calmly, almost casually.

It was amazing what one could get used to.

"Jesus Christ," Steve muttered, when Friar Tuck lookalike Jonathan and another burly aide muscled the brawling kids away, leaving Grant alone with his teachers. "First day back, and already I can't wait for spring break."

Steve seemed to be having a problem catching his breath. Reaching into his pocket, he yanked out his puffer and inhaled. Gradually, his chest stopped heaving, and he stood up straighter.

"Hang in there." Christabel crossed her fingers behind her back. "The kids are just readjusting. They'll be quieter tomorrow."

"Fat chance. At least Grant seems to be all right." Steve spoke in an undertone. "But what's up with Sam?"

Christabel looked away. "She had kind of a relapse over the Christmas vacation. She's on different meds." Christabel couldn't believe how dispassionate she sounded. "Mrs. McKay didn't think she was ready to return to class yet."

Steve raised his eyebrows. "You seem awfully calm."

Christabel didn't answer. After a moment, she went back to Grant's side and sat at an adjacent desk. Here was a teen that might come out the other end of this nightmare with a future. If she could help him, she would.

She started reading over his shoulder, avoiding Steve's stare. Let him walk a mile in her shoes.

After a few more minutes, Jonathan returned to deliver Grant back to his room. The teen scowled, gripping his pen with ferocity. He only rose from his chair when the orderly made a move to manhandle him away.

"That's a wrap, then. A stupendously crappy start to the new year, I must say." Steve started to erase the whiteboard.

"It's bound to get better." *Enough with the platitudes.* Often, things around here got worse.

"Are you going to continue as a volunteer or have you had enough?" Steve asked.

"I'll stick it out for now. I want to see that Grant gets his Creative Writing credit. After the year is up, though, I'm planning to quit."

"Don't blame you." He looked so forlorn; Christabel almost took back what she'd said. But that wouldn't be true.

She gathered up her coat and hat and waited for Steve, who was fussing with paperwork on his desk. Wordlessly, they made their way past the cafeteria and common room. When they reached the exit, Christabel opened her mouth to say good-bye, but Steve shushed her.

"Wait." He looked past her. "Something's wrong."

Christabel turned to see Mrs. McKay racing toward them, all propriety forgotten. Her face was stark white.

"Samantha is not in her room!"

Christabel glanced over her shoulder. Of course, Sam wasn't sneaking up behind them. Was it wrong to feel relieved?

"We haven't seen her." Steve started to cough. He reached for his puffer and gave himself a dose.

"She's got to be close by," Christabel said. "All the doors are locked."

It was strange for unflappable Mrs. McKay to be in such a state. Sam couldn't have escaped. Treffian House was a fortress.

"We have to find her." Mrs. McKay's phone beeped, and she took a quick look at it before putting it back in her pocket. "She's not upstairs. I'll go check the west wing. Could the two of you search the lower floor?"

"Is this really necessary—?" Christabel broke off, reading the panic in Mrs. McKay's eyes. "All right."

Mrs. McKay gave them a sharp nod. As she hurried off in the direction of the cafeteria, Steve and Christabel headed to the stairwell.

"Of course she had to give *us* the basement." Steve went down the steps two at a time, Christabel not far behind.

"What's this area even used for, anyway?" She wrinkled her nose at the smell—mustiness, overlaid with Lysol.

"Not much of anything, nowadays."

At the bottom of the stairs, Steve selected a key from a heavy ring. When he opened the door, the odor got stronger. The sickly green walls glistened, but it was hard to tell if it was from an excess of humidity or just the paint's sheen.

Christabel walked in the center of the hallway, touching nothing, taking shallow breaths. "Dear God."

"Yeah, but apparently everything's up to code." Steve turned a corner.

She was hard on his heels. "The inspectors must have no sense of smell."

He paused to give himself another puff from his inhaler. Under the fluorescent strip lighting his features looked pinched. "Imagine living down here. You can almost feel the despair."

Christabel felt the skin on the back of her arms rise in tiny bumps. She moved closer to Steve.

Their footsteps echoed in the stillness. They walked past the long line of identical doors, set with tiny windows. Steve tried each handle, but none of them budged. Christabel chose a window at random and peeked through the bars. She jerked away, sensing a presence, as if someone were leaning up against the inside of the door. It had to be her imagination.

Steve grabbed her arm. "Sam's not here. Let's go."

"We should at least finish our walk-through." Her voice quavered but she kept moving, tugging him along.

"Fine. But watch out for ghosts and ghouls." He spoke lightly but she felt him tremble as he let go of her.

She found herself taking smaller steps, each footfall as silent as possible. Steve kept trying every door, without success. She let him take the lead again, keeping her eyes lowered.

Steve stopped and peered at one of the windows. "This is odd."

The bars were covered on the inside by cardboard. Christabel brushed past him and twisted the knob. Locked. She took a shaky breath and knocked softly. No answer.

To either side of them, the anonymous cells stretched out endlessly. Steve's face looked bleached around the eye sockets. He didn't object when she took the keyring out of his hands.

The first three attempts to unlock the door were failures. On the fourth try, she felt the key move sweetly in the lock, making an almost inaudible click.

She eased the door open—no creak, just the slight shush of well-maintained hinges. She met Steve's gaze under the hallway's fluorescent glare, and they grimaced at each other, before inching their way into the room's semi-darkness. A lamp in the corner glowed faintly. Christabel groped inside the door and flipped a switch. Nothing.

In the gloom, the space was claustrophobic. She fought the urge to run. As she opened her mouth to call out, Steve grabbed her wrist. He pointed to a second, inner door. It was slightly ajar.

She waited, listening, hearing nothing at first.

And then, there it was. A whooshing sound. Rhythmic, and otherworldly, and almost ... hypnotic.

Steve nodded to her. As one, they crossed silently to the partially open door. They peered around its edge, into a twilit treatment room.

Two tables were positioned parallel to each other, against opposite walls. On the left one, partially covered by a white sheet, a large form sprawled—male adult, judging from the size. On the right, a much smaller person lay, also covered. Female, most likely. Between them, a woman, performing some kind of ritual, her hands flowing through the air. Scooping and lifting over the girl. Depositing over the man.

Christabel pressed her fingers to her mouth. It was Debra, doing her weird Reiki on two patients instead of just one. Her eyes were closed. She was oblivious to everything except her task.

Someone else was there, too, sitting on a metal stool behind Debra, half hidden in the gloom. Ravi raised a warning hand at Christabel and Steve. Rising from his seat, he took a step forward but was hemmed in by Debra, who floated and danced blindly between the two tables. Her face was tranquil as she continued to transfer handfuls of air from girl to man.

Steve began to cough. As he fumbled for his puffer, Christabel ran between the tables, avoiding Debra's swooshing arms. She pulled the sheets aside and stared.

On one side, Sam, lying in a fetal position. So pale.

On the other, Christabel's father. He looked rested and rejuvenated, like a man just back from a relaxing vacation.

"Sam!" She had to wake her up.

Blocked by the swaying, spellbound Debra, Ravi stretched out both of his arms toward Christabel.

Did he think she was a moron? She shook her head at him. "No way!"

He grabbed for her as Debra momentarily moved out of his path. Christabel recoiled.

"Sam!" She jiggled her daughter's ankle. Sam didn't respond. Her eyelids didn't even flicker.

Ravi's eyes were cold, as Christabel grabbed Sam's shoulders and gave her a vigorous shake.

It was no use. Sam flopped back on the table, out for the count.

Steve was no help—bent double, he was trying to get his cough under control. He threw a quick look at Christabel, his eyes streaming. Again, Christabel tried to lift her daughter's shoulders, but in her unconscious state, Sam was a dead weight. Ravi must have realized this, because he dropped his hands and sat back down on his stool. His satisfied smile was obscene.

Debra's eyes drifted open. She seemed disoriented, her hands still rising and falling as if on autopilot. Steadily, her balletic actions began to lose momentum.

Finally, Ravi said, "What are you doing here?"

As if Christabel were the interloper.

"Never mind that—what has *she* been doing to Sam?" Christabel squeezed her daughter's hand, but Sam didn't squeeze back.

"A treatment—approved by Dr. Cheung."

"In the basement, with my *father*?"

Christabel shook Sam's arm. *Please, please wake up.* Steve stood beside her, wheezing. After a moment, he reached out and stilled Christabel's hand.

"We've found her. We should let Mrs. McKay know." Steve said. His eyes were wide. "C'mon."

"No!" Christabel slapped his hand away. "I'm not leaving her alone with these people."

Debra's movements had stopped. She blinked, seeming to regain full consciousness. Behind her, Ravi put a protective hand on her shoulder. Debra's fawnlike brown eyes took in Christabel and Steve, positioned between the treatment beds and the inner door.

"Hello," Debra said, as if they'd come to a tea party.

"Sam is leaving with me. Right now!" Christabel touched her daughter's forehead. It was clammy and cool—almost corpse-like. Why wouldn't she wake up?

"She's my kid, too," Ravi said. "And at least we've finally found a use for her." He began to stroke Debra's hair. The woman leaned back into him, a languid smile on her face.

Christabel tapped Sam's cold cheeks. No response. "I'm going to talk to Paul."

Steve leaned down and examined the base of Sam's treatment table.

"This thing's on wheels," he said, straightening up. "We can roll her to the service elevator."

"Or not." Ravi stepped out in front of Debra, a look of stony determination on his face.

Before she could react, Christabel felt Steve shove her aside. Astonished, she fell to the floor, as he leapt forward to take her place.

He was shorter than Ravi and at least thirty pounds lighter. He didn't have a chance. When Ravi threw a well-aimed jab, Steve went down with a crash.

Chapter 45; January 13 - 3:05 pm

Christabel rose slowly. This was it. The man she had loved and trusted—more than any other person in her lifetime—was going to slug her.

She dared him with her eyes. His face was rigid; his mouth a thin, cruel line. He bore no resemblance to the husband she remembered. But then, he'd never been that ideal man—she'd lied to herself all along.

Ravi remained motionless. He seemed unable, or at least unwilling, to get on with it. His hands dropped to his sides.

"Chickenshit." Christabel's father had raised himself up on one elbow.

He seemed different somehow. The man in the bookstore had been handsome but old, deep wrinkles etched on his face. This new version had the skin of a fifty-year-old and, judging from the shine in his eyes, the vitality of a younger man, too.

"I can't," Ravi said. His posture sagged.

Christabel turned to run.

Halfway to the door, someone grabbed her by the wrist. Intense pain flashed throughout her body. She fell to her knees.

"Let go of me!"

Through an excruciating mist, she swiveled and tried to look up. Debra clutched her viciously by the arm. The woman's eyes were closed and she mumbled something rhythmic.

"Some daughter you turned out to be." Her father had risen from his treatment bed. There was a spring in his step as he walked toward Christabel and Debra. "At least Grace had her uses." His lips parted in a depraved grin. "And even if this one isn't technically mine—" he gestured to the still murmuring Debra, "—she *does* have some special gifts."

Christabel moaned. Flames coursed along her neural pathways.

"And, as for my idiot granddaughter," Christabel's father said, resting a hand on Sam's hip, "at least she's been a valuable resource."

Christabel tried to scream. She could barely breathe. If not for Debra's viselike grip on her arm, she would have collapsed completely.

Her father looked down at her, as if she were a mildly interesting museum exhibit. No pity. No connection. Debra continued her incantations. Poor Steve lay nearby on the tiles, eyes rolled back into his skull. His asthmatic huffing was worse, and there was a blue tinge to his skin.

Ravi stood watching, his back to the wall. Surely he couldn't let this torture continue.

She sought his eyes with hers, but he shifted his gaze. She'd seen that expression a million times. It was the way he looked at Sam.

Christabel swallowed her rising hysteria. She was on her own.

Her father squatted beside her, hunkering down with the easy grace of an athlete. He gave her a mock-sympathetic smile, and patted her head.

"Hurting a bit, my dear?" he asked. He seemed genuinely curious—a scientist with a rat.

"Don't ..." She forced the single syllable through her teeth.

Debra tapped Christabel's mouth, numbing it to stillness. As if in response, Ravi turned his back and faced the blank wall. Moments later, she felt her arm jerk as Debra increased the pressure. It was like being prodded by devils—punished for sins too great to comprehend.

Her father laughed, as he rose. "I don't think you'll be getting any help from your ex, my dear. He's seen the benefits of moving on." He bounced on the balls of his feet, as if testing newly restored flexibility.

"Time to go. It's been a pleasure doing business with you." He slapped Ravi on his stiff, unresponsive back. "Consider your debts settled and our partnership satisfactorily dissolved."

With that, he bent and gave Sam a lingering kiss on her lips, maintaining eye contact with Christabel the whole time. If only she weren't paralyzed, Christabel would have gladly killed him. Filled with fury, she watched him exit, whistling as he went, without a backward glance.

For an instant, she lost hope. They were never going to let her leave this room.

Sam lay on her table. Long, jet-colored hair, streaming across a pale face. Helpless. Innocent. *Abused.*

Christabel had to help her.

She struggled, but her burning, spasming muscles refused to respond. Her eyelids were getting heavy. She battled against the encroaching void. Too late, she remembered the panic button in her pocket.

Across the room, Sam stirred. She turned her head toward Christabel, and opened her eyes halfway, lids drooping. Christabel barely recognized her. Sam had aged ten years—maybe more. A profound weariness showed in the girl's skin—creases and lines, and violet shadows.

"Mommy?" Sam tried to sit up, faltered, and sank back down. "Daddy?"

Ravi didn't budge.

"Stay still, Sam." Debra's voice was strained.

She'd only said three words, but, for an instant, the pressure lifted. Christabel wrenched herself away. She reached into her pocket and pressed the panic button. Once, twice, again.

Maybe someone would come.

Chapter 46; January 13 - 3:20 pm

Debra clamped down, and the agony returned. Once again, Christabel couldn't move—almost couldn't think.

"You stupid bitch." Debra tightened her hold. "And after everything I did for you."

Christabel fought for consciousness.

"She's fighting me," Debra said through gritted teeth. "Do something."

Ravi turned around slowly. He focused on the new woman in his life. As he walked toward them, Christabel sent him a wordless plea—*Help me.*

"You shouldn't have interfered," he said.

Debra released her grip and took a step back. For an instant, the anguish ebbed. Then Ravi wrapped his fingers—that had once caressed Christabel—around her neck.

He began to squeeze.

She couldn't breathe. She raked out with her nails and scored the skin on his wrists. He swore and choked her harder. Her arms dropped to her sides, as large spots blackened her vision. A sound like the howling of wind filled her ears.

From far away, through the crushing pain, she heard Ravi say, "I think she's out."

As the last bit of light faded, footsteps clattered in the hallway.

"Hello? Is anyone in there?" Mrs. McKay's accent had never sounded more musical.

Ravi let go of Christabel's throat, and she tumbled to the floor, air rasping through her damaged windpipe. It felt like heaven wrapped in hellfire.

Mrs. McKay raced into the room, Friar Tuck Jonathan right on her heels. For an instant they froze, taking in the chaotic scene. Then she ran to Sam's side, while he pulled out his phone and punched in some numbers.

"Code Orange; repeat ORANGE! Room 57!"

As he shoved the phone back in his pocket, Jonathan seemed to notice Steve's unconscious form for the first time. "What the hell's happening here?"

Mrs. McKay didn't wait for an answer. She dropped Sam's hand and rushed at Debra, slamming her against the wall with her full body weight, and locking an arm behind her back.

At the same moment, Ravi sprang at the orderly, knocking him down. As Jonathan struggled to get back up, Ravi leapt on top of him, punching him in the face. Jonathan lay motionless, eyes closed, nose oozing blood. Ravi stood up, his eyes wild.

Meanwhile, Christabel had somehow managed to pull herself up onto all fours. Each breath scraped her raw throat. She crawled over to Steve and felt his pulse. His eyelids fluttered. With any luck, he would regain consciousness soon.

Ravi still loomed over the orderly, whose bald dome gleamed in the half light. Mrs. McKay was using her weight advantage to keep the younger woman pinned against the wall. For now, Debra was unable to use her arms, but how long could Mrs. McKay keep her trapped there?

Ravi looked up, as Debra cried out. Christabel struggled to stand, but her legs wouldn't cooperate. She was still on all fours when he charged across the room. He grabbed the metal stool, and bashed Mrs. McKay with it.

There was a ghastly *thump*.

Mrs. McKay went down with a crash. Blood gushed from her forehead, pooling on the floor, and trickling along the grout between the tiles.

The room was horribly quiet. Ravi stared at Mrs. McKay. After interminable seconds he cast the stool away. It clanged against the wall, splattering him with delicate freckles of blood.

The red puddle grew larger. Mrs. McKay never stirred. Her eyes went from faded blue to translucent. Christabel crawled closer and stared into them, praying for them to blink.

"We've got to get out of here!" Debra grabbed Ravi's hand, and he helped her step across Mrs. McKay's body, avoiding the gore.

Sam had finally managed to pull herself up to a seated position on her treatment table. "Daddy?" She scrabbled for her glasses and put them on, cockeyed.

"Daddy!" She heaved herself off the bed and stumbled to his side.

Still weak, she seized hold of him by the waist and sank to the ground, her arms sliding down his legs until she sat on her bottom, holding her father by his ankles. "Don't go!"

Ravi looked at her; his revulsion was unmistakable. Christabel clenched her teeth and began to crawl closer.

"Get off." He kicked out, gently at first, then harder.

"Daddy! No!"

He reached down and slapped Sam across her cheek. The imprint of his hand sprang up lividly across her skin. Still, she held on.

"Stop it!" Christabel cried.

There was no way to bypass the blood on her way around Mrs. McKay's body. She felt it well up between her fingers and soak through the knees of her jeans.

"I'll be good!" Sam was crying, but there was a note of hopefulness in her voice. She looked up at her father. "I promise!"

Ravi glared at Christabel. His face was dark; his eyes were those of a stranger.

He slapped Sam again.

Christabel had thought she had already experienced the most extreme pain possible, but watching Ravi hurt Sam was worse.

She wriggled to the wall. Using it as support, she smeared red handprints over the sickly green paint as she rose. Mrs. McKay's colorless eyes reproached her, over the lake of darkening blood.

Sam reached up an entreating hand. Ravi ignored it and clouted his only daughter on the side of her head. She cowered, a look of uncomprehending suffering on her face.

"Do something, Debra!" Sweat ran down his forehead. He kicked out at Sam again.

Debra closed her eyes and started to chant. Her arms began their graceful rise and fall.

Ravi tried to take a step and almost fell. He stomped down and Christabel heard something crack, like a small branch snapping underfoot.

Sam wailed, a sound that hit Christabel right in the gut. Again, she dragged herself halfway to a standing position. She leaned against the wall, gasping for air, willing her body to move.

All at once, Debra stopped chanting and bent down to touch Sam's wrists. Sam's hands fell limply to her sides, her right pinky finger standing out at an unnatural angle, her mouth open in despair.

Ravi didn't as much as glance at her. He grabbed Debra's arm and the two of them fled, not looking back, to the accompaniment of Sam's whimpers.

Christabel finally managed to stand upright. She took a shaky step toward her daughter. And another. At last, she made it. She gathered Sam into her arms just as she heard the longed-for sound of running feet drawing close.

Chapter 47; January 13 - 3:35 pm

"It's okay, sweetie," Christabel whispered.

Her neck hurt almost more than she could bear. Sam was a dead weight in her arms, but Christabel forced herself to remain standing, propping her daughter up.

"Daddy! Come back!" Sam cried.

On the floor, Steve began to stir. Jonathan was still out cold, but his chest seemed to be rising and falling. Christabel kept her eyes trained on the two men, trying not to look at Mrs. McKay, who lay unmoving in her halo of blood.

Four orderlies burst into the room, crowding the small space, gaping. One young man turned away and promptly threw up. A gray-haired woman with seen-it-all eyes pushed him aside and took charge. She got the two aides who weren't retching to attend to Steve and Jonathan, and, after a cursory check of Mrs. McKay, made a 911 call.

Christabel began to shuffle toward the exit, bringing Sam with her. The girl's thin body twitched. She seemed so much older and frailer than sixteen.

"Hate you," Sam whispered through her tears.

"Oh, Sammie. You don't, really." Christabel kept ushering her along.

The orderly who'd been sick caught up to them, acne scars standing out starkly on his bone-white face. Even now, after all that had happened, Christabel needed to be escorted. Treffian House policy.

But that was all right. She didn't want to be alone with Sam.

They approached the stairs. Christabel couldn't hear anything over Sam's increasingly piercing cries. Not the ghosts of past inmates scrabbling behind their doors; not the sounds of whatever was happening back in that terrible treatment room.

It was over, thank God.

She'd get Sam back to the infirmary and find a member of the staff to set her mangled finger. Then someone could put her to bed—who exactly, she wasn't sure. Poor Mrs. McKay. Christabel shut her eyes for a second, before moving on.

They'd reached the middle of the staircase when Sam balked. Behind her blurry lenses, she squinted at her mother. "You made Daddy go." She yanked away, snarling.

Christabel felt the last particles of her world dissolve. In a state of surreal calmness, she took hold of the railing, and hauled herself up the stairs backward, putting distance between herself and Sam, one step at a time.

With crisp authority, she told the orderly, "Restrain her."

The young man glanced from mother to daughter. He looked as if he wanted to cry.

Sam began to pull herself upward, clawing the railing with her uninjured left hand.

"*Restrain her*, I said!" Christabel yelled out the order, never breaking contact with Sam's narrowed brown eyes—Ravi's eyes, with an insane glitter.

"I hate you!"

Sam's good hand shot out. As Christabel twisted her leg out of her grasp, the orderly finally reacted. He captured Sam's wrists and wrested them behind her back. At a nod from Christabel, he force-marched the girl upward, step by step. Christabel shrank back against the wall as they passed her, Sam screaming and resisting him every inch of the way. The orderly's face was the color of ash, but he didn't let go.

Christabel watched until they were out of sight, her blood-smeared hands hanging by her sides. At that moment, she felt no emotion at all.

* * *

A half hour later she sat in the common room, waiting to be interviewed by the Graysville police. The place was abuzz with people rushing past her, some in uniform, some in street clothes.

She'd scrubbed her hands and face. She'd also done her best to get most of the bloodstains out of her clothes, which clung to her body with distressing dampness.

A staff member—was it Paul?—put a mug of hot, milky tea into her hands. She took the occasional sip without tasting anything. When she finally put it down, sorrow hit her in hurricane blasts—for Sam's tragic, wasted life and for brave Mrs. McKay, who hadn't deserved her awful fate.

Then, she cried for herself.

* * *

After she'd been questioned by the police and examined by doctors, and assured that Steve and Jonathan were going to make full recoveries, Christabel felt other emotions crowd their way into her exhausted being—rage and disgust, along with a fervent hope that Ravi and Debra and her villain of a father would be hunted down. More than anyone else, he deserved to be punished—preferably by a hanging judge.

Strangely enough, she also felt a glimmer of something else. Christabel was never going to be able to fix her broken daughter. From this point onward, she wouldn't even try. She'd seen the hate in her daughter's eyes on one too many an occasion.

It was time to let go.

Chapter 48; January 20

Every pew in the small chapel was packed. Latecomers stood against the walls, murmuring and scuffling their feet. Two old ladies in the row behind Christabel and Steve sang along to a piped-in recording of *The Way We Were*, their wobbly voices painfully off-pitch.

The fusty smell of snow-dampened coats was overwhelming; breathing the thickened air hurt Christabel's injured windpipe, and poor Steve couldn't stop wheezing. He took a deep drag from his inhaler, sputtered for a moment before recovering, and gave her a grateful smile when she patted his arm.

The elderly choristers behind them hit a particularly sour note, making Christabel squirm. Mrs. McKay would have hated this circus of false emotion and voyeurism. Thank God her body was on its way to Scotland–perhaps her spirit was, too.

Eventually, someone turned off the cheesy funeral tunes. A middle-aged female chaplain, dressed in a flowing black robe that concealed her shoes, glided to the altar and opened an enormous bible. She bowed her graying head, and the crowd came to an expectant silence.

"'*Blessed are those who mourn, for they will be comforted,*'" she intoned, with as much emotion as if she were discussing the price of tomatoes at the Graysville superstore.

Christabel tried not to fidget. The gaudy stained-glass window behind the altar portrayed a resurrected Jesus showing His palms to Mary Magdalene. In the background, the other Mary didn't look overly impressed. A wan sunbeam trickled through, illuminating the spot in front of the altar where the casket would normally repose. In its place, masses of white lilies hulked. Occasionally, their cloying scent broke through the smell of wet wool. Christabel wasn't sure which was more nauseating.

Apart from Steve's labored breathing, the congregation was quiet, barring the occasional communally uttered "amen." There wasn't a single sigh or choked-back sob to be heard. Yes, Mrs. McKay had been a starched, proper woman—but, seriously, were Christabel and Steve the only ones here who gave a damn?

In the row ahead, Mandy scanned the crowd, her head pivoting back and forth. A cane was hooked onto the armrest beside her. She looked so much older, as if new wrinkles had been sculpted into her putty-like skin.

But who cared about Mandy or any of the other fake mourners? Christabel was here to pay her respects to a heroic woman. She just wished the service was more moving, but it was obvious the chaplain had never even met Mrs. McKay. Christabel wondered if anyone in the room had really known her. If only Christabel had made more of an effort to do so herself.

The chaplain blathered on. "Audrey McKay was hardworking and kind-hearted. She came from a small town near Glasgow, but as a young woman immigrated to Canada, establishing her home here in Graysville ..."

Across the aisle, Grace sat beside Doby, holding his hand. Her head was turned away, but Doby's expression was doting. At least one positive thing had come out of this nightmare.

Coming to the end of her remarks, the chaplain asked if anyone had words to share about the dearly departed. Nobody was jumping up to volunteer.

Steve jostled Christabel's arm. "Go on. Say something."

Heads swiveled in their direction. She couldn't very well scowl at him, but she managed to give Steve's thigh a secret pinch, and was satisfied to feel him flinch. Trying to assemble a few coherent thoughts, she rose and took hesitant steps toward the front of the church. Somehow, she managed to evade the minister, who was holding out her arms like a shepherd welcoming a lost sheep back to the fold.

Christabel faced the audience. Before gripping the lectern, she adjusted her scarf. She'd camouflaged the bruises, but her neck still ached.

"I can't say I knew Mrs. McKay very well." *Damn throat.* She cleared it. "In fact, until after her death, I didn't even know her first name."

Suddenly, she felt a pang of grief. She rooted around in her pocket for a tissue, before continuing.

"Audrey McKay was wonderful with my daughter, Samantha—endlessly patient, even on Sam's bad days, and always so kind to her. I never once heard her raise her voice in anger."

Christabel paused. She wished she knew something more personal about Mrs. McKay that she could share—something that would honor the woman properly.

"I'm sure Mrs. McKay touched the lives of many other people here today." Christabel hesitated, but nobody met her gaze. Even Steve was looking up at the ceiling with his one good eye, the other still black and swollen.

Christabel swallowed gingerly and gripped the lectern harder. "Mrs. McKay didn't deserve her fate. She was a good person—truly ethical. She protected Sam as best she could, each and every day here at Treffian House—and then, of course, during those last, horrid minutes. She died trying to save others. I believe she was the bravest woman I've ever known."

Christabel had to stop and collect herself. Across the room, Steve nodded. His shoulders were shaking, and he dabbed at his uninjured eye with a white handkerchief. Two rows behind him, Paul was seated, his head lowered so that she could only see the shining black crown of his hair.

"She saved my life—and not just mine. And I want to express how very grateful I will always be to her. For everything—my life, my daughter's life, Steve Dodd's, too. And I do pray that her spirit will live on, because if anyone deserves an afterlife in a better world, it's Audrey McKay."

There. That was all she could manage. Pulling the tissue from her pocket, she patted her eyes as she walked back to her seat. Her steps echoed in the stillness.

She sat back down on the pew beside Steve. He gave her a sideways shoulder hug, jarring her injured neck, but heartwarming, nevertheless.

The chaplain launched into the Twenty-third Psalm. "'*The Lord is my shepherd, I shall not want* ...'" Some members of the congregation mumbled along. Christabel could hear Steve's tentative recitation, but she remained silent, doing her utmost to suppress the surge of sadness that had overtaken her.

"'*Yea, though I walk through the valley of the shadow of death* ...'"

Hands clutched together, Christabel hoped that somewhere, somehow, Audrey McKay was at peace.

* * *

The reception was efficient and unemotional. Slim waiters in black pants and starched white shirts slid through the crowd gathered in the common room, carrying red and white wine on silver trays. A number of the guests were starting to look bleary-eyed. Others huddled around the buffet of mini-quiches, stuffed mushrooms and other savory morsels, raiding it with greedy abandon. For once, the big-screen television was turned off, but every now and then Christabel caught a riff from the Death's Greatest Hits collection that had been playing in the chapel. At the moment, Mariah Carey was bleating out *Bye Bye*.

"Sorry, Mrs. McKay. Audrey, I mean," Christabel whispered, closing her eyes and putting a hand to her pounding forehead.

It was impossible to avoid picking up snatches of conversation as she worked her way across the room, trying to find a quiet corner.

"Here, try one of these." Grace hand-fed a slider to Doby, who gobbled it up like an obedient child.

As Christabel passed them, they kissed, unaware of her presence. She sighed. In the midst of death there had to be life, but surely there was a time and a place.

A few steps further on, Mandy was surrounded by a gaggle of cronies. She was in her element. "Can you believe they haven't caught Ravi Mistry? Or Debra, who I bet is innocent, poor dear. She had magic hands, that one–a real miracle worker. Maybe he kidnapped her. Anyone got new intel?"

Christabel shuddered and kept walking. Until Ravi and Debra were arrested it would be hard to sleep at night.

And then there was her father. She had spoken to Grace at length about reporting him to the police, but her sister was adamant. She didn't want to rake up the past.

Maybe one day she'd convince Grace otherwise. There were innocent lives out there that needed protecting–lives an evil man could yet ruin. Grace should take a page from Mrs. McKay's bravery manual.

Later. Definitely not today–and tomorrow, Christabel was leaving town. She'd never seen a Mayan ruin and she intended to rectify that. She'd walk the beach and begin to heal–spend some quality time by herself and put the past firmly behind her.

"Are you running away for good?" Steve thrust his glass of wine into Christabel's hand. "And don't drink that one–it's mine." He began plying a fork, shoveling food from his loaded plate to his lips.

"Only for a couple of weeks. Sorry to leave you in the lurch."

He chewed and swallowed. "I'll survive."

Christabel looked away as he continued overstuffing his mouth. "I've decided to stay until Grant gets his credit. How about you?"

"Actually, I've handed in my resignation. I'll be leaving the same time as you." Steve turned around and put his plate onto a side table.

He took his glass of wine back, wafted his nose over it, wheezed, and took a swallow.

"Did you find a new teaching job?"

"Not yet." He looked at her intently with his one good eye. "Just decided life is way too precious to spend it in a place that almost killed me."

"You're a gifted teacher. Whoever hires you will be lucky."

"Hey, don't make me blush. But at this point, I'd wait tables. Drive a bus—anything that takes me as far away from Graysville as I can get."

With that, Steve drained his wine. He deposited the empty onto a passing waiter's tray and grabbed two more full glasses, keeping one and handing the other to Christabel. They clinked them together lightly, smiled ruefully at each other, and went in separate directions.

Across the room, Paul leaned against a wall. He wore a beautifully tailored navy suit, but his tie was loosened. Strange—Paul was always impeccably dressed. Possibly it was the effect of the free-flowing wine.

His eyes were lowered; his shoulders drooped. Should she pretend she hadn't noticed him?

She found herself walking over to him. "Hi." She reached out and touched his arm.

He looked up, and his eyes filled with warmth. "Hello, Christabel." He straightened his posture. "May I ask—"

She tilted her head. "Yes, what is it?"

"I'm wondering—have you decided to remain in Graysville?"

"For now. My sister plans to settle here."

He nodded. A smile lifted the corners of his mouth.

"But I'm going to do some traveling first," Christabel hastily added. "It's something I've always fantasized about."

"Ah. Good for you." He stared beyond Christabel, as if trying to read the future.

"How do *you* feel, Paul?" Oh dear, she'd had too much wine. Christabel felt her cheeks grow hot.

"Grateful you're staying, at least for now. Unsure about what's to come." He finally met her gaze. The shadows under his eyes were dark.

"I see."

She didn't, really, but she felt his anguish. He'd lost a colleague. Treffian House was all over the national news, and not in a good way. Things were going to be very difficult for a long time.

He looked down at the tips of his shoes. "And Samantha?"

Her mouth was dry. She took a sip of wine, but it didn't help much.

"I've finally accepted she's a ward of the province."

It was getting easier to say these words. Of course, she'd still make sure Sam got the best possible care—at a distance, with visits, maybe weekly or bi-weekly. Never, ever, unaccompanied.

"Good, good." He paused. "In other circumstances, I'd suggest we get to know each other better."

"I know." She smiled kindly at him. "But who knows what may happen in the future, right?"

His face lit up, the shadows retreating, and for an instant she felt a twinge. No. Wrong time, wrong place. She quickly excused herself, placed her empty wineglass on a side table, and left.

Outside, in the cold January night, she sent a blessing heavenward to Mrs. McKay. It was probably the effect of too much alcohol, but for a split second one of the stars in the sky seemed to glow more brightly.

Pulling up her hood, Christabel walked back to her apartment, past the dried-up fountain with its mourning brass woman. Some fountain of youth. The statue was just an innocuous piece of metal. Real evil lurked, perhaps close by, and it was only too human.

She counted each step, in order to avoid thinking too deeply about the threats that still existed. At home, she packed her suitcase with bright, summer clothes, set her alarm clock, and fell into the first dreamless sleep she'd had in months.

Chapter 49; January 23

Coba, in all its crumbling magnificence, was breathtaking. Christabel had spent the last hour exploring the area on a rented bike. Now, she climbed the 120 steps of the ruined temple, stopping occasionally to catch her breath. When she reached the top, she sat on a rock and looked out, marveling at the view. It was wild with jungle and lush with lakes, and the dome of sky was a vivid shade of blue she'd never seen before.

Her shirt was sticking to her back and one of her knees was skinned, not to mention grubby. She checked her phone for the time, ignoring the emails she had no intention of opening. It was later than she'd thought. In a couple of minutes, she'd have to start her descent or risk missing the return mini-bus ride to her resort.

On a nearby ledge, a young New Yorker was reading snippets from an iPhone travel app to his pretty companion. They leaned into each other with their heads together. Honeymoon, probably—love and lust, certainly. Christabel smiled.

"So what used to happen here? Some kind of ritual?" the young woman asked, running her hand along her lover's thigh.

"Let me see." He poked at the screen with his index finger. "Yeah, here it is. The Mayan priests sacrificed animals—and people." His voice sank to a melodramatic bass. "Even women and girls."

The girl slapped him playfully on the shoulder. "Yuck. *Gross.*"

Christabel got up to leave, took the first steep step, experienced a flash of vertigo, and sat right back down. The stone under her bottom was uncomfortably warm; nevertheless, she felt a chill run the length of her spine.

"I bet they threw them right offa this pyramid," the young man said.

Christabel closed her eyes tightly and concentrated on breathing. When she opened them again, she felt stronger. The tangled jungle spread out before her, interspersed with ancient paths.

She stood and walked down the stairs, one at a time—looking ahead, never back.